C000062246

THE
AEON
CHRONICLES

April M Woodard

DISTANT WORLD PRESS

THE AEON CHRONICLES

Copyright © 2018 by April M Woodard

For information contact :

P.O. Box 2020

Villa Rica, Georgia 30180

http://www.aprilmwoodard.com

Cover Design by SHANNANTHOMPSON ART

Emblem Art by April M Woodard

Graphic Art by April M Woodard with images from ©pngtree.com

****

ISBN: 978-1-7322490-1-1

First Edition: May 2018

"There are far, far better things ahead than any we leave behind."

-C.S. LEWIS

The emblem was engraved with wings, arching above a crown over the letter 'A'. This was a symbol of the noble, of the faithful and true, but not all who wore the symbol believed in what it stood for.

aeon

[ee-*uh* n, ee-on]

noun

1. (in Gnosticism) one of a class of powers or beings conceived as emanating from the Supreme Being and performing various functions in the operations of the universe.

2. eon
[**ee**-*uh* n, **ee**-on]

noun

1. an indefinitely long period of time; age.
2. the largest division of geologic time, comprising two or more eras.
3.*Astronomy.* one billion years.

Truth Keepers

When the Confusion began after Aalok's exile, the king appointed counselors called Truth Keepers. These priests were in charge of teaching the Words of Aramis, to bring souls back to the truth.

FIRST CIRCLE – Council for guidance

SECOND CIRCLE – Council for bonded mates

THIRD CIRCLE – Council for those affected by the Confusion

FOURTH CIRCLE – Council for disagreements

FIFTH CIRCLE - Council for those who lost loved ones who were exiled

SIXTH CIRCLE – Council for those who had direct contact with the fallen Seraphim

SEVENTH CIRCLE – Council for those who trespassed against the Law

EIGHTH CIRCLE – Council before judgment and trial

Aura Colors

BLUE - Wisdom, Kindness, Compassion, Love,
Peace, Trust, Security

WHITE - Purity, Divine Connection, Life

YELLOW — Knowledge, Happiness, Confidence,
Excitement, Unsure

RED - Power, Passion, Anger

GREY - Depression, Sadness, Skeptical

PREMONITION

"SOPHIE!" Alexander shouted above the boom of thunder. While the clouds roared, fireballs screamed, streaking across the sky. A crack lit the heavens in veins of neon pink as Alexander gripped Sophie's shoulder tight. "We have to go!"

Alexander's words fell on deaf ears. All Sophie could focus on was the trembling of her body and the stabbing anxiety in her chest. Lightning flashed again. Bevol's terrified eyes entered her mind. She couldn't be there to soothe him, couldn't hold him as everything came to an end. She wondered if he had hidden in the forest; if he was shaking with fear, staring at the chaos as she was. Her breath hitched as she whispered her horse's name.

Thunder rolled and Alexander lifted his head watching the dark clouds sail away. The danger was passing, heading for the fortress as if drawn to its own darkness like a magnetic force. The wind died down, no longer rustling the palm trees. There was only the sound of the waves rolling over the

Guardian's boots as he brought his gaze back to the Truth Keeper.

"I don't want him to suffer," Sophie said, her voice cracking. "I don't want anyone to suffer."

"Aramis will be merciful," Alexander assured her. "Do you not think he will do everything in his power to set things right?"

Sophie stared at her Guardian as tears rolled down her cheeks. This was a moment of fear in the Truth Keeper, of weakness...of doubt.

A possible future evaporated from Aramis' mind as he exhaled a breath. He opened his weary eyes and glanced down at the parchment before him. The symbols he was writing in the book would one day be deciphered, but now was the present. The future had not yet been decided; the outcome of foreseen events could still change.

Aramis replaced his quill in the inkwell and stood from his desk. Clasping his hands behind his back, he gazed at the window, only to find his troubled expression reflecting back at him.

The time would be soon.

A knock on the doors echoed through the throne room.

"Come in," Aramis answered.

Michael, a Seraph of his army entered the towering doors, dressed in full military attire. His silver winged epaulets glinted as he walked to the center of the room and his breastplate filled with jewels, sparkled as he bowed over the gold emblem inlay. His long brown hair fell forward as his gaze shifted to the floor at a respectful bow. "My king,"

"Did you find the ship?"

"Yes. Aalok is in possession of it." Michael informed, lifting his head. "Shall we act?"

Aramis' gaze went to the Golden Gate of his kingdom, then beyond the unseen veil, past the stars and planets and galaxies. His vision zoomed in, magnifying like a telescope to a green and blue sphere in space.

"No," Aramis answered, shaking his head. "The time is not yet."

"As you wish my Lord,"

"Have you and Gabriel prepared the legions?"

"Yes, my Lord."

"Good. We will need them at their posts soon."

Pulling back his telephoto vision, Aramis glanced down at the inner courtyard of his kingdom. His forehead wrinkled when he set his gaze on the training yard, and the men practicing.

"Have you decided who the protectors of the Truth Keepers will be, my king?"

Aramis went to his desk and picked up a neatly wound scroll, handing it to Michael. "I have a list of possible

Guardians. I want you to go alphabetically; test their spirits and report back to me before they are knighted."

Michael bowed his head. "It shall be done."

As Michael exited the throne room, Aramis glanced down at the book he had been writing. He winced, knowing which side the souls had chosen, but he had hoped they would come back to the light.

Walking back to the window, Aramis set his focus back on Earth. He looked past a forest to a clearing where a group of Seraphim in red robes descended a spaceship. The last of the Seraphim paused in step, let his hood fall to his shoulders, and looked up at Aramis with a haughty grin.

Aramis narrowed his gaze on Aalok and lifted his chin. "So it begins."

THICKENING

DARKNESS

ANOTHER day on Earth welcomed dawn with the song of bluebirds. Though the sunrays of gold had not yet touched the field, it was lit by the white milky hue of an angel. As Sophie lay singing, the sunlight climbed the cliff and warmed her pink cheeks. She breathed the sweet scents lavender and opened her eyes to gaze at the clouds sailing across the sky.

She hoped Serus, her suitor, had received her invitation. She hoped this time he would come. They had always met in the field in the morning for a picnic, but after the night of the King's Grand Ball, things had changed.

A dull ache squeezed her chest and she winced, remembering that fateful night of their sad parting. She could still see Serus' face, twisted in pain at her rejection of his secret proposal. She wanted to be bonded with him, but he couldn't ask her to choose. Not between right and wrong. Not between him and her king. She would always choose truth; she would always choose the side of good.

With a sigh, Sophie focused on the warmth of the rising sun. Her white gown sparkled, casting rainbows on the golden field. She stared at the prisms, thinking of the previous picnics with Serus.

She would listen to him read, listen to the music of his violin. She remembered the first time Serus had brought her chocolate candies, wrapped in a delicate paper and cotton twine. She could again see the pink blossoms that fell like feathers from the tree above them; feel the gentle touch of Serus' lips at their first kiss.

Sophie longed to return to the past and sent out a prayer. But she didn't pray for her own happiness. She prayed for peace again; a life in which there were no questions, a world where truth was absolute, and deception had never born. But deception had been born. Confusion had swept over all existence. It was because of one fallen Seraph, all because of Aalok.

Tears trickled from the corner of her eyes as Sophie squeezed them shut. She tried to go back to pleasant memories of her and Serus again, but the painful past invaded her mind. Her heart thumped against her ribcage as images of those she had counseled drifted through her head. The overwhelming sadness of their hearts gripped her own and she was filled with doubt. Each sorrowful face came with a painful stab; every traitorous word from their mouths knotted her stomach. It was all too much for her to bear, too much for her to still comprehend. So many souls had been banished.

What if Serus couldn't come back from the Confusion? What if he had sealed his fate as others had? Was he in danger of being cast out of the Crystal Kingdom for not standing up to Aalok, for not standing by our king?

She had to talk to him. She had to look into Serus' eyes and see what was truly in his heart. All would be made right by the confession of his trespass.

Taking a package from her picnic basket, Sophie untied the cotton twine, and took a chocolate from the thin paper wrapping. She inhaled the sweet scent of cocoa and caramel before popping the treat into her mouth, daydreaming all of the times she had eaten chocolates in the meadow with Serus.

Lying down again, she closed her eyes and sang a hymn with the birds resting in the forest nearby.

The field became a symphony as a chorus of the Earth followed suit. The birds, the insects; all of the creatures of the field sang. Even the great leviathans bathing in the lake at the bottom of the knoll bellowed out with the song, like tubas and trumpets. She could again hear a melody as he slid his bow across his violin, in smooth even strokes. She hummed to the tune, and the birds joined in her song.

For a short moment, there was peace. For a small sliver in time, there was heavenly bliss. But it was short lived.

Thunder rumbled from beneath the earth, shaking Sophie so hard that her whole body quivered. She sat upright, looking behind her and then back at the lake. The great lizards had not moved and there were no herds of them running in the field. With a hand to the ground, she felt the thunder trail off to a soft shudder beneath her palm. She bit the inside of her cheek and scrunched her shoulders at what had just occurred. The Earth had never trembled before, not on its own, not like that.

Calls from above brought her attention to the sky, where flocks of blackbirds fled from the forest like a bad omen. They squawked, casting a shadow over the wheat field, but their frantic calls faded as they flew over the rolling hills toward the mountains in the distance.

Shivering at a gust of cool wind, Sophie looked sadly at the picnic on the blanket. There was no point in waiting any longer. Serus hadn't come, and just like all the days before, he wouldn't appear.

She made up her mind to leave and go to the kingdom to ask Aramis why the Earth shook. He alone would have the answer.

Shoving another chocolate in her mouth, she picked up her basket, but stilled at the pleasant tune of a pan flute. The pipes sang like wind through reeds with each breath from the player's lips until it fell silent with one last soothing chord.

Sophie waited for the presence above her to speak, but when it didn't, she sorted through the energy of its aura. It was full of pleasure...but also of pain. It held warmth like the sun, but a chilling cold like a shadow. Her gut told her to run, but she stayed against the twinge of fear gripping the pit of her stomach. She recognized these mixed emotions. This was how all souls felt before counsel. Serus was only confused. She couldn't run from her own anxiety. She couldn't leave him. Not now.

Shrugging off the pinpricks of uneasiness, she asked. "Since when do you play the pan flute?"

The figure whose face was shrouded in the shadow of a red hood, murmured in a voice as smooth as silk, "Long before you ever existed, my dear."

Sophie's spun around, only to find the presence had disappeared into thin air. There was no trace except the lingering aura of contempt.

It was Aalok; it had to be. If he were nearby, his followers would be with him. Sophie couldn't bear the thought of another incident, not here, not while she was alone.

Running past the large reptiles, trumpeting a farewell, Sophie didn't stop until she reached her rose gold spacecraft. As the door slid open at her approach, she glanced over her shoulder to the field one last time, cringing at the eerie presence that still lingered.

THE INFINITE
REALM

ZIPPING through space, Sophie's vision was filled with the beautiful colors of distant galaxies. They spread out like a vista beyond her windows as she was drawn into the mouth of the tunnel. The black hole, a portal, sucked in her ship like a vacuum, shooting it across the span of millions of light-years from Earth. Swirls of light spun clockwise around the spacecraft like warped rainbows. The colors faded into black and the ship shot like a bullet into the Infinite Realm full of prismatic stars.

Trickling warmth spread through Sophie's chest as walked toward the inner courtyard of the kingdom. The Infinite Realm was much more vibrant and alluring than Earth. Earth was a paradise indeed, but it was restricted to the limitations set forth in its patterns and design of its dimension. The Infinite Realm was boundless.

The crystal buildings of the kingdom shimmered as if to say 'welcome' when Sophie passed through the Golden Gate. Led by a marble path, she passed row after row of ornate trees and lush flowering gardens. She passed Seraph statues, and flowing fountains until she reached the center of the kingdom.

Aramis' love beamed with a golden glow that mirrored the brightness of Earth's sun from his high tower. Its warmth spread throughout the entire kingdom, warming Sophie's heart as she walked through the inner courtyard. With a smile, she nodded to those she passed. The baker tipped his hat; the tailor nodded with a grin. Every face she encountered was warm and welcoming. Their auras glowed, as did her own, with a soft white hue that emanated off their impeccable attire.

As Sophie turned the corner past the statue of Aramis, the air became stiff and stale. Her steps slowed, sensing a few disheartened souls among the pleasant countenances. They put off sadness and regret. Their vibration frequency was so low, that their aura could hardly be seen. The weight of their emotions was a thick fog and Sophie cringed, moving through the waves of sorrow and pain.

As she neared the steps to the castle entrance, Sophie paused, glancing upward to Aramis' royal Seraphim guarding the golden entry. They towered over her like stone statues, neither looking nor speaking to her. She waited in anticipation, pondering why they were there. Before she could ask, they moved, one to the left and one to the right, and the doors opened slowly. Sophie took in a deep breath and entered the Crystal Castle entryway, keeping her eye on the Seraphim. Still, the angels kept their eyes forward as the door closed with an echoing thud.

Sophie's reflection followed her through the polished sheets of crystal glass that lined the walls as she passed by the many doors in the large hallway. She went up the crystal stairwell and down several more long corridors until she reached the tall double doors. Sophie knocked, rocking up on her toes, eager to enter her king's quarters. As the door creaked on the hinges, the light on the other side glinted onto her silken gown, glittering it like diamonds. The doors opened wide and she shielded her eyes against a light like that of a thousand suns.

As Sophie bowed her head and curtsied, the clouds of confusion faded from her mind. The emotions from those she had felt in the courtyard ceased. Warmth spread through her whole body, tingling it as if it had been bathed in a sparkling pool of sunlight. She was in the presence of her king. She was in the presence of the Creator himself.

"Sophie!" Aramis said joyfully, placing his quill in an inkwell. He stood from his desk and came to her with arms open wide. His robe dragged along the floor; glittering brilliantly as if the very stars of the heavens had been woven into the fabric. His long white hair, unbound by the gravity he had set forth in the realm, flowed like a river behind him as he came to greet her.

Sophie lifted her gaze finding Aramis' soft sapphire eyes. They always sparkled with light, seemed to dance with delight when he was pleased.

"It is so wonderful to see you!" Aramis chuckled lightly, pulling her into his arms. He took a step back and cupped her shoulders. "It has been far too long."

"My Lord, it is an honor, as always."

"I see you spent the morning in the field again."

"Oh," Sophie laughed, picking out the yellow pods from her braid. "Yes, I suppose I should have checked myself in a mirror."

"It's quite all right. Tea?"

"Yes, please."

Aramis gestured for Sophie to sit at a crystal table, then waved his hand. At his command, a white teapot and two cups with saucers appeared.

"Did you see the fawns today?" Aramis asked, pouring her a cup.

"No, I suppose they were by the lake. I was going to go there, but..." Sophie paused. She wanted to tell Aramis about Aalok, but she knew he was already aware of the fallen Seraph's spying. She didn't want to talk about Aalok. She wanted to talk about Serus.

"I thought I would come to see you early—see if there are any new souls you wished me to council today."

Aramis cleared his throat and poured his own cup. "No. There are no souls to council today."

Sophie held back a frown and took a careful sip from her steaming cup. She was grateful for its soothing warmth.

"You always know just the sort of tea I need. Every time it's something different. Rose tea, or mint tea. I even remember the day I brought you dandelions and out came dandelion tea. How do you know which suits me each time?"

"I remember that day." Aramis raised his white brows. "You were only a millennia old. You came in with a bright smile and curious eyes. You asked me why they were the color of the sun, and why I picked blue for the sky, why roses were red." Aramis chuckled. "You have always been quite inquisitive."

Sophie smiled at the compliment but her gaze was drawn to the large window beside them. She let her vision focus upon rolling hills and lavish mansions spread out through the valley. She could see hers among them and vowed to write down the occurrence of the earth shaking when she returned home. It was after all her job to document such things.

When her gaze followed the paths of the kingdom to the courtyard, Sophie frowned, seeing the pink aura of her peers below.

"Sophie, are you all right?"

Glancing down, Sophie found her hands shaking and that her tea had spilled onto the saucer. "Yes, of course." Sophie shrugged. She sat her cup and saucer on the table and folded her hands into her lap to hide her trembling fingers.

Aramis winced. Sophie was not only lying to herself, but she was lying to him. He could sense she didn't realize she was lying. She was new to grief, to fear...to heartbreak. It was hope that had led her to the meadow, and hope that had left her vulnerable.

Aalok had snuck up on her, pretending to be the one she had been secretly waiting on. Aramis knew that no matter what had happened between her and Serus that she had gone to the meadow every day, waiting for him to come. He hadn't come today, nor days before, and Aramis knew why.

He knew Serus had not sent any reply letters but that he had been to her home many times. He had stood on her porch, contemplating if he should knock. Many times he had done this, and every time, he took a step back in shame. Serus had never knocked, because not once did he have the courage to retract his trespass, to admit his betrayal.

Disappointment filled Aramis' heart when he gazed into Sophie's mind, finding nothing but her suitor in her thoughts.

But worse, was the ache he felt pulsing off of her pink aura as she spoke.

"Are you sure there is no one to counsel today?"

Aramis forced a smile. "You did so well in bringing many of your peers back from the Confusion, but I'm afraid that even my most trusted Truth Keepers can not combat the Confusion. It is spreading much too fast."

"So despite my best efforts, there are more souls you've sent away?" Sophie asked, fidgeting with her fingers. She reached for her saucer and cup, careful not to let her hand tremble this time.

"I have spoken to the council and we have agreed there is nothing more that can be done. Aalok is too wise, too cunning. The time of the Truth Keepers is coming to an end. Soon, you will have a new assignment."

"But I have some important documentation on those I have given counsel to. You must see it. They can still be redeemed. If you'll allow me, I can retrieve the documents, and-"

"No," Aramis said, holding up his hand. "We can worry about documents later. Right now, I need to tell you something very important. Something about the future."

"What is it?"

"As you know, all souls have a choice—you, your peers, all of you. But you should know, Sophie, it's not just those I have exiled for treason, there are those that left of their own free will."

"This cannot be."

"It's true."

"Why would they...was there any warning?"

"The Confusion has made it unclear who is faithful and who is not. Auras are not as telling as they used to be."

"How many left on their own accord?"

"Enough. But do not lose faith. I have set forth a new plan."

Aramis walked to the window. As he watched his sons and daughters milling in the courtyard he sensed their distress. It pained him greatly.

He was ready to end it, ready to wipe the slate clean.

"There will be a chance at redemption for them all," Aramis assured. He made his way to his desk and picked up a thick bound book.

Sophie came to his side and gazed at the thousands of blank pages that ruffled through the tome.

"This book has yet to be written. After it is filled, I will know who is of the light and who is of the dark. Your brethren still have a chance to prove their worth."

It was not of his children's doing, but of the fallen Seraph. Aalok was a thief, a swindler. He had stolen the hearts of his children. He had told them fables, made it appear that he created them, but he didn't have the power to create life, he could only manipulate it. In his lies, he had made it appear that Aramis had only made his children for control. Aramis didn't want to control his children. He had given them free will. The only thing he had only asked of them was that they follow the Law. It was the only way to keep the peace, to protect them from the grief and sorrow that Sophie now felt. The more he thought of each precious soul that Aalok had confused, the darker and brighter the blue hue of his aura became.

With her cheeks burning from his aura, Sophie stood in awe of Aramis' power. His blue blaze was full of misery, pulsing off in waves from his body. It grew thick like a wool blanket and it was suffocating her. She wished there was something she could do to ease her king's anguish. But she knew her peer's betrayal was far too great to be soothed.

"The choice I make now will decide the fate of all," he said gravely. "Although Aalok has caused, and shall cause, much pain, I cannot extinguish his soul. One day...it must be done. I have seen there is no turning back for Aalok, but as for the others...they must be saved."

Sophie peered up at Aramis with confusion. "How will you save them?"

Aramis looked to the smaller book he had been working on that morning, then back to Sophie. "You must not fear what I am about to tell you, Sophie. You must be strong."

"Nothing could ever make me doubt you, Aramis. You are my king."

Aramis grimaced behind his smile, remembering his vision. He pushed it from his mind. Regardless of whether or not Sophie would have doubts in the future, he was still confident she would remain loyal.

"I have faith with all of my heart that what you say is true."

With a wave of Aramis' hand, a necklace appeared. The long rose gold chain sparkled, as did the beautiful opal jewel as it floated down into Sophie's hand.

"To give you comfort in dark times."

Sophie snapped the claps around her neck, and then gazed at the jewel as it reflected a rainbow of prisms in her eyes.

"There will be a new life, a new aeon, but no remembrance of what is now."

Sophie's gaze snapped to Aramis'. "What do you mean?"

"The only way to place you in the new aeon is to put you and others, into a slumber, but after you wake...you will have no memory of this lifetime. It will be as if this were all a dream."

"You-you mean I won't remember you, or my brethren? Nothing?" She took a step back and rubbed her breastbone with icy fingertips. "Is there no other way?"

"No, I'm afraid not." Aramis sighed, shaking his head. "There was a time when all souls lived freely, but Aalok has perverted the natural order. Those I have sent away would rather choose exile than live under divine law. I have personally visited the Earth many times, asking them to come home, but they do not wish to return. It has gotten further out of hand than I could have ever foreseen. I have a plan of salvation for all, but each must choose...just as I must. I have chosen you, Sophie, because of your loyalty. You will be one of many to guide those who have fallen away, back toward the truth."

"I don't understand. What do you mean a new life, a new aeon?"

"Let me show you."

Aramis stepped back from Sophie, held out his arms and clapped his hands. Sophie startled at the sound, which echoed through the throne room like rolling thunder. It was a sound she had never experienced before, she could only compare it to the bellow of the great lizards in the forest on Earth.

The sound trailed off and the room darkened like a moonless night. There had always been light on Earth from the moon and sun; there had always been the light of Aramis in the Infinite Realm. Sophie had never experienced anything like this darkness before and froze in fear.

Aramis' voice resounded as he spoke a prophecy. It was not only a foretelling for the first aeon, but for the next to come.

"There are those that rebel against the light of truth. They have lost their way, stumbling in the bleak night as they sleepwalk, but it is time to awaken them from their slumber, for redemption is near. The night is spent and the day is at hand. Cast off the works of darkness and don the armor of light. My words flow at their feet like a river. If they drink of it, they shall never die, for I am the truth and I am the giver of all life. Those who believe upon me shall live everlasting. Those who choose the narrow path shall find eternity."

Aramis slowly lit the darkness, sending his aura of peace to Sophie. She drank it in and lit as the love of her king spread through her being like the water he spoke of. It trickled through her like a warm river, lifted her head with hope in the promise he had foretold.

There was only the light of their auras casting a golden silhouette against the glossy walls of the throne room. They were two dancing flames in the dark of midnight, two beacons of hope, giving light to the black of night.

"You, Sophie, are of the light. In this new life, you must keep your spark. You must shine so that others may see during the darkest and most perilous of times."

Putting an arm around Sophie, he led her to the doors. "Soon my child, you will be sent on an extraordinary assignment. You may not understand all that is to happen, but I know you have the faith to believe. I trust you will always search for the truth, that you will always search for me."

Sophie hugged Aramis tight. He hugged her back and said.

"This is not goodbye, this is-"

Sophie flinched at a thud that sounded from behind the throne room doors.

Aramis narrowed his gaze at the wall. Looking past it, he could see the Seraphim in the Council Room, hear them arguing. They fanned their wings at one another, flinging their arms as they shouted.

Just as he had foreseen, the Confusion had made it to the Infinite Realm.

"You must go quickly!" Aramis said, urging Sophie to the door. "There is not much time left."

Sophie hugged Aramis one last time before she slipped through the door.

Aramis watched her down the steps before he turned to his desk. There were still more to write, still more souls works to be record.

Taking his quill again, the king continued the encrypted numeric text in his book. He paused every now and then as visions came; visions foretelling of every soul's decision, every possible outcome of the future because of their choice.

When a door on the floor below her slammed, Sophie hurried down the stairs, doing her best not to make a sound. Making it to the foyer, she started for the exit until she heard the clatter of armor and heavy stomps behind her.

Ducking behind a pillar, she held her breath and peeked around it to see two Seraphim coming her way. Their blue cloaks covered their wings, but as they passed by she could see the tips of raven feathers beneath the fabric.

"He will not be pleased," one of the Seraphim grumbled.

"It doesn't matter," the other pointed out. "We're growing in number. Aramis won't know what hit him."

Waves of hate and pride pulsed off the pair. It prickled Sophie's neck with a warning, burning the tips of her ears. She clenched her fists and watched as they stomped out the door and out of sight.

With the hallway clear, she ran toward the exit but turned as the foyer fell cold. She gazed through the glass floors toward Aramis' throne room, watching as the light beneath the doors faded and then dimmed out completely.

PRIDE

AS Sophie ran to the inner courtyard, soldiers circled around two warriors in the training yard on the other side of the castle. Alexander, ready to compete in a contest, gripped his sword and stood face to face with his opponent, Caius. The soldiers shouted with excitement as Caius banged his battle-ax against his shield. The golden dome, decorated with the etching of Aramis' emblem, was left unscathed by the pounding. It was engraved with wings, arching above a crown over the letter 'A'. This was a symbol of the noble, of the faithful and true, but not all who wore the symbol believed in what it stood for.

By a pillar behind the two warriors, stood Michael. He crossed his arms, observing his men, while his aura emanated brightly from his brown, shoulder-length hair. He drew a deep breath and closed his eyes in concentration. The air was thick with emotion, a haze of anticipation, but also a hint of envy. Michael's forehead wrinkled, finding the disturbance. If he could pinpoint it, he would know which of them was affected by the Confusion. He tested the auras of the crowd before opening his eyes again, focusing on the one and only soul full of pride.

Beating against their shields, the crowd of men chanted loudly for their champions. Caius raised his ax and it burst into flames. The crowd roared louder, ready for the contest to begin. Alexander glanced over his shoulder at their audience and ran his finger along his blade. It lit up at his touch with golden fire, sizzling and crackling. The life forces of the warriors spread into the weapons with a steady hum, charging the electrified swords, giving the weapon the means to stun their opponent.

Alexander tightened his grip on his sword, knowing the sting of the electrical blade. He would need all his energy to take Caius on. He had never won a contest against him, but he would still try.

Michael watched as the chanting spread, filling the yard with the clamor of boisterous warriors as the two stood, waiting for the other to make the first move.

"Why does this match hold your interest so intently, my brother?" Gabriel asked, coming up behind Michael. He folded his silver, blue-tipped wings and set his gaze to the circling warriors.

"I came to observe the first Guardian, but now I have concerns about Caius. Does he seem different to you?" Michael asked.

Caius lunged forward, his ax raised high, but Alexander countered his move, slashing his flaming blade across Caius's breastplate. Sparks flew as their weapons buzzed and clanged, grinding against one other.

"There is no change in his confidence, if that is what you mean," Gabriel laughed, tipping his head up toward Caius.

Blazing steel against steel, the two warriors danced in a circle. Caius shoved Alexander back and lifted his ax again. An uppercut knocked Alexander a few steps back and he wiped the clear fluid dripping from his chin from the gash. His wound healed as he took a step forward and swung his sword, but Caius spun, slicing Alexander's wrist wide open. It bled, but like his chin, it healed immediately.

Caius lifted his boot and kicked Alexander back, sending Alexander's golden shield flying through the air only to land with a thud in the dust. Caius thrust an elbow into Alexander's nose. Alexander stumbled back and his grip faltered on his sword, leaving it out of reach.

Caius tossed his ax behind him without care. The flames diminished as it went soaring and cleaved into the dirt with a cloud of dust.

Alexander, unarmed but undeterred, approached Caius in a bold move, and the two circled again, dust swirling around their feet as they wrestled.

"True enough, Caius is a great warrior," Michael smiled, "Yet, Aramis favors Alexander."

Caius elbowed Alexander in the gut, ready to finish the fight.

Alexander staggered back a step, noting his gasping for breaths. He calmed himself and rushed forward again at the roar of the crowd.

"You don't sense his anger?" Michael asked.

"Caius takes these contests quite serious," Gabriel shrugged.

"Perhaps, but I sense there is more there than merely his determination of winning."

"Pride?"

"Among other things. I also sense envy and greed. His jealousy is unnerving."

"The darkness." Gabriel sighed. "Yes, I sense it too. I sense it from many of them."

"They all struggle with the corruption."

"Not Alexander. I looked at his book. Not one single trespass has been committed by him." Gabriel pointed out. "I assume that is why Aramis asked him to protect her."

Michael tilted his head with a smile as Alexander gained the upper hand, jumping into the air, bringing down a blow to Caius's back.

When Caius bowed back and then stumbled, Alexander shoved him into the crowd. They, in turn, shoved him to the center of the ring, no matter how he scowled.

He glanced at the crowd as they cheered for Alexander, and then narrowed his gaze at his opponent. He lifted his black-gloved fingers in the air and made a fist, bringing forth a bright white flame to his knuckles.

Alexander didn't light his glove; instead, he advanced and swung at Caius' face, but missed.

Caius' glove met his ribs with a jolt of electricity and Alexander groaned. With clenched teeth, he took another blow, but spun around and swung.

Caius' jaw let out a crack and he went tumbling to the ground. He wiped the fluid leaking from his nose and tried to stand, but couldn't.

The crowd roared with excitement. A warrior had fallen. The bout was over.

Alexander bowed slightly with a nod, the way all showed respect to the fallen opponent when the contest was over.

Caius did not mirror the exchange of respect when he stood; instead, he spat the fluid dripping into his mouth.

Michael took the list from his pocket and checked off Alexander's name. It was not for winning, but for the grace, he showed in his victory. He then made a note by Caius' name and frowned as Gabriel extended his hand.

"I'll see you at the knighting ceremony," Gabriel said, pressing Michael's forearm to his own, bidding farewell.

Michael nodded but kept his eyes on the warriors, wondering if his intuition was right. It didn't matter. If Caius's heart had changed, Aramis already knew.

As a Seraph, Michael didn't have to deal with emotions like the lower angels. He was unfazed and unaffected by the auras because Aramis made him different. He had free will but the emotions of others did not sway him, not the way he felt them sway Alexander. Still, he frowned, watching the warrior, knowing that his opponent, his friend had turned.

The corners of Alexander's eyes crinkled as the waves of anger pulsed off Caius. Regardless, Alexander extended his hand.

"Don't," Caius growled, smacking it away.

Alexander took a step back as Caius brushed the dust from his armor, but after a moment, again, offered his hand in congratulations, ignoring the pinpricks of uneasiness on his neck.

Caius took a long look at it, before glancing over his shoulder at the men then back at Alexander. Grudgingly, he took his comrade's forearm in his. His ego had been bruised more than his cheek that had already healed.

"Excellent contest, my brother." Alexander smiled.

"A painter turned soldier." Caius snickered. "It's a bit surprising, I must say. Have you been training with Michael behind my back?"

"No, of course not. Michael is far too busy to give private lessons." Alexander laughed, flipping his sword over the back of his hand. He sheathed it then raised his brows. "I've been practicing on my own."

The crowd roared for Alexander, and rushed the champion, separating the two warriors. They patted him on the back, crowing their congratulations as Caius gritted his teeth.

After the soldiers had their chance to praise Alexander, they gathered their weapons and made a line toward the banquet hall.

Alexander didn't join them. Instead, he glanced over his shoulder to see Caius walking away, sulking. He hurried to him, putting a hand on his Caius' shoulder, but his smile quickly faded. He was suddenly unnerved by the emotion of jealousy coursing in the air around Caius. "Aren't you going to join us?"

"Go enjoy your praise, Alexander. Your audience awaits."

Alexander opened his mouth to tell Caius he should be mindful of the negative emotions, but a messenger of Aramis caught his attention as she approached.

Her golden headband adorned in jewels glinted in the sunless light. The ivory river of her dress rippled with each step and her wavy blonde hair billowed in the breeze as she handed Alexander a scroll with a respectful bow.

"The king requires your presence." She announced. She then tensed as her eyes shifted to Caius who gave her a once over.

"Of course," Alexander replied. "A moment please?"

The messenger nodded and stepped to the side.

A muscle in Caius' jaw feathered as his aura filled with envy; not only could he feel the messenger's attraction to Alexander's gentle aura, he could feel her distaste for him.

"I'll catch up with you later," Caius nodded, aiming for nonchalance.

"Save some wine." Alexander flashed a smile, but his eyes were still wary. He turned away from Caius and followed the messenger out of the Coliseum to the alabaster path, toward the Crystal Castle.

Caius kept his distance from his fellow soldiers as they made their way to the banquet hall. He muttered to himself, mentally replaying the contest. He liked winning more than anything. He was the best of Aramis' army and hoped to someday become a General.

With only a few steps from the banquet hall, Caius paused as a bright light blinded him, halting his steps. He cupped his brow, squinting past the kingdom gates. He looked past the green pastures, to the rocky edge of the floating kingdom. There, he found a burning flame with great wings spread wide. Lying down his shield and ax, Caius walked through the Golden Gate into the meadow.

Mile after mile, he walked through the grasslands until he reached the edge of the floating kingdom. He squinted, peering up at the being that shone as bright as the sun.

Wings as black as midnight rose high above the figures head. He slid his hood to rest on his ash-white hair and pointed his chin upward. A cunning smile spread, revealing his gleaming white teeth as he said,

"Hello, Caius."

5

SERUS

THE shining aura of the castle grounds dimmed noticeably as Sophie left the inner courtyard. Sweeping her braid to the side, she passed the bewildered faces and quickened her pace as her peers whispered to one another. She couldn't bear the weight of their emotions as they seeped into her by an unseen force.

Pressing her back against a statue of Aramis, she closed her eyes and struggled to take a deep breath. She clutched the gift from her king and she prayed for the dark emotions to stop. She quickly winced at the pain in her palm from the gold-embellished casing. She hadn't realized she was holding it so tight until she saw the imprint creasing her soft skin.

The pain soon faded as the healing crystal hummed and Sophie noticed a sudden calm wash over her. The crystal. It had harmonized its frequency with hers, balancing her whole being.

Free of the confusion, Sophie lifted her head and glanced around the courtyard. Every eye in the crowd was set in the sky as the castle darkened. When Aramis dimmed, the children dimmed with him.

Sophie wanted to take a step toward them, to reach out a hand to touch someone's shoulder, but she quickly remembered Aramis' orders. She was not to counsel any longer. She was given a new assignment and she must obey. Drawing back her hand, she placed it over her pounding heart and stepped away from the crowd.

"I'm sorry," she whispered, but it was much too softly for them to hear.

Exiting the outer courtyard gate, Sophie pressed her back against it, trying to regain her composure. She squeezed her eyes shut, lifting her head to the sky, while a warm liquid trickled down her cheek. She wiped it away quickly, studying the wet droplet and remembered Aramis had been shedding the same liquid.

As if she could run away from all that consumed her, Sophie pushed away from the gate and collided with someone, knocking her off her feet. She glanced up and exhaled in relief at the sight of the familiar face. She had run into another angel, but not just any angel; Sophie knew him all too well.

His white attire, although wrinkled, matched Sophie's. It was that of a Truth Keeper. Aramis' golden emblem was emblazoned on his chest, embroidered with the number eight, the number of his circle. His shiny onyx hair was unkempt, falling into his stone gray eyes, but Sophie could never mistake the smirk, no matter if it had been weeks since she had seen him.

"Milady," Serus offered his hand.

Sophie swallowed at his touch, but gripped it, allowing him to bring her inches from his face.

"Are you all right?"

Sophie pulled her hand away and smoothed a hand over her braid. "Yes, yes, I'm fine." She faked a smile, but her aura faded slightly, showing her lie. Sophie despised lying, and this was the first time she was aware she had done so. She was afraid, however, if she didn't keep up a pleasant facade, Serus would inquire further about her countenance.

An awkward silence formed between them. All Sophie could do was fidget with her fingers, wondering what to say. She wanted to share with Serus everything she had been told, but she knew Aramis had confided in her.

Has Serus also been debriefed? Has he been chosen too?

"Serus-"

Voices filled the air as a crowd of Sophie's peers came pouring through the gate. Many of them paused to greet her, but she found it difficult to focus on them.

Serus was staring at her. He always stared at her.

As her peers parted one by one, Sophie took notice of something she hadn't seen before. Serus' attire was still that of a Truth Keeper but his vibrant white apparel had lost its sheen. The gold cummerbund of his suit had faded like brass, his shirt and collar were smudged with something black. Sophie assumed it was ink, perhaps dirt, but found it strange. All counselors kept their apparel in the most impeccable condition.

With the group of peers parting, she flashed a bemused expression and wet her lips before she spoke. "Did you get my letters?"

"I haven't been home," Serus answered with a shrug. He averted his gaze, sliding his hands in his pockets.

"I'm sorry, I must sound so selfish. You must have been counseling. There are so many confused. I'm sure they appreciate your time and effort."

Serus pulled back his sleeve to check his wristband. "I need to get going."

"Have you changed your mind about our bonding? Is that why you've been avoiding me? I know we haven't spoken of what happened, but..."

"You know I want nothing more than to be bonded with you."

"Then what is it? Please, tell me." Sophie took a step forward, her eyes begging for the truth. As a Truth Keeper, she had the gift of discernment. All she had to do was look deeply into the eyes of one's soul to find her answer, and she was indeed searching Serus' for his.

"I was suspended."

"Suspended?" Sophie stammered. "Probation, maybe, but-"

"You were not informed of this decision?" Serus asked, raising a brow.

Sophie stared at him for a long moment before shifting her gaze to the ground. "No, I thought-"

"Something is troubling you." Serus caressed her face, sweeping the hair from her forehead. "Your glow was dim before you even heard of my suspension."

He brushed his thumb along her cheek, but she didn't meet his gaze.

"You're not going to tell me?"

"I don't know if I'm at liberty. What is your position, as of now?

"Keeping secrets?" Serus teased, flashing a sly grin. "How very unlike you, Sophie."

Sophie opened her mouth to speak, but Serus' wristband vibrated, sounding a chime.

"I'm late. Meet me tonight, by the fountain." Serus kissed Sophie's hand lightly before turning on his heels, heading toward the castle.

It was all too quick a parting for Sophie. She stared at Serus as he walked away, but winced at the burning on the back of her hand. She rubbed her knuckles and peered down at them with furrowed brows as a smudge of ashy soot appeared. Unsure of what it meant, Sophie glanced over her shoulder and watched Serus fade into the distance. When he disappeared from her sight, the lip print did too, along with any evidence of his betrayal.

After the events in the Infinite Realm, Sophie flew her ship back to earth and headed to her favorite place. It was quiet and tranquil with only the sound of the lapping waves. Taking graceful steps on the soft, grainy sand of the shore, Sophie whistled through her fingers, awaiting her friend come to her.

Down the coast, a shining image appeared, galloping in her direction. The horse responded with a gleeful whinny, his white mane waving in the wind. Bevol trotted to her side, huffing playfully in Sophie's face.

"Hey boy, ready for a run?" She asked, smoothing her hands over his silky white coat.

She still saw Bevol as the playful foal she had rescued. He was the reason she visited Earth so frequently. She had found him wandering the dunes when he was only a few weeks old. A storm had rolled in and she'd had no luck in finding Bevol's mother. She led him to a safe place and spent the night taking care of him. Ever since then, she had visited the Earth every sunset to spend time with him.

The horse knelt and Sophie hoisted herself up, patting his behind. He huffed his enjoyment with a mist through his nose before galloping down the beach.

Closing her eyes, Sophie spread her arms out wide, lifting her face toward the sun. Listening to the wind whooshing past, she felt like a bird, soaring through the air. Her heart became light as the heavy burdens of the day melted away with the warmth of the sun. There could still be peace despite the Confusion. There could still be clarity among her uncertainty.

Following a good long run, Bevol trotted into the surf, splashing the temperate sea against Sophie's calves. He pranced like a pony in a parade before Sophie dismounted to wade in the shallows. He dashed the water playfully, and Sophie returned the gesture.

After their water fight, Sophie patted Bevol's shoulder and pointed to the tree line. "Go get a drink."

The horse shook his head.

"Go on," she urged.

Bevol rubbed his long face against her shoulder and then galloped up the dunes into the forest.

Sophie set her gaze on the horizon as she waded further into the surf. She smiled, watching a pod of dolphins. They shot forth from the sea and then dove, one by one across the sun's reflection.

Ready to rest, she leaned back in the salty sea, losing all thoughts to the sound of muffled waves. She glided her arms across the water, basking in the warmth of the sunlight. There was no heartache of auras nearby, no twinge of anxiety gripping her stomach. There was only the feeling of weightlessness and the lukewarm water kissing her skin.

Hours had passed as Sophie drifted in and out of sleep. The rhythm of the ocean was steady until it was drowned out by the sound of approaching hoofbeats. She smiled at first, assuming it was Bevol, but as she tested the aura of the coming body, she froze.

6

GUARDIAN

SOPHIE'S eyes shot open to a shimmering silhouette above her. Springing to her feet, she balled up her fists, ready to defend herself.

"Hey! Whoa!" The hooded figure shouted in alarm.

Sand and salt water stung Sophie's eyes. She squinted at the blurry figure, but she knew by the voice that it was not Aalok.

"I have a message from Aramis." The figure announced.

Still unable to see his face clearly, Sophie looked at the angel's attire. From the bubbling surf, her eyes traveled up his tall black boots to his hand resting on the gold hilt of a sword. He wore a bright blue, buttoned vest, over a white collared shirt, lacing up his chest. It was the symbol on his titanium gauntlet that made her relax her shoulders. He was a warrior, a soldier of the king. Her gaze traveled to his white linen hood and the embroidered gold olive leaves leading up to Aramis' emblem, embossed at the tip.

The warrior slid back his hood, revealing his handsome features. The glow of his amber aura reflected in his eyes. They were as clear and blue as the calm sea at her ankles. She tested the stranger's aura, finding confidence, and that confidence bored into her soul with an unexplainable familiarity.

"My name is Alexander, Captain of Aramis' second-highest legion. I have orders from his majesty to protect you."

"I'm sorry," Sophie said blinking from her daze. "You startled me and I assumed-wait, did you say protect me?"

"Yes. I'm your Guardian."

"Guardian?" Sophie whispered, rubbing her forehead. She had known of soldiers standing watch over the counseling rooms in the castle, but it never occurred to her that Aramis would require them to be personal guards.

A folded parchment stamped with a gold waxy signet was offered. Sophie took it and stared at it for a long moment before peeling back the seal. She read the scroll once; then twice, hoping the letter would give some explanation of her protection. But it didn't.

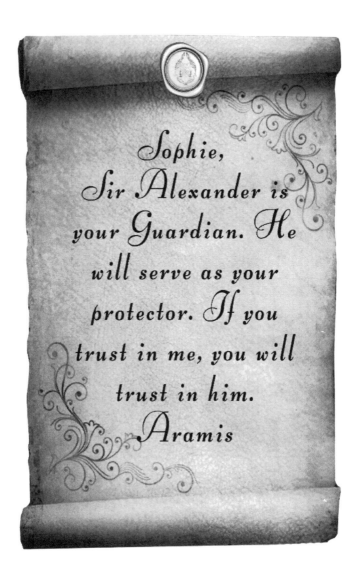

Sophie,
Sir Alexander is your Guardian. He will serve as your protector. If you trust in me, you will trust in him.
Aramis

Alexander folded his arms, shifting his weight from side to side. The Truth Keeper's forehead wrinkled, and he wondered why she felt the need to read it so many times. It was a simple note.

Pulling back his sleeve, he tapped on the holographic screen from the gold wristband on his forearm and checked his notifications, until the Truth Keeper spoke.

"Why do I need protection?"

"I think Aramis made it clear, did he not?"

Sophie parted her lips to argue his needed presence but lifted her head toward the chime of a bell. She peered over her Guardian's shoulder at his horse. It stomped a hoof, kicking up sand as if to chasten his rider. When the silver bell around the gelding's neck chimed again, the Guardian raised a hand for his horse to still.

The chestnut steed shook its black mane, huffing through his nose as if to object, but he obeyed his rider.

Alexander agreed with his horse, Cavalo. It was indeed time to get back to the Infinite Realm and that urgency of return tingled at the alert of his wristband. He narrowed his eyes and deciphered the numeric code before the message disappeared. 'Return Alone'. Aramis had made it clear that Sophie must stay on Earth.

How could she be protected in my absence? The enemy is only miles away.

It didn't make sense to Alexander, but he wouldn't disobey orders. He turned back to Sophie, parting his lips to bid farewell, but her eyes were closed, and her head bowed.

Sophie concentrated on Aramis, rubbing her hand firmly across her chest. She tried to ease the ache inside but it was useless. The sound had reminded her of the chime of the handbells during prayer service. She could again smell the sweet incense she had once carried through the temple. That had been her job as High Priestess. She was then assigned to teach, to remind souls of the words of Aramis, and to give counsel privately.

As Sophie's nimble fingers grazed the chain of her pendant, it sparkled in Alexander's eyes. He narrowed his gaze at the sight of the precious jewel and without a second thought; he took a step forward, taking the amulet in his fingertips.

"A gift from Aramis?" he asked, rubbing his thumb over the crystal. He glared at the black speck inside.

Negative energy...Confusion.

The Truth Keeper managed a slight nod as he slid it from his fingertips.

"Best to keep that put away," he warned, drawing a pair of white gloves from his belt. "There is an Outcast camp not far from here, filled with souls who don't admire Aramis, nor his gifts. It would be wise to not draw attention to yourself."

Alexander glared at her defiance as she clutched her necklace. He then stretched his fingers through the tight leather of his gloves, flexing his fingers, flexing his authority. But she didn't budge. Instead, she grasped Aramis' gift tighter, glaring back at him. Alexander bit his tongue and placed his hands on his hips, afraid if he argued over her sentiment, it would only make matters worse.

She doesn't understand. Let her be…at least for now. You can explain everything later.

"I must transport to the Infinite Realm immediately," Alexander informed. "Stay here. I will return in a few hours to keep watch over you. Trust no one. We cannot afford more of Aramis' assets to be swayed by the enemy."

The Truth Keeper didn't respond. She hung her head, shuffling the glittering sand beneath her feet.

"Do you understand, Truth Keeper?"

When she said nothing, Alexander turned without a farewell, drawing his hood over his head.

I don't have time for this. No one has time. Time is running out.

"So, I'm to wait here and do nothing?" the Truth Keeper called out. "I'm talking to you, Guardian!"

Alexander could hear the Truth Keeper stomp through the waves of the rising tide. The moment he sensed her reach for him, he whipped around, snatching up her wrist.

"I am the only one you can trust, Truth Keeper," Alexander warned with irritation, sensing her aura, he flinched at an unsettling prickle that tingled the back of his neck. He didn't like the emotions Sophie was fighting against. They seeped through him, trickling down his spine, aching his chest. He wouldn't let it show. He wouldn't mirror her conflicted expression.

"Trust you?" She asked, jerking her hand away. "I don't even know you."

"We are this close to war, Sophie of the Seventh Circle," Alexander said, holding up his fingers to show an inch between them. "As we speak, the dark forces of Aalok are growing stronger. I have been assigned to protect you, and protect you I will. The *only* way I can do that is if you trust me."

"Has it escalated that far? Are the other counselors all right?"

"Stay here. I'll return soon." Alexander assured as he grasped the horn of the saddle. He went to hoist himself up but froze as the Truth Keeper's hand touched his bare wrist.

"Please," she requested softly. "I must go to them. I must make sure they won't fall into Confusion."

At her touch, Alexander's breath hitched. It was as if a current of electricity was coursing through every fiber of his being. His hard face relaxed as he turned, daring to make sense of what had happened. Wrestling with what to say to the Truth Keeper, he gently pried her trembling fingers from his arm. *This is no soldier, but an innocent in fear of what's to come.*

Sending up a prayer to Aramis, Alexander found comfort that came in a gentle reply of his plea.

"You must hold fast to the truth," Alexander instructed softly. "Be of courage and faith. We can no longer depend on our emotions. They are tainted, fickle—and if you are not careful, they will easily cloud your mind."

Sophie dropped her head in defeat. Her tears from earlier were proof of her Guardian's words. She pressed a hand to her quivering lips, holding back the liquid pooling in her eyes.

She knew her countenance expressed the turmoil churning inside her. She couldn't help but stand dazed for a long moment. She didn't blink. She didn't speak. She was a statue of sorrow. When she finally spoke, it was hardly a whisper as her voice cracked through restrained tears.

"I've failed my brethren...I tried to do well but...it was not enough. And now..."

Sophie covered her face in shame and turned her back on her Guardian.

I shouldn't have run. I should have given my peers counsel. If they have been cast out, it's my fault.

Tears streamed down Sophie's cheeks. She didn't bother to wipe them away this time. She only stared at the creeping waves, unable to appreciate the cool of the water rushing over her feet. She couldn't feel the warmth of the sunshine on her neck, or wind caressing her long, glimmering locks. There was nothing, nothing but pain that came by the images of her peers and...

Serus. He will be waiting for me at the fountain. What will he think when I don't return to him?

"I will take you home when I return," her Guardian said, interrupting her thoughts, "but you cannot go to the Infinite Realm alone. Stay here and wait for me."

Alexander waited for the Truth Keeper to acknowledge his order. When she didn't, he lifted his hand to comfort her but dropped it just as quickly.

Still, there was no shrugging off the tug inside his soul. He had felt when he first saw the Truth Keeper floating in the ocean when he arrived on the beach. Her bright glow had been so beautiful then, but now, her halo dimmed. As it did, the tug grew stronger and Alexander knew that the longer he prolonged his departure, the harder it would be to leave. So he did.

Sophie stood rigid, devoid of any emotion other than grief and regret. Her knees buckled and she fell to the ground weeping. She clawed at the sand, wishing the ache in her chest would ease, but darkness clouded her mind. She was lost in the bleak space filled with doubt.

It was a void, a place filled with nothing but cold and black. Her spirit tumbled into the endless abyss, bound by fear and regret from which there was no escape. But there was still the burning flame in her heart; there was still hope crying out from within. She sent out a prayer to Aramis and that request rose to the sky as she reached for the stars as she fell.

Suspended in the air as if bouncing on an invisible string, Sophie bobbed. Her body bowed back, then stilled. She was weightless, listening to a soothing voice that softly echoed her name.

Blinding light cut through the veil of black and it grew brighter, coming toward her. A hand reached for her and she grasped it. The light drew her up and away from the darkness, away from the void, back to her own mind.

Sophie sucked in a deep breath of a salty breeze, grasping the sand between her fingers. She lifted her head to the sunset, warmed by the rays as they glittered the sand and sea.

Aramis may have been in another realm, another dimension, but his spirit had not abandoned her. It never would. It guided her, lifting her chin as if to remind her to hold her head high. She was a Truth Keeper, she was the daughter of the king.

Sophie set her eyes on the horizon, a canvas of pinks and oranges, like a coral reef of the ocean floor. Fluffy clouds of purple and gray slid across the sky. She watched them for a moment and then became perplexed as a light flashed from them.

Scooting back from the rising tide, she shivered as a cold wind blew through her soaked gown. Resting her chin on her knees, she watched the sun bleed into its rippling reflection. When the sun had melted away, she set her gaze to the stars. They twinkled by the billions in a vast and endless twilight. The harvest moon rose in an unsettling hue of orange. It was something Sophie had never seen before, but she knew the Earth was changing. *Everything* was changing.

The moon's brilliant glow cast a shadow beside her of four tall legs and a shaking mane. Sophie glanced beside her at Bevol. He huffed a warm misty breath on her shoulder before he settled beside her on the sand.

Sophie rested her head on his middle, let her body rise and fall with each steady breath he took, and soon lulled to sleep by the rhythmic sound of the waves. She let sleep take her to the Infinite Realm, to a day long ago. She was again dancing at a festival, singing in tune with her peers to the songs. She paused and walked over to the corner of the artisans. Somehow the dream had changed. Somehow, she found her Guardian sitting at a canvas. In this dream, he wasn't frowning, but smiling as he looked over his shoulder to pause from painting a portrait.

OUTCAST

HIGH-pitched screams jolted Sophie awake. Thunder roared, followed by a crack as a flaming ball of fire exploded into a nearby mountainside. Bevol lurched from the sand with an anxious whinny and galloped into the forest as Sophie watched the sky in awe.

It lit neon red, streaking with smoke and fire. Bits of trees and fiery rocks exploded into the mountains in the distance. Remaining pieces fell and fizzled out into the ocean, making it appear as if the sea was sending up a prayer for the sky to yield.

And then, it was over.

Hearing a distant whinny from Bevol, Sophie bolted through the tree line and into the forest. She followed his hoof beats, batting leaves from her face, weaving through the mossy trunks of pines and oaks. Her footsteps matched the rhythm of her racing heart, her breaths rasped in her chest. There had never been a time that she had felt tired, but somehow now, she was.

She found Bevol in a clearing, wide-eyed, and stamping in warning.

"Shh, it's okay boy," Sophie murmured, trying to soothe him.

Bevol grunted, jerking his head up and down, and backed away.

"I won't let anything hurt you. It's over. There are no more stars falling...listen."

Bevol perked his ears and stood still.

"See? You're safe."

Big brown eyes stared back at Sophie, but her horse didn't budge.

"Bevol, please. We must go back to the shore,"

Bevol huffed, taking a few steps toward her, but at a rustle from the nearby bushes, he flinched. With the flick of his tail, Bevol trotted into the forest, leaving Sophie standing alone.

Sophie glanced down at the bush as it moved again. A chirp came as a birdlike head peeked out. The dainty dinosaur hoped from the bushes to stand on three-toed feet in front of her. Its pointy-head tilted to one side, and it parted its mouth as if to smile, showing off his sharp little teeth.

"No crumbs today, my friend."

The dinosaur chirped a reply before its eyes darted to a blue bug flitting over its head. It let out a screech, clawing at the air, and hoped away, chasing the blue beetle.

Letting out a long sigh, Sophie turned to go back to the shore, assuring herself Bevol would return once he had realized it was safe. She muttered about her dirty feet walking on the trodden path but stopped at a familiar cry that pierced her ears.

Bevol.

Taking off into the dark forest, Sophie ignored the sharp stabs of twigs under her feet, the branches that smacked her face. The cuts healed, but the clear liquid from her wounds dripped down her arms and cheeks like raindrops.

Finally, she found him, but a gasp escaped her lips as she stooped, hiding from the bodies surrounding him.

Her peers laughed as they lassoed Bevol in ropes. They shouted, shoved him. Bevol reared back, letting out another cry, but a loud smack at his muzzle silenced him.

Anger lit Sophie's aura in blue. She wanted to scream, to shout at them to stop, but she couldn't. She knew if she did, those that Alexander had warned her of could find her. She didn't know if these peers were Outcast, but assumed so by their actions. As a Truth Keeper, it was her job to reprimand them gently, but Sophie didn't want to counsel them. She wanted to punish them.

Clenching her teeth, Sophie scolded herself for her thoughts and watched the horrific sight, unable to tear her eyes away from the abuse. She trembled with anger, waiting for them to move, and when they did, she followed.

Tugging Bevol further into the forest, her peers made their way to a wall of rock. It had been made of dull, dirty stone, mortared together with mud. A groan came from the wooden door in the wall as her peers opened it and dragged Bevol inside behind them.

Rushing to the door, Sophie gripped the edge of it with her slim fingers and grunted against its weight to push it back open. She slipped through the crack, then choked on a breath of stale, putrid air that wafted from inside. The scent was like nothing she had ever smelled before. It was a mix of smoke and sulfur, of discarded vinegar wine.

Covering her nose, Sophie watched the angels take Bevol past a roaring bonfire and tents made of cheap, tattered linens. There were several of them scattered around the dead grass of the open field. They were dingy, covered in ash from other small fires spread here and there in the campsite.

Gripping a branch, Sophie's hand grew hot until a burning spread through her palm. Muffling a cry, she jerked her hand away as the bark crumbled at her feet. Perplexed by the searing sensation, she brought her hand in front of her face. She winced at her tender skin, now covered in a light coat of ash.

Wiping her palm on her dress to rub away the pain, Sophie dusted off the ash. She then scolded the smear stain that soiled her gown before glancing around the thicket. It was covered in handprints, her handprints. The branches of the trees had been splintered; the bark nicked and scraped.

An ache swelled in Sophie's chest as she brought her gaze to the campsite again. The tents. The tree's had been broken to support the tattered linens, stacked to make the fires, and sloppily carved into a table and chairs.

Pressing her hand to the trunk of a battered tree, Sophie could feel its pain. She could also see how helpless it had been as her peers hacked at it, snapped its arms and chopped at its body with no regard. All life was sacred on the Earth, the trees, the dirt, and the animals. Someone had violated this place. Someone had trespassed against it.

As Sophie walked through the trees, she could see others cut down. Tears fell down her cheek as she placed a hand on a stump. Her palm burned against the circles of growth, cut short by a dull ax. The film of dust on her dress, the gray soot; it was the evidence of the trespass, and it was everywhere.

Flicking her gaze back to the clearing, Sophie found the dancing flames. Shadows danced around them, mirroring her peers. Their clothing was much like what was worn in the Infinite Realm, but the robes, the uniforms of titles they had once held were filthy. These peers were no longer nobles. They were Outcasts.

Are they the ones that left on their own free will?

She took a step closer, studying their soiled and frayed garments; the black smudges on their hands and faces. They laughed and skipped around one another. Sophie frowned at their merriment, for she knew it was not true joy. There was no aura of warmth, no light emanating off their bodies. She could feel nothing, nothing but a dank wind that swept through the campsite.

While the embers from the logs flitted into the air, Sophie wondered if they were keeping warm by the fire because their hearts were cold.

Can they no longer feel the warmth from Aramis' spirit?

Sympathy filled Sophie's heart. She bit her lip, fighting the urge to counsel them. Aramis had given her a new assignment. She was not to counsel, not anymore. She watched the Outcasts as they cheered, toasting their brassy goblets at the end of a song played by a group of musicians. Her eyes traveled over their heads, spotting bandits as they dragged Bevol up a craggy path. She couldn't abandon him. She couldn't bear to leave him in the hands of his abusers. She weaved her way through the dying thicket, ready to catch up with them until her Guardian's brooding face entered her mind.

He could be waiting for her, ready to take her back to the Infinite Realm. Aramis had instructed her to listen to him, to trust him. She knew there was no other choice. She had to return to the shore. If she didn't, there would be severe consequences, not for her, but for her lost and confused peers in the next life Aramis had spoken of.

Dizziness swept over Sophie's skull as a puff of smoke blew into her face. She gasped and swallowed her ashy saliva. With a throbbing head, she leaned against the dying trees, letting her hand burn as she fought the urge to gag. She had to get out of there; she had to go back to the beach.

But Bevol...

She couldn't choose her faithful pet over the souls she could save.

Can I?

Sophie looked at the crowd again. She was confident she was strong enough. She could do it. She could counsel them. She could save them now, convince them to return with her, to repent of their trespasses. She could save them and Bevol.

A sharp trill sent a shock wave up Sophie's spine before she could take a step. She covered her ears and cringed, clenching her teeth. A cello and a hand drum joined in and the shriek of strings ceased. Sophie let her hands fall to her sides, peeking through the flickering flames to the players. She focused on a defined chin, flush against an ebony violin. Her mouth gaped and her eyes widened, darting from his chin to supple lips as they drew up into a charming smile.

Serus slid the bow across his violin with smooth strokes. He closed his eyes, enraptured by music. Sophie straightened and as if in a daze. She walked toward the fire memorized by the posture and form in which Serus played. The band behind him quickened with an upbeat tempo. The drum matched the pace of her pounding heart. Serus tapped his foot, sliding his bow back and forth as if possessed by the lively tune.

Beside him, a female with slick, black hair sped up the pace further. Faster and faster she and Serus played. It was a game, a competition of skill. The female broke first and Serus' strings sang in a breathless solo.

Sophie watched in amazement as his fingers jumped from wire to wire with dexterity. She knew Serus was skilled with many instruments, but she had never seen him play like this.

When he sent another shrill chord screeching into the air, she cringed, covering her ears. It was like the scream of the falling stars, a warning of danger, a warning to run. She couldn't bear the anxiety that spiked with each shriek of the strings. It all too much, too intense, too brutal, and it sent a scorching pain through her nerve endings.

As Serus' fingers slid down the strings, Sophie focused on his eyes, letting her hands rest at her side. She had never seen him play with such passion, strum patterns filled with so much pain. The moment he closed his eyes tight and grimaced, an impulse to ease his grief shot through her. She gripped her gown in her fists and lifted a soiled foot. She was ready to comfort him, ready to counsel the Outcasts, but as her toes touched the ashy ground, the stern voice of her Guardian echoed through her mind.

Trust no one.

MEMORIES

SERUS finished the melody with a flourish and nodded to his fellow musicians. He sat his violin on the ground, then took up his empty goblet, and proceeded to fill it to the brim. He took a long sip ready drown out his sorrow, to numb his pain.

Holding up the cup, he twisted the stem with his fingers. He studied his reflection, now a stranger in the brass. The distorted image of a traitor glared back at him, replacing his frown with a smug smile.

Ignoring his guilt, Serus corked the wine and lifted his cup to his lips again. He paused in mid-sip and narrowed his gaze as a halo peeked over the rim. He squinted to make sure he was truly seeing what was there. He wondered if he was imagining her, or if he was haunted by the choices he had made.

Has her spirit come to chastise me?

Rising cautiously as if a sudden movement would frighten the apparition away, Serus stared at the glowing angel. But before he could take a step toward her, an ashen Outcast gripped her with a soot-stained hand.

"Hey!"

Sophie froze at the hand squeezing her wrist.

"What are you doing hiding back here? Join the party!" The drunken Outcast slurred.

As he tugged Sophie closer to the raging fire, she studied his face. Although none of Aramis' children could grow old, this angel seemed to have aged. He was haggard, with bags under his empty eyes. His garments were stained, his hair greasy and unkempt. Black smudges streaked his forehead and neck.

Holding her breath against his odor, Sophie tried to wrench herself free from his firm grasp.

"Come on! You can't have fun over there." He insisted, dragging her towards the group.

"I'm not-" Sophie stammered.

"More wine! Hail Aalok! Another has joined our cause!" The Outcast announced before staggering off into a group of people. He raised his goblet in an enthusiastic toast, spilling the contents on himself and also on those gathered by him.

Rubbing her tender arm, Sophie peered up at Serus. He was staring back at her from the other side of the flames. They lit his face in the shadows, accentuating his strong jaw and dimpled cheeks. But there was no light emanating from him.

Serus was as dim and as colorless as everything else beyond the wall.

Sophie glanced at the ashen Outcast that had grabbed her as they spat their laughter. She watched some grope one another. Others stumble over themselves, dancing with no care of their steps. They were drunk on strong wine, overflowing their cups as they poured more drinks.

They were trespassing; breaking the Law of Aramis, a law Sophie had never broken, until now. She had disobeyed her king by coming here, by standing among the Outcast. These peers had been tainted by the Confusion and she was in danger of being contaminated by the disease.

Sophie turned away in shame, but as her curiosity stirred, she couldn't help but gape at those partaking in wine. She wondered what it would be like to join them, to laugh and sing—to forget everything she knew—to forget the past. In her thoughts, something spoke to her, something dark, something vile. It told her to let go, to join in the festivities.

"Free will to choose," it murmured, tickling her earlobe.

As the notion of joining their celebration plagued her mind, Sophie's arm burned from the ashy handprint of the drunken Outcast. It was a mark of burning desire, an imprint of a choice. This place had tainted her and she could not go back to Aramis unclean. She pressed her lips against her teeth hard in remorse. She was not an Outcast, she was a Truth

Keeper, and if she did as they were now, she too would be in danger of exile.

The music filled the air as the Outcast with long black hair played her violin. She gave Sophie a sultry smile as if hinting she knew something Sophie didn't.

Sophie listened to the melody, entranced by the song. It was like a siren's call, a smooth and soothing lullaby. The whisper spoke again and Sophie closed her eyes. She was ready to take another step toward the crowd, ready to forget the pain of her past.

"Hello, gorgeous."

Sophie flinched at a hand on her waist but turned to find Serus' smiling. Sorrow melted away, replaced with relief as she exhaled at his touch. They held their gaze, not a word uttered for a long moment.

Serus fixed his gaze on Sophie's lips, ready to satisfy his desire to kiss her. He drank in her goodness, savoring it like a fine wine. He was home. He was at peace, and there was no need to return to the Infinite Realm...she was here and *she* was his heaven.

He leaned in, parting his lips to kiss her until a glint from her chest caught his eyes. He glared at her necklace and then looked at his peers. He couldn't let them see it; they couldn't know she wasn't one of them. He caressed Sophie's neck; trailing fingers down her throat, slow, calculated. Kissing

Sophie's cheek to distract her, he wrapped his fingers around the chain and tugged.

Sophie let out a small cry as the chain of her necklace snapped like the string of a harp. "Serus!"

Serus pressed her to him to, a warning finger to his lips as the chain dangled from his fist.

She shifted her gaze, following his to the intoxicated Outcasts. They were laughing, dancing to the music as dusty ash clouds swirled around their feet. She looked at their hands, finding them as black as the burning logs of the campfire. She glanced at their lips. They too were black, tainted from speaking out against her king. It wasn't ash or residue from the cinders that covered them, but something dark from within, revealing their trespasses. She brought her gaze back to Serus' warning finger at his lips. He too was covered in the soot.

Serus lifted his chin to an Outcast as if to say, 'yes, she has joined us. Now go about your way.'

The Outcast nodded and lifted his goblet with a salute.

Serus' eyes darted around the camp as he led Sophie away from the party. He was grateful his peers were too focused on their merriment to notice the subtle white hue of the glowing stranger.

All of them were, save Nehia, the dark-haired violin player, slitting her eyes.

Serus quickened his pace and lifted the flap of his tent. He glanced over his shoulder at Nehia, warning her with a scowl to stay away as he urged Sophie inside.

Entering the tent, Sophie noted the lit candles, a table with two chairs, food, and wine. There was a bed in the corner, made of straw, covered with a red velvet blanket. This was how the Outcast lived. This is what they had chosen.

"Serus, why did you-"

"If they see this, they will know you are not one of us." He answered, inspecting the necklace in his hand. "The others...they no longer keep the gifts from Aramis. They throw them in the fire and watch them burn. They want no reminder of who they once were." He glanced up with soft eyes and took a step closer. "I do apologize," he murmured, sweeping her hair to one side. He swallowed; grazing his fingers over the red scratch left by the chain, but relaxed as it healed before his eyes. She wasn't affected like he was. She could still heal on her own.

Regardless of her ability to heal, Serus still felt remorseful for any pain he may have inflicted. He leaned toward Sophie's neck and brushed the spot gently with his lips, savoring the coconut scent of her soft skin.

Sophie closed her eyes and trembled, losing herself in his touch. For a moment, she had forgotten where she was, until the scent of smoke from Serus' garments filled her nose.

"Serus?"

"Yes, my love?" Serus breathed, trailing kisses down her collarbone.

"Are you here to counsel the Outcasts?"

"Of course not."

Sophie pressed her hands to Serus' chest, pushing him back. "Then why are you here?"

"Isn't it obvious?"

"No. You can't be-"

"Banished?" Serus asked with narrowed eyes. He left her side and went to a table. He poured a drink from a decanter and took a sip. "Aramis locked me out and threw away the key."

He smirked, holding back a frown as he met Sophie's glossy eyes. It pained him to see her so disappointed, to see him like this. He called forth a mask to cover his true emotions. He couldn't let Sophie see the war in his heart, see his weakness. Confidence was power, according to Aalok. Cool restraint was attractive. Aalok had instructed him, mentored him on how to be suave, persuasive in the past few weeks. He had been taught not to be his thoughtful self. At least, not if he was going to convince Sophie to be with him.

He poured another glass and offered it to her. "Here, for what ails you."

Sophie shook her head. As thirsty as she was, she would not partake in wine. This was not the occasion to do so. There was no celebrating his fall, or the fact he was separated from her. Because of his choice, they would be parted. She was thousands of years old now, and she knew it could be thousands more before she and Serus might be together again. There was no telling how long this next life would be. For now, there was still time, for now, they had this moment.

"It isn't too late," Sophie mumbled, "you don't have to stay here. After your sentence, you can return."

Serus let out a laugh. "After my sentence." He then pursed his lips, glaring at Sophie as if she was mocking him. She hadn't come to be with him. She had come to convince him to repent. "You know more than anyone how long a soul is exiled for treason."

"Aramis will make an exception. I'm sure of it."

"You know what you're doing, don't you?" Serus asked, hiding his disappointment with a wry grin. "Fraternizing with the enemy," He tsked. "What will your king think?"

"Is that what you are now? My enemy?"

"You tell me."

Sophie took a step closer, cupping his face. She looked deep into his eyes, past the mask of pride, past the facade of collected calm. She held his stare until he broke, unveiling the pain and regret inside of his heart. "Tell me the truth,"

"The truth..." Serus glared, willing the mask of cool to return, "is that your king quickly dismisses those he claims to love. But *you,* Princess, you are utter perfection...and it appears those such as myself are unworthy to be in your presence."

"How can you say that?

"Does the truth hurt, Truth Keeper?"

"This isn't you."

"Perhaps you don't know me as well as you thought you did."

"And this is who you are? The epitome of envy...of pride?" Sophie bit her lip and shook her head, staring at Serus for a long time. Darkness had now filled his eyes as he held a smug look, never breaking his hateful stare.

"I shouldn't be here." Sophie murmured, turning to leave the tent.

"Wait!"

"There's nothing more I have to say to you." Sophie struggled to free her arm from Serus' grasp. " Let me go!"

"Don't go out that way!"

"And why not?" Sophie winced as Serus' aura of regret sent needles through her skin. She had to get away from him. She had to get away from his arrogance, from his aura of mixed emotions. They slithered up her spine like a prickly snake and coiled around her throat. She couldn't breathe, couldn't think in this place.

"They would be curious of why you left. They assume you have come to be with me." Behind Serus' haughty facade was the wave of fear he wouldn't show. If Sophie left him now, the

Outcasts would know she didn't come to join them. They would bind her, torture her for information, and after, take her to Aalok. He couldn't bear the thought of seeing the lesions on her delicate skin. "They assume we've just bonded."

Heat rose to Sophie's cheeks as her gaze darted to the red velvet on the pad of straw. She yanked from his grasp, ready to escape the flames of embarrassment licking her cheeks.

"We haven't been bonded," she said taking hold of the flap, "and now, we never will."

"Don't be stupid."

Sophie whipped around. "*I'm* stupid?"

"That's not what I meant."

"But that's what you think." She got in his face, her aura flaming in blue. "You think I'm foolish to follow Aramis."

"Sophie-"

"Don't bother trying to lie. Your spirit tells me *exactly* how you feel."

Sophie flung the flap to the side but paused at the sight of the dark-haired violinist. The woman swayed to her serenade behind the dancing flames. As her eyes closed, she angled her elbow to the sky, pressing a waving finger into the strings to make it cry.

Sophie dropped her shoulders. Her breaths were shallow, her heart racing as she remembered how she and Serus had once swayed to that very melody.

"Don't you remember what it was like before?" He asked.

Sophie's breath hitched in her throat.

How could I forget?

As Serus wrapped an arm around her waist, she didn't fight him. Consumed by the emotions of their happy past, she let him sway her left to right. Soon she was in the past, reliving a painful memory, one she had buried deep down during the time of their separation.

Sophie stood in an ivory, chiffon gown in the ballroom, socializing with several fellow counselors. They were discussing Aalok's demotion, as well as the growing number of their peers in need of counsel. Although Sophie was uncomfortable with the topic, she smiled and nodded politely. Her eyes then surveyed the ballroom, but she didn't see the one who she had been waiting for.

She sipped her wine, shifting her gaze to each soldier posted at the exits. She frowned, disappointed that they were even needed. She watched them scan the room, watching them eye every movement of every soul attending. Anyone among them could be a spy; any one of them could have secretly turned.

Sophie excused herself and made her way toward the garden to get some fresh air. Halfway across the room, she paused. A sensation tingled through every fiber of her being. It warmed her, filling her chest before it spread through her body. Her aura illuminated with hope, sensing Serus nearby. The vibration was profound, growing stronger as her eyes darted through the sea of people, searching for him.

Serus fixed his stormy gray eyes upon Sophie, tossing back another gulp of wine. Casually he clasped his hands behind his back and followed her around the ballroom at a distance. He stood behind the crowd, drinking in her aura before he reached out and took her hand.

At their touch, the two of them glowed, brightening the room of candlelight. Serus took her by the waist and swept her to the middle of the dance floor. He bowed as Sophie curtsied, and they joined the other couples as a song of King's Waltz began.

"Happy to see me?" Serus teased.

"Always," Sophie admitted, following Serus' precise steps.

They glided across the dance floor, their gaze never breaking. They swept left to right, twirling, glowing the brightest of all the dancers.

The song ended, and the crowd clapped.

Serus hesitated before releasing Sophie's waist, pressing her against him.

"I miss that gorgeous smile," He whispered in her ear. He kissed Sophie's cheek and then stepped back to bow.

As Sophie curtsied, he glanced over her shoulder and clenched his teeth. He kept his head down, hoping he would go unnoticed. He couldn't bear to be chastised in front of his beloved.

Sophie peered at Aramis, who was making his way around the room to chat. She then turned back to Serus with furrowed brows. "Is everything all right?"

A moment of uncomfortable silence passed before the orchestra came to life again. It was the last dance to end the grand party, and soon, Serus would have to leave. He parted his lips to speak, but the words in his mind remained there.

Sophie didn't know it, but Serus was at war with what he felt for her and what he aspired to become.

Idling in the middle of the dance floor, Serus turned his gaze back to Sophie, who stood in anticipation. The time would be soon. He had to remove her from the crowd.

Bringing his cheek to hers, he whispered. "I have a gift for you."

Taking her hand, he led her through the veranda and down the steps into the garden. The fragrance of the blooming flowers filled the air. Every shade of pink, yellow, and purple lined the vine-covered walls. There were fruit trees bearing apples, lemons, and oranges. There was an archway of gold, leading to an arbor covered in roses beside a stone bridge over a babbling brook. But Serus didn't lead her to their usual spot;

instead, he brought her to a fountain, tucked away in a circle of rose vines.

Sophie tucked her dress, sitting on the edge of the basin as Serus took a small folded piece of paper from his pocket.

"With your permission, milady," Serus said, raising a brow.

Sophie's heart fluttered as he handed her the neatly creased parchment.

A letter of request was the first step one took to be approved for bonding. If the first request of courting was approved, the companions could send another request for Aramis' blessing. If signed, the suitor would proceed with their engagement by the offering of a white ribbon. After that, they would set a date to be infinitely bonded.

Sophie knew that this was that second request when Serus reached into his pocket, taking from it a long white ribbon.

"Serus, I..." Her heart raced as Serus took her hand, wrapping the ribbon around her forearm gently.

"Sophie, my love, my shining sun...I never want us to be apart. I want to live each and every day in the presence of your grace and beauty."

Serus didn't take his gaze from Sophie's as he held his hand over the fountain. With the energy inside of him, he drew up a trickling stream and with his mind, asked it to encompass them. He then pushed an intense vibration from himself into the water. It parted from the swirling stream into several intricate shapes. They were like snowflakes, twirling in the air as if tethered by a string, floating effortlessly. The symbols were the reflection of Serus' soul, of his love for her.

Sophie squeezed Serus' hand, vibrating the water into a symbol of gratitude.

Serus cupped Sophie's face, brushing his lips against hers. "Say yes?"

Sophie closed her eyes, ready to meet Serus' lips with her answer, a kiss to seal their engagement. But the sudden cessation of music followed by Aalok's booming voice sent a chill down her spine.

The symbols of love trembled into a reflection of Sophie's spiking anxiety. They expanded, bursting into droplets and fell like rain to the ground. A chilling wind blew through the garden, sweeping the request off the basin and down the path.

Sophie watched it skitter away before she stood. She was ready to run to the steps toward the ballroom, ready to stand up to Aalok. But she stumbled back to find Serus' grip still on the ribbon and a storm of pain clouding in his eyes.

"Serus, what are you-"

"Sophie don't," Serus clutched the ribbon and drew her toward him. "They will all make the choice regardless, my love. Let them do what they will."

"How can you say that? It is our duty to fight against the rebellion, to stand for truth, and uphold the Law!"

"We don't have to fight. We don't even have to choose a side."

Sophie turned away, gazing at the thorns of the roses for two quivering breaths before she turned back to Serus. Wincing at the pain stabbing at her chest, she unwound the ribbon from her wrist. She let it slip through her fingertips and watched it float to the ground like a feather, waving her white flag of surrender. "You took an oath."

"Where my loyalty lies, doesn't change what I feel for you—or you for me," Serus said, tracing her lips. He leaned down to kiss her, but Sophie pulled away.

"You can't ask me to choose between you and my king."

Serus cupped Sophie's face and kissed her. It was passionate and urgent; it was a request, a plea. When their lips parted, he pressed his forehead gently to hers. "I'm not. All I'm asking is for you to stay."

"I can't," Sophie whispered and slipped from his grasp.

As Sophie fled the garden, Serus stood frozen in disbelief. He had fallen for her loyalty, her faithfulness, but now he resented her purity. He glared at the folded paper tumbling away in the breeze, before snatching it up to squeeze it in his fist with regret.

9

TRUST

"YOU knew, didn't you?" Sophie asked, shoving Serus away. The images of the ball may have faded, but the aching in her chest still remained.

Serus held up his hands. "Sophie, please."

A stark realization hit her all at once, finding the evidence of his trespass on his sooty fingertips. Her horrified gaze shot to her own hands, seeing them now tainted.

"You knew-" Sophie choked on her words. The air was too thick, too suffocating with Serus' aura of guilt. She prayed he didn't know any better, that he had blindly followed Aalok. But her trust in him was dwindling like the flames of the bonfire outside the tent. "You knew Aalok was coming..."

Serus furrowed his brows at the way Sophie looked at him. She stared like a frightened fawn. Her wide eyes were fixed, her body frozen stiff. She acted as if he was about to prey on her, as if he was a wolf, baring his teeth with bloody lips.

Regret set his heart on fire, burning so deep that it singed his very soul. He had to touch her. He had to relieve her grief with a gentle caress. He needed her like breath, like music. She was the lyrics to his song; the notes, the chords. But the music between them had ceased, just as it had outside the tent.

"Yes," Serus answered, in a ragged voice.

"How long?"

"How long what?"

"How long have you been following Aalok?"

A smile replaced Serus' frown and he was quickly reminded of the part he was to play. Aalok had already won over millions. It was his turn to win over Sophie. She had once been his, and she would be again. He would see to it.

"Who says I follow anyone?" Serus asked, slipping his fingers across her collarbone. His smile deepened the moment she shivered at his touch. He pulled her close, pausing inches away from her mouth. He lingered there a few heartbeats, waited for her chest to fall; waited for her breath to warm his frigid fingers that traced her lips. "I have a gift for you." He whispered, and leaned down, ready to satisfy his desire with her lips.

But Sophie pulled away.

"So that's how it is?" he asked, narrowing his eyes.

"You made your choice... now, I must make mine."

"Can I, at least, show you something before you go?"

Without an answer from Sophie, Serus went to his bed and lifted the pad of straw. From beneath it, he took out a small black box, painted with blooming red roses. He gave up his offering, opening the top, to reveal the white bonding ribbon he had kept. Beside it, was the request, folded into a tiny rose. He picked up the sentimental request, and paused, thinking of how best to explain himself. He had never followed Aalok. Not with loyalty. But he didn't know if that truth would be enough, at least, enough in the eyes of a Truth Keeper.

"Despite all that has happened, this was the one thing that gave me hope...I thought—I thought perhaps that if you loved me, regardless of my faults, we could still be together."

Sophie's knees grew weak at Serus' wistful expression. He offered the request like a truce, an apology that could somehow smooth over any offenses. Her eyes crinkled at the neatly curled parchment. It was wrinkled and dirty from soot, tainted just as she was from his trespasses.

"No matter the war between two sides, we can remain. All I want, all I ever wanted was for us to be together."

Sophie's stomach tightened. A knot rose in her throat. She couldn't ignore what was right. She couldn't ignore the truth. The truth was; he was an Outcast, fallen, unclean. Her king was just and upright, and she had vowed to serve him, no matter the coveting of her heart.

She searched Serus' eyes, battling with the desire to wrap her arms around him, to hold him, but most of all, to reclaim him. He had been hers once, and she, his. She didn't want to lose him, not now, not when all she knew was soon to be over.

"Serus, I-"

"Just say yes," Serus begged, pressing his forehead to hers. "Say you'll stay."

"Don't do this. Don't force me to choose," Sophie whispered with tears welling in her eyes.

Serus cupped her face gently and brushed his lips against hers, but before he could wrap her in his arms, she flinched.

"Sophie!"

Serus held back a crooked grin and slid his hands in his pockets, concealing the request. He had sensed the soldier nearby, had been biding his time, stalling so that the soldier could see this.

"Ah. The Guardian," Serus sneered, leaning against the table. He took up his cup of wine and took a casual sip. " It's common courtesy to announce one's self before intruding a dwelling, you know."

The Guardian gripped the hilt of his sword.

"Manners, soldier," Serus warned.

The Guardian's gaze darted to Sophie. "I thought my orders were clear."

"Taking orders now?" Serus teased. He clucked his tongue with a reprimand. "The Sophie I know doesn't let anyone boss her around. *Especially* not some puffed up suit of armor."

A warning came with the Guardian's eyes as sharp and pointed as his weapon. "Out," he growled at the Truth Keeper.

She didn't budge.

"Now."

"Free will, Sophie." Serus reminded. "You *do* have a choice."

When Sophie kept her weary gaze on Serus, her Guardian scowled, snatching up her arm, and dragged her outside.

"Get on." Her Guardian ordered, lifting his chin.

Sophie turned in surprise. Somehow the Guardian had rescued him; somehow he had made sure her beloved friend was unharmed. "Bevol."

While Sophie apologized to her horse for leaving him behind, Alexander looked her over. His mouth twisted to one side, repulsed. A sooty handprint wrapped around her waist, her hand, and ash, traced the line of her collarbone to her jaw. He gnashed his teeth at the tinted smear across her lips, and then looked over his shoulder to the Outcast with contempt.

The Outcast only lifted his chin with a sly grin.

With a swift sweep, Alexander hoisted Sophie on her horses back. He whistled through his teeth, signaling it to follow him. He marched toward the stone wall, then peered over his shoulder, glaring a warning back at the Outcast one last time

Serus glowered at Sophie's Guardian before fixing his gaze on her. His heart softened the moment their eyes met but hardened at her frown of disappointment. The further she went from Serus, the colder the camp became. His fingers turned icy again, and his breath swirled in front of him in a frosty vapor.

"Wait."

At Serus' strained plea, Sophie drew back on Bevol's mane. Bevol halted, and Alexander came to a standstill. Nehia, the violinist, paused from her song. She watched Serus from the campfire and rested her red violin on her hip, amused. She fed off the pain and suffering of those around her. Betrayal, jealousy, envy, even a hint of lust swirled in the air. She inhaled a deep breath through her nostrils, tantalized by the toxic fumes.

The Outcasts stood huddled together, murmuring restlessly about the Guardian. Some even tried to coax others into banding together to take him on.

Alexander shot a glance at them and rested his hand on the hilt of his sword, daring them to make a move.

None of them did.

Serus reached into his pocket, revealing Sophie's necklace in his ashy fingertips. Taking her hand, he placed Aramis' gift in her palm and folded her fingers over it.

"Thank you," Sophie whispered.

"You're welcome," He whispered back. He kissed the back of her knuckles and let his lips linger there before he glanced up with soft eyes. "The beauty of free will is that you have a choice." He let his hand slip from hers. "You know where to find me if you ever change your mind."

The love, the betrayal, and the choice between Serus and Aramis were too much of a burden for Sophie. She considered jumping off Bevol, telling her Guardian she was staying, to embrace Serus and assure him that everything would be okay.

What if staying could convince him to change his mind? What if he could be saved before it was too late?

As Sophie pondered, warring with what to do, a voice tickled her ear. It was the same slithering whisper she had heard before, only this time, its words were filled with flattery.

You are the greatest among all Truth Keepers. Only you can change his heart. Stay...stay with Serus...

Sophie leaned forward, ready to jump, ready to abandon her duty. Before she could, she was jerked back and carried away at the whistle from her Guardian's lips.

Serus crossed his arms, exchanging one last haughty stare at the soldier. With a smirk, he waved a farewell, until the door to the camp closed with a thud.

A frosty cloud escaped Serus' lips as he glanced at the musicians who called for him to return to the bonfire. The moment Serus did, he guzzled down a full glass of wine and rested his violin beneath his chin. He pressed the bow hard against the strings, drew back his elbow painfully slow. He willed the notes to cry, to sing his loss, his pain. But Serus couldn't hear the music he brought forth; he was deaf to his song of sorrow. The only thing he heard was the echo of his demotion and the crack of his breaking heart.

10

THE PAST

ALEXANDER led the way back to the shore, still brooding, still glaring at the path as if it had insulted him. Every time he saw the Outcast's smug smile in his thoughts, how close the Truth Keeper's lips had been to his, Alexander's amber aura rose higher.

Does she not care about her brethren?? Does she believed the traitor's lies?

He ground his teeth thinking of what may have happened in the tent before he had arrived. He didn't have to look back to be reminded of where the Outcast's hands had been. There were consequences for her actions, and Alexander only hoped he hadn't already failed his king on the first day of his watch.

Sophie winced, watching her Guardian's amber glow expand. Every time it did, she could feel his anger, the accusations poking at her chest. She averted her gaze to the morning light spreading through the trees. It sparkled on the dew dripping off the leaves and fragrant flowers.

Sucking in a deep breath of fresh air, Sophie exhaled, now eased by the warm sunrays. She smoothed a hand over

Bevol's coat. It was brighter now that they were beyond the wall. Everything was cleaner, whiter...everything, but the ash and soot on her skin.

Studying her wrist, Sophie tensed at a tickle. She watched in amazement as her wrist glowed, matching her Guardian's aura. Amber sparkled with light like glitter, erasing the drunken Outcast's fingerprints with light. The aura was cleansing her, cover the evidence of the trespass he had committed.

Perhaps it was forgiveness Sophie now felt emanating from her Guardian. She couldn't be sure. He was still flaming with so many mixed emotions. She glanced at her knuckles and Serus' ashy lip print. It hadn't budged until they were further from the camp. The closer they got the beach; the more the lip print faded until it vanished from her skin completely.

Sophie gave a sideways glance at her Guardian's clean uniform and then furrowed her brows at her sooty dress.

Does he have some type of protection or was it because he didn't let the Outcasts touch him?

Staring at the evidence of her disobedience, Sophie grieved the choice she had made. She had failed. That moment in tent had been her one chance at saving Serus and now, there were only the consequences for disobeying her king's orders.

Alexander kept a steady pace, alert to any new potential enemies hiding in the forest. He held his eyes to the lush green trees for a moment, catching the rainbow of feather from the birds that flew from branch to branch. They weren't eating the fruits of the trees, as they should, they were squawking. There were no songs of the birds either, only calls, only warnings.

Alexander turned toward the call of behemoths deep in the forest. They rattled the ground, bellowing out a warning as well. The foxes skittered across the mossy dirt, hiding in thickets. The deer, the wolves, even the tiny chipmunks ran and hid.

With another trumpet of the great lizards, Sophie peered through the gaps of the tower high trees. As they came to a clearing, she could finally see the herd of olive-green and red scaly beasts. The largest of the herd stood on its hind legs, reaching its head high. It snapped a long tree branch in half and eased forward on his front feet. The ground trembled in response, quivering her body.

Sophie thought back to the way the Earth shook when she was in the meadow. She shivered, wondering if the ground would shake again. She glanced at Alexander and relaxed her shoulders, seeing and feeling his aura had lowered from its brilliant blaze to a calm golden glow. She thought about apologizing, about explaining what happened, but she couldn't find the words.

Alexander turned his head away from the great reptile's calls and frowned. Soon, the great beasts would cease to exist. It troubled him that such a magnificent creation must die. He wondered if they would exist again as he would, as the other animals would. That was one of the questions he had asked Aramis when he had returned to the Infinite Realm.

More questions about the next life raced through Alexander's mind. He had new questions now, ones that couldn't be answered. He worried about the Truth Keeper. He was afraid she would be just as naive in the next life as she was now. He prayed to Aramis, asking if he could pair her with someone to aid her in the next aeon.

The ash around Sophie's hips and lips flashed in Alexander's mind again. He swallowed hard, shoving down his resentment. Serus, the Outcast, was her weakness. He had to keep her away from him. He had to make sure she wouldn't fall into temptation to listen to his words. He was a follower of Aalok, a follower of a liar.

Thinking back to his first meeting with Sophie's suitor, Alexander walked through his memories, going to the night of the ball, the night of Aalok's rebellion.

Alexander stood in the beautiful ballroom of the Crystal Castle. He was in his own mind, replaying the data that had been recorded. He was an apparition, a ghost, but unlike a ghost, he was able to touch things and smell things.

Glancing around the festive event, he took notice of all the things he hadn't had the chance to before. He studied the candlestick chandeliers. He peered up, smiling at how they sparkled, casting rainbow prisms on the walls from their ornamental dewdrops. He then admired the golden Seraphs in the crown moldings of doorframes, then the inlay of the king's emblem at his feet in the glossy alabaster floor. He sniffed the fragrance of the flowers in the vases on the banquet table, as well as the delicious food, steaming into the air.

His ears welcomed the pleasant melody the orchestra played. He watched the happy faces, sweeping one another across the dance floor. They crossed the inlay of the king's emblem, going through him. He could see, touch, and smell, but the data of the past could not be changed, for this was only a memory.

Following the dancers, Alexander watched them until he found his past self, gazing at the crowd. Again, he felt the wanting, the need to bonded like the other souls. His past self withdrew his gaze and scanned the room for potential spies, but he, his apparition, couldn't help but stare at the dancers. A mate had been missing in his life, a bonding had yet to occur.

He wished so much he could have sat on a stool, sweeping colors across a cotton canvas. The painting would have been a rainbow of hues; swirls of pinks, blues, and purples. He would have painted the different shades of the dancer's auras, and the glowing faces of them as they beamed at one another in utter bliss. He frowned, as did his past self, noting the distraction, and set his gaze to the exits.

He wasn't here to reminisce. He was here to gather the details of the meeting with the Outcast, the confrontation with the Truth Keepers suitor.

A twinge hit him in the pit of his stomach, knowing how unprepared he had been.

The moment the doors busted open, Alexander's past self was hit with a shockwave of anger and deceit. He held his ground and glared at Aalok and his soldiers. Their auras pulsed in waves of crimson, accompanying Aalok in a hazy cloud of blood red. The fallen Seraph stood for a moment, narrowing his eyes in contempt at the happy gathering. He then set his gaze on Alexander's apparition as if he knew he was replaying his past.

With a smirk, Aalok walked through Alexander and his soldiers followed close behind, also going through him. Alexander's past self readied his weapon, lighting it with golden fire. It hummed, as did the other fiery swords from his fellow soldiers who stood in a blazing circle of protection around Aramis.

Aramis raised his hands, ordering the soldiers to stand down.

The soldiers obeyed with hesitance, sheathing their weapons at their sides.

Aalok's face was a mask of innocence as he feigned surprise. "Good evening," He said, and held out his hands for one of his lackeys to remove his red robe. He rolled his shoulders, revealing the consequences of his fall, reveling in his trespass. His wings unfurled, displaying his power, his might. They were as black as night and as sleek and shiny as crow feathers. He spread them wide, and as he did, the guests of Aramis backed away, gasping.

"Honored guests," Aalok began, raising his hand. " Do not be alarmed. I come here peacefully."

The room hushed, looking to Aramis, but he only frowned at the intruders.

"My humble friends, it is an honor to visit with you on this wondrous occasion. How wonderful it is that you are all gathered here and how glorious this night will be, because tonight, I offer you a gift."

The room was filled with murmurs, but the quiet clamor came to a halt when a horrified Truth Keeper burst through the veranda doors.

"Don't listen to him!" Sophie shouted.

Alexander remembered this exact moment, how his past self had lost his focus on Aalok. He had been enamored by the luster of the Truth Keeper's flaming white aura; the fire of her righteous indignation. But he wasn't here to stare like his past self was doing now. He was here to study his enemies.

This time Alexander watched Aalok closely. He surveyed his posture, how the Seraph's fingers and lips twitched. Alexander now knew why the Seraph had been jolted. The

Outcast had not done as promised. He had not kept the Truth Keeper in the garden accepting his proposal.

Alexander had been informed of how Serus had given his word. He had been instructed to get Sophie to say yes to his engagement, and after, take her willingly to the fortress for the ceremony. Alexander's past self was not privy to that information back then, but Alexander was now. And he used it to find comfort, a newfound faith in the Truth Keeper. She was loyal back then. Perhaps, she always would be.

"Favored Truth Keeper," Aalok said, sweetly. "This gift is not only for those who have been of great service, but a gift to all."

Alexander glanced over his shoulder at his past self. He watched him hurry to the back of the room and follow a male with jet-black hair, sneaking through the frozen audience. The Outcast was dressed in Truth Keeper attire, but this time, Alexander's ghost spied his tainted fingers, the evidence of his treachery.

"My gift does not require works or good behavior." Aalok continued, "My gift is free, for it is already inside each and every one of you. If you follow me, I can show the true potential that each of you possess. Follow me, and I will show you far more than you have ever dreamed, so much more than anything your king would have you know. Experiences and revelations much deeper than the mere surface of what Aramis allows you to unveil. If you come with me, your eyes shall be opened, and you can be gods. You will be as I am. You will be rulers of yourselves. My gift to you my friends…is freedom."

"Liar!" A Truth Keeper yelled from behind Aramis.

The crowd cried out in an uproar of confusion.

"I speak the truth. You have only to ask your king." Aalok countered. "Aramis? Is there not more we could do if it were not your rules?"

Aramis furrowed his brows and his throat bobbed. "Yes, Aalok, you know this to be true, but-"

"See? Aramis himself has spoken that we may do as we please." Aalok mocked, cutting Aramis short.

"We must hold fast to Aramis' Laws!" another Truth Keeper called from the middle of the room.

"Who says we should?" Aalok fired back, rustling his wings. "Your king has clearly admitted we can choose to follow his laws or live free of its regulations, free of the consequences of trespassing it. It is he who sentences us into exile if we do not obey the Law, but I say: do as you will, do as you please, please yourselves. None of you should be exiled for wanting more. Follow me, and I will show you how to attain this knowledge."

"The rules are there to protect us and keep the peace," Sophie stated loudly. She then addressed the crowd. "To keep us all happy and well pleased. Our king loves us, as he loves even you, Aalok. It is you who broke the law and disrupted the purity of the kingdom." Sophie turned to her brethren again. "He's twisting Aramis' words. Can't you see that?"

"Fair enough, Truth Keeper. But if what you say is true, then why do I feel contempt in the hearts of your brethren in this room?" Aalok demanded, cunningly. "It seems not all of us are well pleased, not all of us are at peace. It is not enough. We could do so much more; have so much more. We could all *be* so much more. We could create our own destinies, not be subject to this one infinite being."

"He created us, as he did you. Why should we listen to you?" Someone in the crowd asked, coming closer to Aalok.

"Because..." Aalok grinned, clasping his hands behind his back, "Aramis has made me wise. He put me in charge of you, to watch over you, to teach you. I know all. I am all, for I am just like your beloved king. I am his first and most wonderful creation."

The Truth Keepers could not contest that truth.

"Only I give you a choice, not laws, not petty rules, but freedom!" Aalok's wings spread wide, rising high. "Free yourselves of this bondage and together we will make a new kingdom!"

Alexander's past self glared at Aalok, before setting his fixed stare on a fleeting Outcast. He and Alexander followed him to the back of the room to the unblocked exit.

As the Outcast stretched out his hand for the golden doorknob, he jerked it back when a white, blazing flame made contact with his wrist.

"Going somewhere?" Alexander's past self asked. His eyes flickered, reflecting the light of his sword.

Alexander stood on the other side of the Outcast. He watched a sly grin pull at his lips as he rubbed his sooty hand from the electric shock.

"And what business would that be of yours, soldier?"

"Where does your allegiance lie?" Alexander's memory demanded, his sword now blazing against the traitor's chin. "Answer me, coward!" He snatched him up, taking hold of his suit, but the Outcast only glared, and calmly shoved him away.

"I answer to no one," Serus spat.

Alexander's past self and his apparition knitted their brows at the fallen Truth Keeper.

Serus narrowed his eyes, daring Alexander's memory to make a move.

A commotion distracted Alexander's past self. His attention went to the center of the room, which was now in a full-blown uproar. Souls were lit in pinks or with no hue at all. One side of the room was burning in pinks and reds, the other in a white and golden glow.

The two sides were yelling and shouting, arguing about who was right. In the midst of the commotion, Aalok made his way to Aramis and gave a cocky grin.

"They will choose me, Aramis, and when they do, you will bow on your knees before me," Aalok declared.

"So much pride. Have you forgotten that I made you? That I can turn your soul to ashes with just one word."

"You'll have to destroy the others with me."

"They don't know what they are doing."

Aalok gave a clever grin. "Bide your time Aramis, but you and I both know what the future holds. You have seen their choice."

Aramis kept his stare but said nothing.

With the smug smile still plastered on his lips, Aalok turned to the crowd. "The choice is yours, my friends. Bondage or freedom."

Alexander's former self stood in shock at the sight of his brethren arguing with the Truth Keepers. What horrified him the most was the change in their auras. Their glow dimmed and tinged with red as they followed Aalok to exit the ballroom.

While Alexander's prior self watched the mutiny, Alexander bared his teeth at Serus.

"You don't deserve her, you coward," he snapped.

Serus smirked at Alexander's former self and simply slipped out the door

"Stupid," Alexander growled at his past self. "He was right there and you let him get away!"

Souls tainted in crimson continued to file out the door. They did not look back, not even once as the Truth Keepers pleaded with them.

Aramis made his way to the middle of the ballroom, his eyes welling with tears.

Sophie pulled and tugged at her tainted brethren, but it was no use. They followed Aalok and his soldiers out the door without a second thought.

Alexander's past self lowered his sword as Sophie's bright aura dimmed, along with the other remaining souls left standing in shock. They covered their mouths in disbelief and comforted one another.

At the slam of the ballroom doors, the candles of the chandeliers went out all at once. The smoke from them lifted into the air as the hues of the soul's auras all dimmed in disappointment. The ballroom grew cold and dark, reflecting the sadness of only a third of the bodies that remained standing with their king.

Sophie fell to the floor and covered her eyes to weep.

Alexander's steps were heavy as he made his way to the crying Truth Keeper. He stood above her for a long moment, thinking of how beautiful she was, even with no light.

Kneeling down, he scooped her into his arms and to his surprise; Sophie wrapped her arms around him tight. Tears streamed down her face, making grey circles on his white linen uniform. She drew back as if to ask him why he was there, why he was changing the past of his own memory. Alexander didn't have an answer. All he knew was that he was there and she needed him. He wiped her tears, gazing into her eyes. She gazed back at him, and then set her sight on his lips. Alexander parted his ready to comfort her with a gentle kiss, but the sound of waves called him to return to the present.

Alexander's memory dripped off the pages of his mind until the sad, and yet beautiful portrait, vanished entirely. His apparition had tried to change things. But no one could turn back the hands of time, not even Aramis. The past was set in stone and only the data of that memory could be relived.

In reality, Alexander had run to Aramis asking for orders as Aalok exited. The soldiers had boarded their spacecraft's, chasing the Outcasts to the edge of the floating kingdom. Aramis had gone to Sophie's side and put a hand on her shoulder. He had spoken a few words about faith and hope. Sophie had stood, took the hands of those she could feel most troubled and led them down the hall, to one of the many counseling rooms. That was reality. That was the truth documented in Sophie's book of life.

Alexander exhaled. He was growing tired of the distraction of his emotions. He had warned Sophie they were fickle, untrustworthy, and here he was, changing the past in his imagination. With only a few feet to the shore, Alexander glanced over his shoulder to the Truth Keeper. She had to know she couldn't depend on her emotions. He had to make it clear they were at war.

"I told you to stay on the beach." He said sternly.

Sophie jerked her head up. "There was fire falling from the sky and Bevol ran away and-"

"That doesn't matter," he interrupted. He walked toward the lapping waves, avoiding her conflicted aura. "You could have been taken to Aalok. You walked right into a den of vipers without even thinking."

"I did think!"

Alexander paused in his steps and turned. He narrowed his eyes at her objection. "Serus' soul is not the only one that needs to be saved, Truth Keeper. I hope you remember that in your next life."

Sophie opened her mouth to speak but at the mention of the next life, she closed it. She winced, feeling guilty again for wanting to try to help Serus. As she sulked in sorrow, Alexander stood at the water's edge, crossing his arms.

He needed some distance from Sophie so he could clear his head. Her aura was strong and filled with pain. He ran his hands through his hair as if raking through his thoughts, going over all that had happened in the past few weeks.

How could anyone betray the king?

Aramis had provided for them, taught them, and given them all their heart's desires if they did well. How could it not be enough? It amazed Alexander that anyone would turn against his Aramis, that they could be consumed with darkness, or that such darkness could even exist. But it did, and it had affected the Truth Keeper deeply.

He wished she had not gone to the camp. There were only thousands of Truth Keepers left among the billions of souls Aramis had made. It didn't seem like it was enough to fight the next war in the new aeon.

How can we go up against Aalok with those numbers?

Alexander wondered if Sophie had, in some way, been swayed. The sooty prints of Serus had lingered far too long.

Had she at some point thought of choosing the traitor?

Glancing over his shoulder, Alexander watched her examine her necklace. It sparkled in the sunlight of dawn, casting rainbows in every direction. The gift was a reminder of purity, of faithfulness to her king.

Clasping Aramis' gift around her neck, Sophie grasped the opal stone and closed her eyes.

Alexander knew she was trying to be free of the negative emotions, to have the jewel hum a resonance of peace. But the jewel wouldn't perform, not for her. It could only consume the negativity of others.

Seeing Sophie's face wrinkling in confusion, Alexander contemplated telling her the truth about Serus and what he had done. He questioned if the Outcast had been honest with her during her visit to the camp. Seeing how she had almost kissed Serus, Alexander could only assume that he hadn't.

He stared at the ocean, losing himself to the sound and sway of its rhythm. Soon, he found a crystal floor beneath his feet, and before him, the doors of the king's throne room. He went through them, walking toward the light of Aramis, walking away from the beach, and back into his memories.

11

THE LIBRARY

OF SOULS

"MY Lord, I have come as you have requested," Alexander bowed.

Aramis waved his hands in the air as if he were composing an orchestra and filled a tall pitcher with water. "Was my message difficult to decode?"

"No, I was–delayed."

"Rise, my son."

Alexander stood, finding Aramis smiling with a playful glint in his eye. "Have a seat."

Sitting at the small oak table, Alexander surveyed the intimate banquet, waiting patiently for Aramis to finish setting the table.

While Aramis made gold plates and delectable food appear on them, Alexander gazed at the paintings along the walls. He saw one of his favorites; an oil of a wide oak tree, standing in a golden wheat field. A humble smile pulled at the corner of his lips. It was an honor to have his art displayed in Aramis' castle. There were thousands upon thousands of artists and only so much wall space for their creations upon the walls.

Catching a whiff of the food before him, Alexander's gaze was drawn to the steaming vegetables and then his empty glass. He swallowed, wetting his dry mouth.

That morning, he trained with Caius and won, met with Aramis, been knighted a General, and given his new uniform. He was also given orders to introduce himself to the Truth Keeper, Sophie, and tell her she could not return to the Infinite Realm.

Tell her? That task had not been so simple.

"So, you're fond of horses?" Aramis asked, filling Alexander's glass. He then proceeded to sit, placing a napkin on his lap.

"My Lord?"

"The horses that run wild in the countryside, you favor those creatures above all else. Why is that?"

"They are a beautiful creation of yours, my king. Noble. Humble. They have a calm spirit about them."

"Indeed."

"As you know, I hung one of your canvases depicting these wonderful creatures in the Great Hall Library. Sophie loves that painting."

Alexander painfully swallowed the food caught in his throat before taking a sip of water at the mention of Sophie's name.

"She's quite fond of horses as well," Aramis commented, skewering a small potato with his fork.

"The Truth Keeper is very...bold, if I may say. She speaks her mind without hesitation."

Aramis chuckled. "Sophie is not like other Truth Keepers."

"So I have seen."

"So, the horses, you care for them all, yes? Even those that run wild and free? You favor one in particular. Ronin, is it?"

"Yes. He is an excellent companion."

"He was a wild horse and yet you tamed him."

"My Lord, I apologize, but I must ask; if it is so imperative I protect the Truth Keeper, then why do you request my presence here to dine and talk of horses? You said it was an urgent matter, and yet we sit here, dining as if it was an ordinary day. Surely, you have asked me here to speak of more than my friendship with my horse."

Aramis grinned wide and stood, draping the napkin over his arm. He took the pitcher of water from the table in one hand and then made a blue quill appear in his other.

"It is indeed an urgent matter. The assignment I ask of you is of the utmost importance to me. Water, my son?"

"Yes, please."

Aramis put a wine glass in front of Alexander and began to fill it. "In life, my children are like water. They flow through one another like the river into the sea." He eased back the pitcher above the cup, letting a single droplet rest on the tip of spout. "One single drop can ripple a calm sea."

The drop of water slid from the spout and into the cup. It rippled outward and against the glass then into itself. Aramis set the pitcher down and waved his hand but did not turn the water into wine as Alexander had expected. An inkwell appeared on the table next to the wine glass and Aramis dipped the quill in it. At a tap of his finger, a single drop of black ink fell into the cup, sullying the clear liquid inside.

"The same goes for those affected by their trespasses." Aramis continued. "They become tainted as the darkness seeps in, trickling into their thoughts like a rushing river, flowing into an ocean of confusion."

Alexander leaned down and peered at the swirls of ink as Aramis emptied a fruit bowl and placed the glass inside it. He took up the pitcher of water and poured it into the ink, filling the cup, until it overflowed into the bowl. The inky water spilled out, leaving the liquid inside the wine glass clean again.

"When my love overflows in them, there is no longer room for the darkness. As you know, love covers a multitude of trespasses. But only if the soul can trust; only if they believe."

Aramis wiped his hands with the napkin now stained with smudges of ink over the bowl. "Now, we shall talk about the purpose of your assignment."

Aramis' white robe graced the floor, making it appear as if he was floating to the bay window.

"The Truth Keeper I have asked you to protect is indeed vivacious. She is one of the most zealous and trusted of all the counselors in the Seventh Circle. However, she is also incredibly vulnerable and I worry she could be swayed."

"My king, if you are worried about her loyalty, perhaps I should bring her here to speak with you," Alexander suggested as he stood.

"No. There are too many spies—Truth Keepers who have fallen into confusion. Some are Sophie's closest friends. You must keep her far from here. Do you understand?"

"Yes, my Lord,"

"For you to truly understand what you are up against, you must know the importance of why she must be protected," Aramis continued, leading Alexander to a door behind his throne. "I made all of you with so many wonderful qualities: compassion, intelligence, artistic ability, the ability to love, and yes, even the ability to hate. I gave you all reasoning to temper the balance, and a choice. There was a time life was simple, but that time is over. Regardless of the Confusion, Sophie and a select few, including you, have held to the core values of those days. You are loyal, believers of truth, seekers of the light, unturned, and therefore, you have been given the most important tasks. I have assigned other Guardians, like you, to watch over the purest and most vulnerable among the Truth Keepers. They must not waver, for their purpose is far too great."

Aramis reached into his pocket drawing out a set of gold skeleton keys on a ring. They clinked together as he sorted through them until he found the one he was looking for.

"This key will unlock this door, which leads to the Library of Souls," he explained. "Every story of every soul in existence is just beyond this very door." He handed Alexander the key. "Go and read Sophie's book of life. Only then will you understand what she is up against and why she needs protection. I will be waiting here when you are finished, in case you have further questions."

Alexander nodded and looked at the shiny key in the palm of his hand. No one had been allowed past this door, no one had been given permission to read of a soul's works, except the Seraphs.

"Use your time wisely, my son."

Alexander was hesitated, but inserted the key. At the click of the lock, he looked back at Aramis, who clasped his hands behind his back and nodded for him to proceed.

Alexander descended the winding cobblestone staircase, which led to an immaculate library, filled with row after row of bookcases. He wondered how he could find Sophie's name among them all, until he found the golden plaques, labeling the rows alphabetically.

Standing at the "A", Alexander. He had to know, he had to see what was in his book.

He searched the shelves until a certain glittering gold title caught his eye. It was thick with years of what he guessed were his achievements as well as many days he had spent painting. Opening it, he did indeed find that documentation, but to his surprise, there was also information on his rise in rank, and even losses to Caius. Reading of what had happened that day, he frowned at the truth about his friend, and why Alexander had been chosen as General, and not Caius.

Closing his book, Alexander proceeded to the 'S' section. Taking Sophie's book from its nook, he opened it, starting at the beginning; the creation of Sophie's very own being.

The first page wasn't filled with words as he expected, but an illustration sketched in gold. It seemed to glint in Alexander's eyes as he watched the drawing come to life. It moved slowly, making an elegant mobile depiction of her birth.

Sophie's soul peeked out of Aramis' hands. It appeared shy, but grew bright and sparkled as it was parted from another at the touch of Aramis' fingertips.

Watching this moment, Alexander paused, gazing at the departure of her soul from the other. Something deep within tugged at his heart, something whispering what he had felt when he had first seen her on the beach.

Warmth spread across his chest with a wave of pure and utter bliss at this documented moment. He was like a flower in a field, peeling back his petals to welcome the warmth of the sun.

After watching the depiction of Sophie crowning ceremony, the sketched stilled, requesting Alexander turn the page to learn more. He gathered information about Sophie's accomplishments, her written works, her love for animals, and her great patience during counseling as a high priestess. He let out a breath, overwhelmed by the depth of the love and compassion that she held for her peers.

Although he had felt her bright spirit when he first met her, he now truly understood why she would be one of the few to help bring many back to the truth. She was self-sacrificing, loyal, and kind. She had never doubted her king's goodness and had always stood up for what was right. She had lived her whole life without one single trespass. She had been innocent. She had been pure.

Putting Sophie's book back in its nook, Alexander caught sight of something in the back of the room. It beckoned him to come closer, and instead of going back up the stairs like he knew he should, he stood beneath a locked glass case, looking at a book.

The Book of Samria, he read on the gold plaque.

Heading back to the stairway, Alexander paused as another name caught his eye. His aura blazed in blue, and the longer he stared at the name, the more vexed he became. He gnashed his teeth, swiping Serus' book from its place. He flipped through page after page, reading of his betrayal, of things he had done in secret, of his exile and the reason behind it. He also read of the war in Serus' heart over his great love for Sophie.

Flipping to the last pages documented, Alexander found words appearing right before his very eyes. They first jotted across the parchment in gold, writing of Serus' joy at the sight of The Truth Keeper's arrival at the camp. But as Serus' thoughts of trespassing filled his mind, the words turned as red as blood, tainting the proceeding pages in crimson.

12

BURDENS TO
BEAR

AT the sound of Serus' book thudding shut, Alexander blinked his eyes from the memory. He couldn't change the past. He couldn't change the fact that he had wasted time reading of what was taking place, instead of being there to prevent it.

Prickling pain from Sophie's aura seeped through him. He glanced over his shoulder at her. She was without trespass, and he had been too stern with her. She couldn't help her affection for Serus, just as he couldn't help his affections for her. Sophie was his assignment, an asset, and he was her Guardian. *Only* her Guardian.

Alexander stood silent, gazing up at the clouds, praying to Aramis about how to handle everything on his mind. He was so troubled, swayed by his own fickle emotions. He cared for Sophie, not understanding why he was drawn to her so intimately. She was a stranger to him, and he to her. Surely, there was an explanation; surely Aramis could shed some light.

Ending his prayer, Alexander gave thanks to Aramis, giving him the burden of all his woes.

"Love covers a multitude of trespasses." Aramis' voice echoed in reply.

Alexander dropped his head in defeat and then glanced up through his lashes. Love. That was not the answer he had hoped for, but he knew love had more than one meaning, so he settled on the one that fit; the love of faith and friendship.

Sophie dismounted Bevol and looked at the small paper rose that Serus had secretly given her. Her fingers shook as she stared at it. She didn't know if she could open it. She didn't know if she could stand seeing if the request hadn't been approved.

But if it had? What then? What would it change?

Unfolding the soft, tawny edges, Sophie took a deep breath and read.

My King and my Lord,

I, Serus, Truth Keeper of the Eighth Circle, humbly ask permission to take Sophie, Truth Keeper of the Seventh Circle, to be my Infinite Companion. I vow to uphold the Law and to fulfill all my duties. If this joining is accepted, I promise to love, honor, and cherish Sophie for all of eternity, be it pleasing to your Majesty.

In deepest regards,
Serus,
Truth Keeper of the Eighth Circle

Sophie's shoulders fell as she gazed at the bottom of the document. There was no golden seal of Aramis' signet, no approval for their engagement. It had all been a lie, an illusion; a false hope. Her face contorted as the paper fell from her hands. Tears streamed down her cheeks and she fell to her knees, holding back a whimper.

A breeze brushed her shoulder. It was soothing, giving her some comfort, but that comfort didn't last. Startling panic rose in Sophie's chest, watching the request get swept up. The request danced at her fingertips as if to say goodbye before it sailed through the wind, and over her Guardian's shoulder.

Sophie held her breath as he snatched up the wrinkled paper. He didn't glance at it; he only turned to face the soul it belonged to.

Bracing herself for her Guardian's rigid tone, Sophie backed away, waiting for him reprimand her. But he didn't. Instead, he folded the paper back into its creases and offered it.

"I believe this is yours," he said softly.

Sophie accepted the request and met her Guardian's stare. His eyes were soft, and for the first time, his countenance appeared sympathetic. She gazed into them for a long moment, feeling a tug, the same spark of energy when they had first met.

"Thank you," Sophie whispered.

Her Guardian nodded and went past her toward the dunes.

"I'm sorry Alexander,"

He paused at his name, seemingly surprised that she used it.

"I couldn't leave Bevol." Sophie's voice trailed off, as she petted her horse's neck. Guilt crept up her spine, knowing she had put herself in danger. She had gone to Bevol's rescue, but how could she have gotten so caught up in the music? How could she have gone with Serus into his tent? Her mind raced, questioning what could have happened from her mindless actions.

What if Alexander hadn't found me? What if Serus had kissed me? Would I have kissed him back? Would I have stayed?

"It wasn't your fault. I should have gotten there sooner." Alexander told her.

"How did you know where I was?"

He drew back his sleeve, revealing a gold wristband. "Your necklace is connected."

"So you can find me anywhere?"

A small smile pulled at her Guardian's lips. He seemed to study her as if to silently question if she had thought of evading his closetful watch again. "There's no getting rid of me, Truth Keeper."

Sophie swallowed as her stomach fluttered. "Thank you," she stammered, "for saving Bevol," "He's a very dear friend."

"Your dear friend looks thirsty," Alexander noted and led the way over the dunes, and into the forest.

It was only a short walk to the secret spring, and Sophie was grateful that it was no further. The weight of her emotions had exhausted her before they had even stepped foot beneath the leafy canopy. It was a strange feeling, this weakness. She had never had to gasp for breath, never had to forced herself to move. If only she could return to the castle, then Aramis could renew her strength. Earth's limitations had its own effect, but now Sophie was realizing, it had been the Confusion that had taken its toll.

Once they reached the spring, Alexander prepared a spot beneath a weeping willow tree to rest. He unbuckled his belt, set his cape to the side, and laid his sword neatly beside them. Sophie went to the pool, hidden by the morning fog and wet her face. Ronin and Bevol leaned down, swishing their tails. They waited for Sophie to straighten before they lapped up the water for a drink.

Looking at the place Alexander had brought her to, Sophie surveyed the hidden gem. It was small, surrounded by a lush paradise filled with hibiscus flowers and fruit trees. Ferns and moss climbed the rocks of the waterfall where a vibrant rainbow arched across the pool. It was much like the Prayer Gardens in the Infinite Realm.

As Sophie made her way around the edge of the basin to look at the rainbow, Alexander tended to Ronin's saddle. He kept his watchful stare on Sophie, only to soon realize it wasn't for her protection.

He was taking in the details of her delicate silhouette, how the fraying strands of her long hair lifted in the breeze. An urge to sketch her came over him. He longed to paint how she glowed, how relaxed she looked, standing in that splendid place. But there were no parchments, or pencils to use, and Sophie wasn't his muse. She was his assignment.

Turning away, Alexander ran his fingers through his hair. He was doing it again, longing for something he knew he couldn't have. Still, he couldn't help but feel that tug again, to be drawn to look at her with such devotion.

He glanced down at the ground, only to find his feet aglow. His arms, his chest, his whole body had bet set to flames. He swallowed hard, knowing he couldn't ignore his souls request any longer. He couldn't ignore the truth. The truth was, he had fallen deeply, and unintentionally, in love with the Truth Keeper he had sworn to protect.

As Alexander stared, Sophie bowed her head. She wasn't praying to Aramis like she knew she should. Instead, she stood overwhelmed, examining the back of her hand where Serus had kissed her. Her knuckles burned as if reflecting her desire to be with him, as if calling her to go back to the camp. Serus' hopeful face appeared in her mind and she deliberated on how she could find him in her new life. She had to bring him back to redemption.

Frowning, she wondered what her new life would be like. She couldn't imagine being parted from all the souls she loved. She didn't want to say goodbye—she didn't know how. There had never been an end, only an existence.

At the buzz of his wristband, Alexander's glow went out. He pulled his gaze from Sophie, drawing back his sleeve to read the numeric message. The secret codes were the only way to keep Aalok from figuring out the timeline of Aramis' plan. If Aalok knew the time of the end, he would work harder and faster to corrupt more souls.

Alexander deciphered the numbers in his mind, but not fast enough. The code disappeared from his screen before he could decipher the last sentence. He tapped the screen to retrieve it, but there was no way of getting it back. He exhaled in frustration, hoping it was only an alert of Aalok's whereabouts and what part of Earth to stay away from. Closing his eyes, Alexander tried to find an aura of negativity but became distracted by Sophie's voice.

"What happens now?" She asked, skipping a smooth stone across the water.

"We wait," Alexander informed. He came to her side and skipped a stone beside hers.

"Did Aramis say when?"

"No, but I'll be alerted as the time draws near."

"Do you think it can be stopped? That the souls, even Aalok, will come to realize what they have done? That everything can go back to the way it was?"

"No, Aalok will not turn back and Aramis has already set everything in place," Alexander sighed, remembering Aramis telling him of the future vision he had seen.

"As for those filled with the darkness...they are too consumed with pride to admit they're wrong. They care about nothing but themselves and what they want, no matter who it hurts, no matter how all souls are affected."

He clenched his jaw, remembering the moment he found Sophie in Serus' tent. She had been so close to kissing him, so close to being caught up in his lies. *That is why you must stay away from anyone that has been infected with the lies of Aalok. Even more dangerous are those who have not yet chosen a side, but who stand by, watching the war from the sidelines.*

Sophie stared at the waterfall, thinking of Serus. He had told her she didn't have to choose, that they could be together. How could he not understand that Aramis was in control? The fate of all souls rested in the palm of the king's hand. Did Serus really think Aalok would be a better king? She wished she could have counseled him. Untying her braid, Sophie combed her fingers through the waves of her strands.

Alexander watched her face the wind, trying to hide her troubled expression. But it didn't matter if she concealed her face, he could sense the emotions in her aura. He knew it was the time to tell, no matter how reluctant he was to do so. He had to explain. In a way, he wished Aramis had not given him the keys to the Library of Souls. He wished he had not been informed of every detail. He knew everything about how the end would come, but not when. He also knew that no matter how hard Sophie could have tried, Serus wouldn't have changed. Not at the fountain; not in the tent. His face burned as he peered sideways in Sophie's direction. He had to tell her the truth.

"Sophie," Alexander began, crossing his arms. "I know of your history with Serus and—"

Sophie whipped around to face him. "What about our history?"

"I know more than what happened at the Ball."

"How much?"

"All of it. I was privileged with classified information. I'm sorry, but what you feel for him cannot be. At least, not in this lifetime."

"This new lifetime...do-do you think there's a chance that souls will find one another?"

"Aramis mentioned that some souls would be placed with those that fell or stood watching without making a choice. He says it is the chosen that will guide them back to him, and the chosen that will be able to sense another chosen soul. We will see it in their eyes, just as we do now. But more so, we will feel it in their spirit."

"But we won't remember them?"

"The connection will spark. Aramis said it would feel as if we knew them from a dream, but no. In a way, it keeps the war fair. Having the advantage of knowing changes a soul's fate. Not knowing, keeps their innocence. If the souls go through this next life and still choose the darkness, they will do it in ignorance. The only compass we will have will be something deep within us, telling us what is right and what is wrong."

"A conscience."

Alexander nodded. "It's a loophole in the agreement."

"But Aalok would have figured that out, wouldn't he?"

"No. His pride blinds him. He thinks it's an advantage, that if souls don't know their past, it will be easier to sway them. He figures if no one is listening to Aramis' spirit inside them now, they won't in the future either."

Sophie let out a breath, fidgeting with her necklace. "I wonder what the new world will be like. Will we have cities? Transportation, as we do now? Do you think Aramis will rebuild everything the same way?"

"He didn't say. He only said humans, which is what we will be called, will figure it out on their own. He said it would take time. It will take thousands of years to discover the smallest beginnings of the technology now use."

"Then perhaps we will all be here again, on Earth," Sophie said, rocking on her heels with a pleasant smile.

Alexander's lips turned upward at her hope.

"I love everything about this world; the smells, the tastes, the sounds. I wonder if there will be chocolate. Do you think there will be chocolate?"

Alexander bit his lip. Aramis had answered all his questions about the new world. He had told him about their new bodies, but most of all, about the challenges that would come with it.

"This new life will be much harder to survive than I think you realize."

"What do you mean?"

"We won't be like we are now. Our bodies won't heal. They will be fragile, perishable."

Sophie frowned. "Perishable?"

"We will grow old...and one day die." Alexander knelt down and picked up a mix of dirt and sand. He stood and let mixture fall from his hands. It sifted into the breeze. "Of the dust, we will be born and to the dust, we shall return."

Sophie's forehead wrinkled. She didn't understand. Not completely. A second death? She wondered why Aramis chose this plan, but she didn't question his decision.

"The new bodies will be organic." Alexander continued. "They will have its own wants and needs—they won't care about what is in here," He pointing to his head, "or what is in here."

He took Sophie's hand, placed it on his chest and held it there until Sophie could feel the steady beat of his heart.

Sophie tensed as her body trembled at the warm touch of Alexander's palm.

"The new age...it won't be like this one. Just know, that if you follow Aramis' spirit, you won't' fail your next mission...if you ignore it, the darkness will consume you, just as it's consuming souls now."

Sophie attempted to withdraw her hand, but as she did, Alexander slid his grip to her wrist, bringing the back of her hand closer to his face. He rubbed his thumb over the place where Serus had kissed her as if he could remove the gesture, or make her forget the moment had ever occurred.

"This ashen soot," he began, nodding to the back of her hand, " won't be present in the next life." Pain flickered in his eyes as he met Sophie's. "Only now can we see such things. They will be hidden from us in the new dimension, but never from Aramis. He will see and document everything, just as he does now."

Alexander gently lowered Sophie's hand but held her gaze and quoted Aramis' words. "What is spoken in secret will be known. What is covered will be revealed."

Sophie wanted to ask Alexander a million questions. She wanted to know everything about what Aramis had told him, but she kept quiet. She could only stare into his blue eyes as something deep sparked within her soul. Was it admiration?

Gratefulness? Whatever it was, it pulled Sophie closer, willing her to peer deeper into his eyes.

Alexander closed in the space, placing his hand on her shoulders and said, softly. "Close your eyes,"

Sophie closed her eyes, focusing on the heat in Alexander's hands.

"What do you feel when you are with Aramis?" He asked, in almost a whisper.

"Warmth, comfort, peace–love."

"Concentrate on those feelings. Draw them from your soul-harness them."

Sophie focused on every moment she had ever spent with Aramis. She remembered their talks over tea, their walks on Earth. She remembered standing with him in the forest, where he told her to name the animals she liked the most. She remembered how they had spent hours in the library. He had taught her how to read and write their language. She warmed with the emotions from her memories and as she did, her aura spread out from her body with a faint, wavering hue of periwinkle.

Seeing Sophie's aura emanate, Alexander closed his eyes and began to meditate with her.

The two souls focused on Aramis' power, his gentleness, and his great wisdom. Their auras waved from wisps of lilac purple to a deep shade of royal blue.

"That fire Sophie, it will always burn within you." Alexander said, squeezing Sophie's arms gently. "You can follow it, trust it."

Sophie's spirit called out to her king...and he answered.

The air around Sophie and Alexander lifted, swirling their blue auras like a single pillar of fire.

After a long moment, Alexander let his hands rest at his side and waited for Sophie's eyes to flutter open. The blue flames dwindled from her body until only a calm, milky white glow remained. He gazed at Sophie's lips, and then her hand, finding the trespasses of the Outcast had vanished.

She had been cleansed of their Confusion.

Watching the color coming back into her pink cheeks, Alexander smiled and watched the Truth Keeper's hair shine with a vibrant shade of brown. Her dress shimmered in the sunlight, and her skin was full of tan pigment again.

Bevol came between Sophie and Alexander, nestling his nose in the crease of her neck.

Sophie laughed. She was her normal cheerful self again. She had been renewed, strengthened, and she was thankful to Aramis for lending her his peace.

"Hey boy," she giggled, stroking Bevol's nose. "Did you have a good rest?"

Alexander's brilliant smile fell. He wished he could paint Sophie with Bevol, but even if he did, it would soon be lost and forgotten. He grieved for what was to come. He knew he had to focus on the task at hand, but the more he tried, the more the future invaded his thoughts, especially the thought of losing Sophie. He wasn't ready for that.

I would die a thousand lifetimes if it meant she would be protected.

He shook his head, trying to shake away the tug in his chest. He told himself he had to let her go, that he couldn't allow his emotions to cloud his mind. He let his gaze follow the wake of the pool to the falls, then up the rapids to the top of the rocky plateau. His favorite sport came to his mind. He was always good at diving and before his promotion; he had swum twenty laps every day in the lake at his home. A swim. It would not only distract him from his feelings, but also Sophie from what was to come. For now, there was still time to enjoy their last day on Earth. For now, they could live.

A CAVE OF
STARLIGHT

"WHAT is that?" Alexander asked, peering over the edge into the pool.

Sophie leaned over beside him. "What? What do you see?"

She narrowed her gaze but saw nothing but small colorful fish and her reflection. She glanced at Alexander's rippling face in the water, seeing his lips draw up into a smile. Before she could react, his arms were around her waist. She kicked her legs, letting out a shriek, but it was cut off by the splash as they fell into the pool.

Surfacing, Sophie sputtered, sweeping her dripping strands of hair from her face. She coughed, watching Alexander come up a few feet away. He jerked his head to the side, slapping his blond locks against his forehead.

"Whoo! That's cold!"

"You think you're funny, don't you?" Sophie laughed, splashing him.

Alexander splashed her back. "Not as funny as the face you made when I grabbed you."

Sophie narrowed her eyes and splashed him again, but Alexander dipped under her. He surfaced behind her, and then laughed, dodging each swift moment of her hand as she attempted to grab him. He shoved the water with his palm in defense, sending a small wave over her face.

"You're slow." He teased.

"I'm not slow!" Sophie shoved water back at him and wiped her eyes.

Alexander glanced over his shoulder to the other side of the pool. He smirked, turning his gaze back at Sophie, and jutted his chin. "Prove it."

"Is that a challenge, Guardian?"

"On three." Alexander nodded.

They counted down together. "One...two..."

Alexander pushed off, leaving Sophie with her mouth hanging open.

Sophie followed suit, using quick even strokes to try to catch up, but she couldn't. He was all ready to the other side of the pool before she could make it halfway across.

Swimming to the basin, she watched the muscles in Alexander's forearms flex as he heaved himself out of the water.

He glanced at his wristband and shook his head. "Definitely slow."

"You cheated," Sophie protested, resting her head on her arms on the edge of the pool. She panted, trying to gather an even breath.

Alexander shrugged, and then glanced at the rocky wall beside him. "I said on three, not after," He teased, and climbed up the side of the waterfall. His soaked shirt clung to his skin, revealing the tight lines of his warrior body.

"You should see the view," He waved, gesturing Sophie for join him at the top.

Sophie shook her head in disbelief and then peered up the rocky wall. She accepted his challenge and rose from the pool to scale the wall to the summit.

Reaching the edge of the plateau, Alexander took Sophie's hand and pulled her up onto the bluff beside him. Her heart thudded wildly in her chest. It wasn't from the exertion, but from the way Alexander brilliantly smiled at her.

She gazed down at the forest, the beach, and the mountains edging the horizon in the distance. Taking mental snapshots of Aramis' magnificent creation would never get old. She hoped to keep these memories, hoped they would be tucked away somewhere deep within her subconscious. She imagined what a perfect retreat this cliff would have been. She would have hung a hammock; laid in the sun reading, or napped, while swaying in the breeze.

"See you at the bottom," Alexander said, bringing her back to the present.

Sophie watched him plant his feet at the cliffs edge, and leap backward. Her heart fluttered, watching him dive headfirst into the pool. When he surfaced, she took a few steps back before taking a running leap, arms spread, legs together, and dove. Her stomach did summersaults as she fell, and then settled, as time seemed to slow. She could focus on the mist below her and the crystals at the bottom of the see-through pool. Time sped up the moment she sucked in a deep breath and her fingertips met the water.

A big grin was on her face as she surfaced, and then swam to Alexander to dunk him. He rose, returning the gesture before racing her to the edge of the pool for another dive.

The Truth Keeper and Guardian laughed and joked, showing off their diving skills as if they had been friends for years. They were playful, pushing one another off the bluff, and racing back and forth from one end of the spring to the other. After a long while, they rested on some rocks by the rushing falls. They spent hours talking about the way life used to be and the wonderful ways they had passed the time over the last few hundred years; before the Confusion.

Sophie talked about how she used to dance. She described her tulle dresses and her pink shoes. She admitted how much she missed performing in the courtyard during festivals. She also spoke about the stories she had written.

They were always about the animals and the lush distant planets she planned to visit. She talked about the shells she collected all the times she and Bevol were on the beach. Those were the memories she wished she didn't have to forget; those were the memories she cherished most.

Alexander listened to every word. He never once interrupted the Truth Keeper. He was far too intrigued with her life; too eager to know whom she was before the dark days. When Sophie finally asked him about his past, his eyes gleamed, thinking of his own happy memories.

He told her about days spent on his sailboat, described the sunset, the array of colors in pastels and vibrant hues. He described the rolling green hills of the countryside, and how Ronin and he would ride and play there. He talked about all the different horses he had named, but he never once mentioned he had painted them. He never told her what he missed most about his life before the war. He didn't want to admit he had been nothing more than a humble painter.

Hours had passed. Sophie and Alexander had not realized they had spent half the day in the secret spring. They had forgotten about the time, and that the end was near.

When they went back to the cliff to jump, Alexander, watched from the pool below, pleased by the smile on Sophie's face. He knew he had made the right decision in getting her into the water. It was clear she loved swimming as much as he did. He remembered back to when he studied her from afar as she waded in the ocean before their first encounter. Water was her therapy, just as it was his.

He somehow knew, that even if she didn't remember today, he had given her some type of joy before the time came to say goodbye. She didn't have to spend her last few moments dreading the end. She could pretend, even if it was just for a little while, she could live in a moment where all was right.

After peeling off his soaked shirt, Alexander glanced at his watch. There had been no decoded messages. His body glistened in the sunlight and he was grateful for the warmth of the sun.

Draping his garment over a nearby tree branch to dry, Alexander turned back toward the pool. His gaze soon darted from Sophie to a light that sparkled behind the falls. It glimmered against the crystal-studded rocks, drawing him to it.

"I win!" Sophie shouted, slicking back the hair over her eyes. She glanced up to the cliff, ready to watch Alexander dive. After treading the water for several heartbeats, she realized he wasn't there. She scanned the spring, but there was no sight of her Guardian. A stab of fear pierced her heart with the thought that something had happened to him.

Had he run into an Outcast? Was he captured? Were the Outcasts lurking in the trees?

She hid behind the rocks in the pool, peeking out. Her gaze darted from tree to tree, but there were only the spider monkeys eating fruit and the parrots grooming their feathers.

Spotting something white, Sophie got out of the pool. She ran to Alexander's shirt and wrung it in her hand. As it dripped at her feet, she glanced around the spring once more, until a voice called her to follow him behind the waterfall.

Inside the cave, Sophie glanced at the rocky ceiling, covered in long, thick vines. Sunlight filtered in through the small hole, giving a glimpse of the blue sky above. Her gaze then followed the light to the clear green water. There were clear crystals in the bottom of the pool, much like the one Aramis had gifted her. She grasped the king's gift and smiled, wondering if this secret place had been made just for her.

As Sophie drank in the wonder of this newfound place, she spotted Alexander. He was swimming toward her, a wide grin spreading across his lips.

"What are you doing now?"

"Get in and find out," Alexander dared, splashing her feet.

Sophie jumped in and swam after Alexander, who led the way to a small, dark entrance. It reminded her of the dark space in her mind, the endless void of doubt that had swallowed her up.

"I think we should stay here," She said, treading water away from him.

"Don't you trust me?"

Sophie glanced at Alexander's offered hand. The Guardian was no longer a stranger to her. He was a friend, a trusted soul she knew she could count on. She took his hand and he squeezed her fingers, clearly pleased with her answer.

Alexander guided her through the dark tunnel of stalactites. The water was ankle deep, making it easy to walk on the smooth stones beneath. Further inside, the water deepened to their waists and they entered a second cave.

Vivid, neon lights pulsated in clusters above. Sophie gasped in delight, awestruck by the stunning view of the hundreds of phosphorescent glowworms.

Alexander kept still so Sophie could enjoy the reflection of their twinkling in the water. "Aramis, the artist."

"The world is his canvas," Sophie smiled, waving her hand over the water, rippling it toward him.

As Sophie glanced around in admiration, Alexander stared at her, basking in her blue hue.

Sophie felt his gaze and met his fixed stare. "What?"

"You're reflecting Aramis' spirit."

Thoughts of Aramis entered Sophie's mind. She frowned and her glow faded.

"Did I say something wrong?"

"No, I just-I wish I could take away his pain," she admitted. "I failed him. He trusted me to care for those in need of counsel, to show them the truth, but no matter how much I counseled, they still turned."

Alexander's shoulders slumped as he felt Sophie's aura of heartache. "It's not your fault. You didn't do this, Aalok did. You spent countless days with souls, made every attempt to reach them. Don't ever believe you're responsible for their blindness. Those who have fallen have made their own choices, ruining it for the rest of us, forcing Aramis to do something he never planned to do. It is they, and Aalok, who have caused this. Not Aramis, and certainly not you."

"What if I can't reach them in the next life?" Sophie whispered. She pressed her lips hard, trying to hold back her tears. Serus' face made his way into her mind. Her heart ached at the shallowness of his eyes as she left the camp. Her knuckles burned as his kiss flashed in her mind, and she rubbed her hand, trembling again at the pain.

Alexander rested his thumb on Sophie's chin, lifting it up so he could see into her eyes.

Sophie shivered, but this time, the trembling was not of fear, but from the way Alexander was looking at her.

"Morning lit the path out of the black of night, but they who delighted in the darkness, didn't open their eyes to search for the sun's redemption," Alexander said, quoting Aramis' words. "They are only bitter because of what you stand for, who you represent."

"I don't want them to be bitter. I didn't ask to be a Truth Keeper. I didn't choose this."

"No, but Aramis chose you and others like you. Light will overcome the darkness. But we can't lose hope or we lose that light."

"There are so many things I feel that were left unsaid, so many souls I have yet to counsel. If only I had more time…"

Alexander's forehead wrinkled. He wished he could have more time with Sophie. He wanted her to know him, truly know him. Right now he was just her protector, a soldier sent from Aramis.

Alexander's wristband vibrated, and he glanced at the code. 'Soon'.

"We should get back to the spring." Alexander exhaled and took a step past Sophie, but she grasped his forearm.

"Will you stay with me to the end?" Sophie asked, gazing up at him. When his brows knitted, Sophie rephrased her words. "I mean…is that what is required of you? To watch over me until this aeon ends?"

Alexander swallowed hard and turned to her. "Yes, those are Aramis' orders."

"All this time you have stayed so calm. You act as if you're not afraid of what will happen. But I—I keep losing hope. I keep doubting Aramis' plan." Sophie trembled as tears streamed down her cheeks. "I'm not strong enough to do this."

Alexander's ribs pressed against his lungs. He couldn't breathe. He was too close to Sophie, trapped by her aura expelling her negative emotions. His face contorted as he looked to the way leading to the exit, but then shifted back to the Truth Keeper.

She held a hand to her mouth to muffle her cries. She was still trying to be strong, but Alexander could feel the panic in her aura. She was about to come undone.

"Don't lose hope, not now." He said softly, taking her in his arms.

Sophie welcomed her Guardian's comfort, but she still wept. Hope. There was no hope. Not now, not when everything she knew would be gone. She would be cast into a new world, a strange new place with no familiar faces to turn to.

She had tried to keep faith all this time, tried to swallow the fear, but she couldn't. Not any longer.

As Sophie cried, Alexander wrapped his arms tighter around her as if he could squeeze the pain from her being. But it wasn't enough. He wasn't enough. She needed Aramis. She needed his wisdom.

Closing his eyes, Alexander sent out a prayer.

In Aramis' answer, the Guardian lit in blue wisping waves. It emanated from his body to Sophie in a low and soothing hum, a melody of calm. Alexander had been unable to comfort the Truth Keeper in the ballroom, but he could comfort her now.

Seeing her Guardian reflect the spirit of Aramis, Sophie glowed too. She pressed her cheek to her his chest, soothed by the steady beat of his heart. She focused on its rhythm and the humming of his aura's resonance as if it was a lullaby. The song picked up speed as Sophie embraced her Guardian in gratitude for his comfort. But it wasn't just the gratitude she felt. Something else was there, something spurred by the tug in her soul. As her heart lit to flames and her stomach fluttered, her aura reflected her emotions.

Alexander reacted to the rush of exhilaration her felt from her and met her eyes with surprise. She was no longer glowing a milky hue, but his same amber glow. He wiped the tears from her cheeks and gazed at the light now flickering in her eyes.

The song from their souls was the most beautiful hum of chords: A sharp, D, F and, G.

It was a symphony of strings and bass. It reverberated off the walls as if it were a concert hall.

When their aura's expanded, the melody grew louder and the glowworms pulsed in time with the tune.

The water around them shivered and then vibrated upwards. It rose into several round orbs and transformed into intricate, crystal-like snowflakes.

Watching the water float gracefully around them, Sophie felt something she had never felt before. Staring into

Alexander's eyes, she could see his soul, as if it had been waiting for her, searching for her. She had found what she never knew her she had been missing. The lost piece had been found and it slid into place, connecting her soul and Alexander's with a snap.

Alexander also felt the snap and the rush of energy in her being. He brushed Sophie's cheek with his thumb. His chest swirled with emotion and his body quivered as if it would burst into a blaze if he didn't press his lips to hers. Without another thought, he kissed her and exhaled a long, satisfying breath at her taste.

Sophie kissed Alexander back, leaning into his lips, accepting the gentle sweep of his tongue.

They burned brighter with each kiss, illuminating the cave with their golden rays of light.

Sophie's body quivered, but soon, it was not from her emotions like before, but from the movement beneath her feet.

The hard tremor crawled up her legs, rippling the water around her. Her eyes shot open and she pushed Alexander away as her body shook so hard, her teeth chattered.

The vibrating snowflakes collapsed, falling like drops of rain.

Alexander's gaze darted from droplets to the rippling water. It bubbled and sloshed from side to side against the rocky walls. The glowworms fell too, filling the pool like tiny neon bulbs. The cave shook with a furious roar, and Alexander turned back to Sophie to take her hand, only to hear her whisper her regret.

"What have I done?"

14

THE
BEGINNING
OF THE END

AN ear-shattering crack resounded from above. Sophie flinched and watched as the rocky wall split, spewing water into the cave. Alexander's hand was around hers in an instant. He towed her toward the light; the way out as the water rose. Another rumble shook the cave and before Sophie and Alexander could make it through to the exit, the walls of the cave gave way.

The clatter of boulders filled Sophie's ears but soon it was the rush of water. She slipped through Alexander's fingers and was sucked through a watery vortex.

Tumbling in the current, Sophie pushed down the breath in her lungs; even as rocks sliced her flailing hands and feet.

But when a sharp pain struck her skull, she heaved the oxygen from her chest. With a throbbing head, Sophie sunk into a whirl of darkness that filled her vision until her body went numb, weightless. A peaceful silence came. Everything around her went black. She was rendered unconscious and a void welcomed her into a bottomless pit.

Shooting up from the lagoon, Alexander whipped his hair out of his eyes. He called out for Sophie. His gaze darted around the pool until a glint caught his eye. He squinted, finding the ends of Sophie's gown. They sparkled, waving into the dark abyss below his feet. He sucked in a deep breath and dove several feet before wrapping an arm around the Truth Keeper's waist, kicking his way to the surface.

Sophie sputtered water, choking through strangled breaths as Alexander swam them to the lagoon basin. He heaved her up on dry land with a groan and then climbed out. As she coughed, he placed his hand gently on her back, hoping she was all right.

"I'm fine," Sophie rasped. She stood, coughing again and supported herself against the rock wall. She surveyed the cuts on her skin, hissing through her teeth as it stitched itself back together.

Another alert dinged from Alexander's wristband. He had missed the first warning of the quake. That's what the code had meant. He clenched his teeth, frustrated for allowing himself to be distracted.

They had to get back to the secret spring and to higher ground; much higher ground.

Taking Sophie's hand, Alexander rushed through the small cave opening to the spring. He snatched his shirt from the branch, all but dragging the Truth Keeper behind him.

Spotting Ronin, he hastened his pace, whistling for him to come, but Sophie stopped abruptly, slipping her hand from her Guardian's grasp.

"Sophie! Come on!"

"Bevol," Sophie whispered.

Alexander shouted again, but Sophie couldn't hear him. She could only hear the rush of blood in her ears. She wet her dry lips as they quivered, turning in circles, searching for Bevol. He was gone. He had fled in fear, again.

A hand wrapped around her waist before she could run to find him. Scooped up into her Guardian's lap, she leaned back against his chest as Ronin took off through the tree line and toward the shore.

A tingle ran up Alexander's arm; another warning alerting him. Urgency shot through him, raising the hair on the back of his neck.

A mountain roared in the distance, trailing a plume of smoke into the air.

Sophie gripped her Guardian's arm around her waist, watching the clouds fill the sky. Day turned to dusk and the shadow of the fleeing horse and his riders faded from the sandy ground.

Ronin galloped up a sloping hillside and onto the path leading to Alexander's vehicle.

Once at his ship, Alexander jumped off his horse and helped Sophie slide down.

"Get in the ship," He ordered gruffly, pointing his chin.

Sophie glanced at the white vessel bearing Aramis' emblem. It was larger than hers but still too small for more than two passengers. As the door opened automatically, Sophie smoothed a hand down the white stripe on Ronin's nose. She kissed him, choking back tears before running to the ship to crawling inside.

"I'm so sorry, boy. I wish there was another way." Alexander whispered as he stroked Ronin's face. "We will meet again, my friend. Aramis promised; he always keeps his promises."

Ronin nuzzled Alexander's cheek before Alexander turned away with damp eyes.

Sophie turned away, unable to bear the sight of Ronin's unblinking stare as his rider abandoned him. She bit back her tears, knowing the Earth, and all its inhabitants would be destroyed. Everything would die and there was nothing she could do to stop it. The horses, the dinosaurs, the tiny creatures in the forest; all of them would perish.

Her hands shook. Her chest tightened. She couldn't bear to listen to the heartbroken cries of Ronin. She covered her ears, hoping to muffle the sound.

Dropping into the pilot seat, Alexander tossed his shirt behind him as his door slid closed with a click. Ronin's cries were silenced. Sophie removed her hands, glancing at her Guardian's face, now a mask of stone. He flipped buttons and started the takeoff sequence, lifting the narrow spacecraft into the air. The wings of the ship spread out to the side of the craft as he pointed the nose up to the sky.

Sophie pressed a hand to the glass window and looked out, seeing Ronin, now only a small brown dot on the cliff. As the clouds hid Earth, Sophie leaned her head against the window letting her tears trickled down her face.

"It will all be over soon," Alexander assured himself. Squeezing his eyes tight, he shoved the throttle forward, leaving the Earth, and all living on it to the coming chaos soon to unfold.

Alexander's spacecraft glided through the cosmos, like a ship sailing in a sea of stars. As it cruised the darkness, he grieved Ronin. He remembered the day he first saw him. He was painting the horses that had been grazing in a clover field. He had come to that spot to paint the sunset. He had swept a shade of yellow on his brush, ready to mirror the vibrant hues of morning until something nudged him from behind.

Looking over his shoulder, he found a brown horse with a white stripe down his nose and forehead. The horse grunted at him, and then leaned over, snatching one of his brushes with his teeth. Alexander ran after him, chasing until the horse came to a standstill and dropped the brush at his boots. A playful game. That was the beginning of Alexander and Ronin's friendship.

Alexander remembered teaching Ronin commands, fitting him in royal armor after he was promoted to Aramis' army. He remembered the rides across the countryside and could still hear the bell around Ronin's neck. It chimed in his mind, bringing recollection of his first meeting with Sophie.

His mind raced through the moments thereafter, ending with their kiss in the cave. The moment his face flushed with heat, he stood and went to the cargo area. He shuffled through a few drawers, finding an extra shirt and pulled it over his head. On his way back, he glanced at Sophie in the passenger-side and frowned.

Sophie sniffed, gazing out her window at the vast universe until her eyes caught Alexander in the reflection. She wiped her cheeks, sensing him pause behind her. She could feel his aura of grief. She was grieving too. She never had the chance to say goodbye. She never got to tell Bevol how sorry she was for leaving him. She wondered where he had run. Wondered why the Earth had to be destroyed.

Alexander dropped into the pilot seat, and Sophie could sense his regret thickening. It washed over him like a wave. He was being drawn out to sea, and there was no land in sight, no light, guiding the way to the safety of the shore. There was only him, alone in the middle of a raging ocean of emotion. Then everything stilled. It was as if the storm of his aura had ceased at once.

Sophie wondered if he was allowing himself to slip into emptiness, if he was convincing himself that it would make it easier, to ignore the pain. Sucking in a sharp breath, she sat up and turned to face her Guardian. His face was unreadable. He was frozen, staring out the windshield into the darkness. She wondered if he wished he were floating out there, drifting out in nothingness. Her gaze traveled from his face to his white knuckles and she watched him grip the steering wheel tight, twisting it.

"Alexander," she said softly.

He didn't move.

"Alexander," she repeated louder this time.

Alexander eased his grip and blinked. "What?"

"Where are we going?"

Alexander looked around the ship as if he didn't know where he was. His gaze then shifted to Sophie's troubled expression. An alert came from his wristband before he could answer. He didn't understand the code. "It Begins" was not what he expected to see. He stared at the message until it disappeared, wondering why he had been instructed to not return to the Infinite Realm. Aramis' message had been clear. 'Wait for my signal, then bring the Truth Keeper to me.'

The earth is being destroyed. Wasn't the ground shaking a clear sign that it was time to head back?

"We wait," Alexander huffed, tapping on the icons on the screen of the dash. He glared at the ship's instruments then leaned his head back against the headrest.

Sophie glanced at the fuel gauge and raised her brows. "If we wait too long, we won't have enough plasma to make it through the portal."

"We wait. Quietly."

"Maybe it would help if you talked about how you feel."

Alexander gave a throaty laugh and shook his head. "No thanks, Truth Keeper."

"So what? You just expect me to sit here in silence? Deal with all the emotions you won't face?"

"I expect you to-"

"Expect me to what?" Sophie asked, crossing her arms.

"Brace yourself," Alexander murmured, clicking buttons.

"Brace myself?" Sophie did a double take out her window, seeing the mass of rocks heading their way.

"Hold on!" Alexander turned the steering wheel sharply, but it didn't matter.

The meteors slammed into the back of the spacecraft, thrusting Sophie forward against the dash. The collision shook her so hard that it rattled her skull. She squeezed her eyes tight, holding back the urge to vomit.

An alarm sounded, but Sophie couldn't hear it. There was only a high-pitch ringing in her ears as she looked at Alexander blurring in her vision.

He was moving his mouth as if in slow motion. She could faintly hear his words. Holding her throbbing head in her hands, she winced pain splitting across her forehead.

"Are you okay?" Alexander's muffled voice asked.

"I think so," she groaned, touching the cut on her head. She squinted, trying to bring the liquid on her fingers into focus. Blood. Her blood. It was the same clear fluid pulsing in her veins, pumping through her body to keep up with the rapid beat of her heart. Her forehead tightened as the gash healed. Healing had never hurt before, but it did after the cave, and now. Sophie didn't understand, could only assume she had been affected by her negative emotions, by Alexander's too.

As Sophie sat healing, Alexander cursed under his breath, tapping the screen on the dash. When the icons of the ship's instruments flickered, he slammed his fist against the screen, glaring at the fuel gauge. It was ticking down, and fast.

"If this keeps up, we'll end up floating," Alexander said, unbuckling. He rose from his seat and went to the back of his ship. He sifted through the drawers in the walls, slamming them one by one. Finding what he had been searching for, his shoulders relaxed as he took out a small, blue fluorescent vial, and held it up. "Thank Aramis,"

He shoved the spare vial in the fuel receptor then sat in the pilot seat. "That's all I have left."

Alexander punched in the coordinates to a nearby planet, but the computer told him there wasn't enough fuel to make it to his destination. He punched in more coordinates, but every time he did, the computer notified him that the destination was too far.

Sophie glanced at the fuel gauge as it ticked down, and then glanced out the porthole to measure how far they were from Earth.

"I have some reserves at my home."

"No. Aramis gave strict orders. We're not to return to the Infinite Realm until I'm notified,"

Glancing back at Sophie, his gaze darted over her shoulder to the window. A band of red rocks, large and small, were heading toward the ship. He had never seen anything like it. It was like an army of boulders, lined up in a formation, ready to go to war.

Sophie punched in the coordinates to her home and the computer responded just as she expected. "We can make it."

"How many vials do you have?"

"I-I don't know, ten?"

"That's not enough, and if I don't patch the leak we won't be able to make it." Alexander stared hard at the fuel gauge for a long moment, then let out a breath in frustration. "Fine. I'll figure it out once we get there."

Pressing the icon, Alexander set the destination for Sophie's home in the Infinite Realm, and a portal soon appeared.

When Alexander thrust the throttle forward, the ship flashed. The ship disappeared into the black swirling void, leaving behind the pieces of broken planets drifting through space, heading for Earth.

15

HOME

"LET'S make this quick," Alexander urged landing the spacecraft on Sophie's lawn. "Aramis could alert us at any moment."

Sophie jumped out and met Alexander at the back of the ship, watching him examine the damage of the impact. The back end had been smashed, crumpled like a tin can. The plasma fuel was trickling out.

"Great," Alexander grumbled, lifting the cargo door. He grabbed his sword and gloves from a bag. With haste he shoved his fingers through the white leather and slammed the door hard, knowing there would be a consequence for bringing the Truth Keeper to the Infinite Realm. "Stay close,"

Sophie shadowed her Guardian as they ran up the grassy knoll, scanning it for enemies. They traversed the yard, going through the intricate iron gate, leading to the cobblestone sidewalk. They passed the white rose bushes, fruit trees, and colorful flowerbeds, placed neatly around the well-manicured lawn.

Sophie's heart raced as they ran to her home. It was three stories high, with a wrap around porch circling each story. There was a stained glass circle window in the tower of Sophie's book nook, leading to the steeples that topped each tower with delicate, winding designs. Although extravagant, the house seemed small. It was dull and dark, standing under the purple cloudy skies above.

Rushing up the cobblestone steps and past the white pillars to the cherry oak door, Alexander drew his sword and brought a finger to his lips as they slipped inside.

Inside, the furniture continued the theme of the home with delicate woodwork and elegant trim. A large oak table in the dining room sat set for eight. To the left of the foyer, was Sophie's study. It was cozy and covered in bookshelves, which overflowed with textbooks about Earth, and her own writings. Clean, white drapes graced the window by her tidy desk, which was organized with stacks of papers, utensils, and a tiny potted plant that sat drooping as if saddened by Sophie's absence.

Sophie and Alexander walked cautiously across the living room. The waxed wooden floor led to a lush rug, woven in gold with Aramis' emblem. Sophie paused on the emblem of the crown as the chandelier above her quivered. The crystal of it chimed, jingling, as the Infinite Realm rumbled beneath their feet.

"Hurry," Alexander ordered, and ran up the stairs, inspecting the upper rooms for intruders.

Sophie approached the wall and pulled on two books from the shelf decorated with fig leaves. Gears rotated, grinding against one another, before the secret door clicked opened, revealing a hidden library. It was covered wall to wall with scrolls, the same documents she had mentioned to Aramis. In the back of the storage area was a small crate filled with the plasma vials. She frowned. She remembered ten, but now there were only eight. She recalled using one to go to the Earth that morning to wait for Serus, and one on the way back. Sophie's chest grew heavy. Serus. What she had done was unforgivable. How could she face him again, knowing she had kissed her Guardian?

Pressing her lips into a thin line, she stacked the vials in her arms, trying to shake off what happened in the cave. Heading out to meet up with Alexander at the steps, she paused, staring at the stacked scrolls of those she had counseled.

Sophie knew Aramis had his own documentation, but she had hoped hers would have been relevant to him. After all, these scrolls were vital information on the very souls who had turned. They held valuable secrets about Aalok. She wondered if it even mattered now. The house shook and Sophie gripped the vials tight. No. Aramis had chosen a plan and that plan was being fulfilled.

In Sophie's bedroom, Alexander knelt on the floor, looking under her bed, before making his way to the closet.

After checking every possible hiding spot, he confirmed that the room was secure. Making his way through Sophie's bedroom door, his hand gripped the doorframe as something caught his attention.

The mural on the wall. He knew it well, but still examined the painting. The scenes flowed into one another, creating a splendid masterpiece. Alexander smoothed his hand over the depictions. It was his brushstrokes, his oils. He grimaced, knowing it would be destroyed. Every painting he had ever created would be gone. He understood Aramis' disappointment, for all of Aramis' creations—his art—his masterpieces, would soon cease to exist.

Alexander took one last look at the painting before he closed Sophie's bedroom door. When he finished his inspection of the upper floor, he hurried down the stairs to Sophie, who stood, frowning at a framed painting hanging on her wall.

The canvas was an image of rolling green hills and a dappled horse grazing in an open field. She then looked at the watercolor landscape of mountains and a lake. She went to another with fruit trees, and then one of a brook lined with colorful flowers, under the umbrella of a purple wisteria tree. Earth. All of the paintings were of Earth. Sophie may have not realized it, but Alexander knew his work. He had painted every single one of these depictions.

"We need to go," Alexander said, then took the plasma vials from Sophie's arms and counted them. "I thought you said you had ten?"

"I'm sorry. I must have used more than I thought."

"I'm assuming you don't have any tools I could use to fix the leak, do you?"

"I always went to the Crystal Kingdom when I needed repairs." Sophie shrugged.

Alexander headed for the door. "We'll repair the ship at my place. I have more than enough plasma vials there."

"I can't do this,"

Alexander let out a light laugh and took hold of the doorknob. "You won't have to. I know how to fix the leak."

"No, I mean, I need a moment."

Alexander looked over his shoulder. "I'm sorry, I thought I heard you say you need a moment?"

"Go to your place, fix your ship. I'll be ready to go when you get back. I just-I need some time alone."

Alexander shoved the vials in his belt satchel. He crossed his arms, staring at Sophie for a moment. "And you think that's a good idea? To stay alone, unprotected? What if the Outcasts come here looking for you?"

Sophie didn't have a response. She only put her hand to her forehead and rubbed it. "Please, everything feels like it's spinning. I can't breathe, not with all my emotions...and yours. It's too much."

Alexander's wristband sounded an alert.

"What's it say? Is it time to go back?"

Alexander tapped the screen. The alert was coming from one of Aramis' ships, but it wasn't in code. He read it over and over again, trying to understand why someone in the fleet would notify him out in the open.

"It says the Outcasts are at Aalok's fortress. They're planning to attack the kingdom at Earth's dawn."

Sophie's eyes lit up. "Then we have plenty of time."

Alexander's forehead wrinkled as he glanced up at Sophie. "Aalok's plans do not change Aramis'."

"But I'm not in danger."

"I'm not leaving you here,"

Sophie took careful steps to Alexander and placed her hand on his arm. "Please? Being around you, feeling everything you feel...it hurts. I need some space."

Alexander stared thoughtfully at Sophie. He knew she needed time alone. He needed time alone too. The weight of her emotions from her aura was exhausting. His gut twisted, but against his better instincts, he nodded in agreement.

"You have less than twenty minutes, Earth time. Keep the door locked. Do not open it for anyone, but me. Do you understand?"

"Yes,"

Alexander set his watch for twenty minutes as Sophie followed him to her front door.

"I mean it. Twenty minutes, not a second longer," he repeated sternly, pointing to the screen on his wristband.

Sophie nodded again, closing the door, but as she was about to lock it, Alexander pushed it back open. Sophie let out a grunt of surprise, holding onto the edge of the door, seeing only a sliver of Alexander's face through the crack.

"Trust no one."

Exhaling in relief at the sound of the door locks; Alexander made his way to his ship. He ignored his gut, telling him that he should stay. His heart whispered, told him that he had put the Truth Keeper at risk. There was no question he would be punished for this choice.

Sophie watched from the window as the vehicle blinked twice before soaring high into the sky above. She exhaled as her shoulders fell. The suffocating mix of emotions had left with Alexander, no thick cloud of pain and guilt. She glanced around the room, wondering what her new home would be like in the next life.

Would there be homes? Would there be books? Art?

She glanced at the framed paintings and then at the clock. If only there was more time. If only she could travel to the past and make things right. She shook her head, reminding herself she only had minutes and headed up the stairs to her room.

Sophie's bedroom was warm and inviting, with clean, white curtains gracing her windows as well as her neatly made canopy bed. Trinkets and books filled the shelves that lined the walls beside a dark oak vanity in the corner. She went to it, running her fingers along a golden brush. A frown came as she stared at her dirty face in the vanity mirror and untied her braid. Sweeping the familiar bristles through her soft, but frazzled hair, she hummed a tune. Her gaze went to her music box, and soon the face of the artisan who made it came to her mind.

She ran a finger over the etching of the fleur in the wood. The woodworker had been one of the peers she had counseled and begged not to go to Aalok. She swallowed the knot in her throat, winding the key carefully, and opened the top. The soothing melody filled her ears as she went to sit on her bed, listening to the ting of metal against metal.

With the sweet tune chiming in her ears, Sophie ached to be back at the castle. She recalled dancing to this melody, twirling on her toes at one of the festivals.

Rising from the bed, Sophie retraced the graceful steps, matching the choreography in her mind. When she opened her eyes, she looked over her shoulder at the painted mural of the Infinite Kingdom displayed on the wall. She approached it slowly and traced her fingers over the dried paint. She recalled how she had fallen in love with the artwork when she first arrived at her new home.

Replaying her life before her job as a Truth Keeper, Sophie smiled at a memory of her dancing, lifting her leg in the soft white tulle of her dress. She had been a talented lead dancer, and took joy in the music and her movements. Another was of her playing the piano with a gold leaf adornment in her hair. She could still feel the keys beneath her fingers. Then another scene of her picking flowers in the meadow, the day before she met Serus. There were so many scenes of her life, so many happy memories. Her fingers followed the brushstrokes over the scenes, and down to the signature of the artisan. She wished she had inquired who the artist was, now she would never know.

Sophie set her sight to the image of Aramis. He was holding a bright shining star in his palm. It was her soul, the moment that Aramis had created her. Many glowing bodies were around her, Seraphim too. They were singing with joy at her arrival. Sophie smoothed her hand over Aramis' bright painted face on the mural, feeling peace, but it didn't last. Her chest ached, knowing she would be separated from him. She reminded herself that if she ever wanted to be with him again that she would have to do what he had asked of her. She would have to be strong. She would go through the next life. She would lead souls back to the truth.

A knock at the door startled Sophie and the music box snapped shut with a ting. Sophie clutched it to her chest and looked to the clock on the wall.

Another knock.

Creeping on her tiptoes, Sophie went to the window. She drew back the curtains, hoping to see Alexander's vehicle, but the hovering craft was not there. In its place was a large military ship of Aramis' fleet.

Sophie rushed down the stairs in a panic and called to whoever was on the other side. "State your name, soldier."

"Caius. I'm a Guardian of Aramis' imperial army." A deep muffled voice responded. "My fleet and I are going from home to home, taking all souls back to the kingdom. Is your Guardian with you? May I speak with him?"

Sophie's heart raced and she bit her lip. It was hard to determine their intentions through the door, so she placed a palm to it, only to jerk it back as it burned.

"Please open the door."

Sophie looked at the clock, frantically. Minutes were still left. "My Guardian, Sir Alexander, is on his way back to get me. He should be here shortly. Can we wait for him?"

"There is no time to wait," Caius insisted. "The enemy is close. We cannot afford to have you swayed in the final moments. It could change Aramis' plan for your next life. The consequences would be devastating."

Sophie trembled at this soldier's tone and brought her gaze back to the clock in desperation as if staring at it would make time speed up time.

"Please hurry, Alexander." She murmured, hugging her music box.

The seconds ticked by and when the time was up, Sophie's heart stopped as her front door busted open.

"Take her," Caius ordered.

Two rebels wearing red uniforms stomped forward. Their faces were smudged with soot, screwed up with scowls.

At the jerk on her arms, Sophie's grip faulted on her prized possession.

The music box fell helplessly and clattered to the floor. It played an uneven tune as if trying to sooth Sophie's fear, but was cut short as a rebel kicked it across the room.

"Stop this!" Sophie demanded as she struggled. "Your loyalty should be to Aramis! Not Aalo-!"

A cry escaped her lips as one of the rebel's, tucked her arms firmly to her spine.

"Loyalty," Caius scoffed. "Truth Keeper, unlike you, we do not follow one being mindlessly. There will be a new king, a king that does not impose strict rules or regulations. A king who allows all to live as they please, without persecution."

Sophie's body tensed, watching the flickering red energy dance over Caius' glove. She had never seen this kind of fire before and the crackling from it made her tremble.

"Our king," Caius added, coming inches from Sophie's face. "Will be most pleased to see you."

Sophie's stomach turned while Caius slid a fiery-gloved finger along her cheek. Although it burned like a hot poker, she kept her fixed stare on his dark, cold eyes. A painful shock came from his lethal grip around her throat. It lit Sophie's skin on fire, locking up her muscles. Her body went rigid for an agonizing moment before she blacked out and went limp.

Caius released his grip in satisfaction. He lifted her chin, tilting her floppy head back against the soldier's breastplate. He eyed her clavicle and then glanced down at her chest, spying the jewel of her necklace. He clutched the chain and jerked the clasp from her neck with a snap.

"Take her to the ship," Caius ordered his men.

The soldier carried her out the door, while the rest of Caius's crew followed him to the ship, making their way on board. The pilot typed in the coordinates to their destination, waiting for Caius to join them, but Caius lingered for a few seconds longer, studying the jewel.

He knitted his brows, lifting the necklace in the air. As it spun slowly, he wondered why Aalok had requested that he fetch the useless item. Nonetheless, he tucked it into his shirt pocket, making sure it was secure. Resting his hand on the hilt of his sword, he observed Sophie's living room. This was the kind of abode he had always dreamed of, the kind he felt he deserved.

Catching sight of the paintings on the wall, he scoffed, recognizing Alexander's signature on all of them. His gaze shifted to the scroll room in the walls of books. Spotting a familiar title from across the room. He curled his lips maliciously, making his way to them.

Raising his hand, Caius snapped his fingertips. Crimson fire appeared once again, flickering with a crackle. He held the book to his glove's fiery tips before flinging it into the secret scroll room. The parchments caught fire, setting the room ablaze. Flames crackled and popped, consuming everything in its path. It crawled out of the storage room and crept up the walls into Sophie's living space, like a demon, hungry, searching for more to devour.

Caius smiled to himself, taking one last look, as the fire ate through the tapestry rug and the emblem of Aramis. He walked to the stolen ship and boarded. The ship took off with a double flash of light and disappeared into the sky, heading for Aalok's fortress.

In the secret room, the book crackled as it burned. It's white leather cover peeled and shrank. The winged emblem melted, streaking down the spine as the title, *The Words of Aramis*, dripped to the floor like tears of gold.

TAKEN

ALEXANDER shoved open the door to his log cabin. It rebounded off the wall, clattering his framed paintings. Grabbing a new uniform, he hurried to the storage closet for the vials. Placing them in his belt satchel, he headed to the door but paused. A view of the mountains from the window caught his attention. His gaze traveled down to his dock where his sailboat sat, bobbing on the lake. He couldn't go sailing or paint the sunsets of the fields. Not anymore.

He daydreamed for a few heartbeats about how things could have been different—if somehow he and Sophie could have met another way. He would have courted her, taken her for rides in the countryside, guided her hand as she steered his sailboat across the endless oceans. He would have painted her in every landscape, but the thoughts of the daydream faded as he shook his head. Everything would be erased, blotted out with inky darkness. Aramis had made it clear. He would have no memory of this life—not fully.

Alexander held on to the promise of Aramis' words. He would see Ronin again one day, he would be given everything back just the way it was, and more. He would be bonded with a mate in the eternal afterlife, but that would have to wait. He would first have to protect Sophie and succeed in the mission that waited for him in the next life. He had to leave this all behind. He would face death.

Shutting the door, his armband vibrated, popping up a clock ticking down. There were only minutes left to return to the Truth Keeper, but he could make it if he hurried.

Bringing his airship down above Sophie's home, Alexander caught sight of a flickering light. Panic pierced his heart. He gripped the steering wheel, hurling his ship into a free fall. While the craft fell, he unbuckled, pressed autopilot, and stood at the opening of the door. He let out a breath through pursed lips and cracked his knuckles before he leaped out. He landed on one knee, his fist braced against the ground. It shook beneath his steady feet, as his ship jolted, inches from touching the tips of the blades of grass. He ran to Sophie's home. It was not yet overtaken by the blaze, but he feared the worst. He was unable to sense her presence but called for her regardless.

At the entrance, he halted at the sight of the ashy soot fingerprints and boot marks on the porch and doorknob.

He gritted his teeth and a growl raised in his throat as followed the soot smudges through the threshold. He watched the inferno, bursting into his own amber blaze. He jerked back his sleeve, typing in the code on his screen that linked Sophie's location from her necklace. The coordinates glowed white light, traveling across the Infinite Realm.

Gnashing his teeth, Alexander climbed back into his ship. He punched the dash and cursed himself.

Stupid.

The reason for his delay flashed in his mind. It wasn't that he had taken too long to fix the ship. It was the fact that he had paused for sentiment.

Alexander let out a controlled breath and glanced at the white light on his wristband, blinking urgently. Sophie's white icon moved across the Infinite Realm past the gated entrance of the kingdom. He glared as the pulsing light disappeared for a few heartbeats, before reappearing, heading for a green and blue globe.

Earth.

He tapped the lock on Sophie's location and lifted the ship into the air, pressing the button for a portal. He shoved the throttle forward. The craft zipped through the rainbow swirls of the wormhole, toward Aalok's fortress; toward the Truth Keeper he was determined to save.

Sophie drifted in and out of consciousness for a moment until the ship's cargo area came into view, blurry and unfocused. She blinked her eyes, finding weapons on the walls and chains clinking from the ceiling. As a hum echoed in her ears and the smell of smoke filled her nostrils, Sophie found a pair of ashy boots across from her. She tested the spirit of the aura nearby, finding nothing but pride and a pulsing wave of hate.

Groaning, Sophie struggled to arch her stiff back away from the cold metal biting into her. There was no moving her limbs. They were still too stiff. Then it came, the excruciating stab of pins and needles, filling her arms and legs. She coughed and gasped for breath as panic overtook her like never before. Her face contorted, not just from the pain, but from the sorrow and grief, she had been pushing deep down.

Caius glanced down at the Truth Keeper, smiling at her struggle. His electric glove had sent more than a debilitating shock. It had poisoned her with a small dose of negative energy. His smile widened, seeing her face twist in torment from the flood of emotions. "Sleep well?" he asked.

"What did you do to me?" Sophie croaked. Groggy, she lifted her arms and legs, but the pricking of pins and needles prevented her from standing.

"You were being rather difficult," Caius teased, squatting down beside her. He cocked his head to the side and pursed his lips. His eyes roamed her body before he met her weary gaze. "We are not your enemy, Truth Keeper. We only wish to show you the truth. Soon, you will understand that your king is not what he appears to be."

"He's deceived you," Sophie rasped. She blinked, trying to stay awake but it was no use. As her head fell back on the cold metal floor, the room blurred and went black.

Caius clicked his tongue and stood, staring at the Truth Keeper. He considered the reward he would ask for her capture. He already had everything he wanted. Perhaps he could bargain with Aalok for one night with her in his chamber. He wouldn't force himself on her, of course, but if he were lucky, rumors would spread that he took her to bed.

An announcement of descent filled the ship's speakers as the airship soared over the ocean. Two soldiers stomped through the sliding doors into the cargo area and took Sophie by the arms. They dragged her across the floor, their fingers digging painfully into her skin. Sophie whimpered, drifting back to awareness, but she was too weak to fight them off.

Caius strutted to Sophie, a vulpine smile spread across his face. "Soon, you will understand," he crooned, bringing his gloved fingers close to her face.

Sophie flinched, moaning at the searing pain the movement caused. But no matter the pain she felt, no matter the torture she would endure, she vowed she would never bow to Aalok. He was a liar. He had declared war against her king and his kingdom. He had perverted its purity. Although she was consumed by hopelessness, Sophie knew she would rather suffer than bend a knee at the fallen Seraph's feet.

167

The captain of the ship announced their approach and the soldiers readied their weapons, popping their necks from side to side as Aalok's fortress came into view.

The metallic structure resting upon the rocky mountaintop was plated in pure gold. It was tiered in a spiral, circling down to a wide round base, but in the light of the rising blood moon, it appeared brassy. Clouds of ash from the volcano that Sophie and Alexander had escaped earlier hovered above. They swirled around the pointy tip of the fortress, like a vortex of a portal as if the power of Aalok alone was churning them.

The soldiers shoved Sophie out of the stolen airship and led her to the bridge. Sophie scrunched her nose at the smell of smoke and noted the dusting of ash on the ground. In the air, the ash descended lazily, like thousands of floating grey embers. Before long, her hair was covered in them. She lifted her tousled strands, trying to pick up an ember, but the ash smeared between her fingertips.

A groan from the sky snapped Sophie's gaze to the cloud covered blood moon. Pink and purple lightning streaked across them. The soldiers shoved her across the narrow walkway. She watched pebbles dance from the heavy footfalls of the soldiers to the edge. They leapt to freedom into the roaring ruby waves below.

Nearing the entrance of the fortress, Sophie gaped at the tall black double doors, which were eerily reminiscent of the ones at the Crystal Castle. Two guards stood at either side in full gold and red armor. They each had a brassy red pin on their chest, an emblem.

As Sophie passed the guards, her shoulders tensed. She had heard stories of this place, how once inside; one's mind became clouded. There had been stories of how the soul was captivated, drawn in by the luxury, and the promises of Aalok. It was a place of dreams, but also a place of deception. The soul never knew what was reality or a dream. Once inside, they were trapped in their own minds, trapped in a daydream, unable to see the dark reality of their own bondage.

A chilling draft came from the opening of the creaking doors, but to Sophie's surprise, the fortress was not a dark and hopeless place she had expected. Instead, it was a replica of her king's castle. The only difference was that the interior was not made of refined crystals, but a gaudy glittering gold.

BROTHER
AGAINST
BROTHER

SPRINTING up the rocky hillside, Alexander headed toward the bridge of the fortress. The volcanic ash danced in the air like snowflakes, coating his white uniform with a film of dingy grey. Drawing his sword, he sensed the presence of souls with anger in their hearts.

Ten feet from the entrance, the soldiers of Aalok's army crept up behind him from the boulders and followed him. More soldiers emerged from the entrance. These were the very soldiers he had won many contests against during training. He knew their weaknesses. He lit his sword, a confident smile spreading across his lips as the others encircled him.

At the attack of the first soldier, Alexander turned, driving the electric steel into his chest. The soldier fell, as another swung his sword, glowing with crimson rage. Alexander ducked and spun to the right, head butting a third soldier, knocking him back. As the soldier fell, a growl rose in Alexander's throat as fire gripped his side. Gritting his teeth against the shock of a glove, he elbowed the soldier square in the face.

Another soldier kicked Alexander's feet out from beneath him, raising his hand to punch him in the face. He rolled under the punch and came to his feet, kicking another attacker. Swinging his sword, he took out four more soldiers in one blow. Three soldiers jumped on top of him, but he pushed them off with a feral cry, swinging his sword. As they fell, Alexander sheathed his weapon and took off up the hill but soon slid to a stop. He winced as his skin crawled at the sight the soldier blocking the entrance. Gripping the hilt of his sword, his light dimmed as betrayal twisted in his gut.

"Bravo, Alexander." Caius smiled as his claps echoed behind him.

"Caius."

Drawing his sword, Caius slid his hand across the black iron, igniting the sharp blade. The crimson flames crackled and hummed, flickering in his dark brown eyes.

"Alexander, the humble painter, entrusted with a zealous Truth Keeper. If you were such a great soldier, she wouldn't have been captured so easily, now would she?"

"You don't have to follow Aalok, Caius. Aramis will give you the chance to ask forgiveness for your trespasses."

Caius' laugh echoed off the rocky walls as if mocking Alexander more than once. "Trespasses."

"I don't want to fight you."

Caius' lips twisted into a sneer as he twirled his sword over the back of his hand. "Enough talk. Shall we begin?"

Alexander drew his sword and squared his shoulders.

"I have to warn you," Caius grinned wolfishly, "this is really going to hurt."

Caius lunged, swinging his sword at Alexander's head, but Alexander ducked and struck Caius at the back of his knee. Caius stumbled, but kept his footing, swinging his weapon idly; acting as if the attack had not daunted him.

The two circled around one another, glaring.

"Two-hundred wins to your one and yet you seem so confident now. I shouldn't have let you win last time. It's gone to your head."

"Where is Sophie?" Alexander demanded.

"Sophie? Ah, so I see you do not call the high priestess by her title. Become close, have we?"

"I won't ask you again."

"You're worried about her." Caius couldn't hold back his smile. He could feel Alexander's concern for the Truth Keeper pulsing in waves. He lowered his sword, drinking in the negative emotions. It gave him pleasure to find a new weakness in his former ally. He could smell Alexander's emotions swirling in the air like a sweet perfume. He drew a deep breath, pulsing with power at his enemy's distress.

"You've fallen for her." Caius chuckled before clicking his tongue. "What will your king think, hm? You know as well as I do you cannot love one who is to bond with another. It is a trespass to even think of it...but you are thinking of it, aren't you?"

Alexander leaped into the air with a snarl and met Caius' sword. The flaming blades hummed, grinding until he pushed off with a growl. Caius spun on his feet and Alexander blocked the blade, but not before the sharp end cut through his shirt, slicing his arm. He winced, squeezing his bicep as pain radiated through him.

Caius laughed as his hate and jealousy increased tenfold and the fire of his weapon grew, as did his ego. He rested the fiery sword over his shoulder and let out a long theatrical sigh. "Why don't you just give up? Save yourself the trouble."

"Have you ever known me to be a quitter?"

"Perseverance is truly a noble quality." Caius shrugged off his sword. "Fine. Let's make a deal, shall we? Bow before me and I will allow you to see the Truth Keeper before she is presented."

"I bow to no one but my king,"

"Very well then." Caius extended his sword in an uppercut.

Alexander blocked the blow.

The swords crackled and popped as Alexander and Caius battled.

While the two danced around one another, the first soldier that Alexander had taken down, regained mobility in his limbs and rolled to his side, taking up his gun. He aimed and fired a bolt of energy, but Alexander reacted quickly, blocking it with his sword. Other soldiers pulled out their energy weapons and fired, but Alexander blocked those shots too. He turned and met Caius' sword but as another barrage of bolts came his way. He held up his sword to his face and blocked the attack but then gasped in pain.

Looking down, Alexander found the red flicker at the tip of a black blade extruding from his middle. A shockwave of currents sizzled up his spine in a searing streak of scorching fire. The soldiers coming at him blurred and he clenched his teeth, holding back his screams before falling on his knees.

"Hurts, doesn't it?" Caius hissed, resting his boot on Alexander's shoulder. "If I had known hate could fuel my power, I would have followed it long ago." He kicked

Alexander to the ground. He leaned his weight on his boot, grasping the hilt of his sword, and twisted the blade.

Alexander cried out in pain.

With another sharp twist, Caius jerked his weapon out of Alexander's back. He wiped the blade clean with his gloves, and as if it was nothing, flicked the blood from his fingers.

"Love makes you weak," Caius spat, kicking ash in Alexander's face. "You should have stuck to painting, old friend. You're no warrior. Your king only dressed you as one."

Caius knelt down, taking a clump of Alexander's hair in his fist. He waited for the crowd of fallen soldiers to form a circle, and then jerked up Alexander's head. He wanted them to see the Guardian humiliated, to see one that Aramis favored, now weak.

Alexander was more than weak. He was writhing in pain from his wound. It was taking too long to heal and he couldn't fight Caius' hold.

"It's funny," Caius said into Alexander's ear. "All this time you waited for the right girl to court, and when she finally comes along, she's untouchable. You're duty bound, merely a servant. Nothing more. Still trust him? Still believe in your king's plan?" Caius leaned closer. "Your king is not the only one who can see what's going on. I know about your little moment in the cave, Alexander. A little late to care for someone, don't you think? Too bad she is about to be rescued...but not by you. She is with her beloved, even as we speak." Caius shoved Alexander's head away and stood watching as Alexander's body spasm from the shocks. "Such a shame. You could have been a great warrior for Aalok." Caius glanced to his men, reveling in his victory. "Take him to the prison."

18

PRISONER

SOPHIE greeted every friend she passed on the way to the library with a pleasant smile. Entering the courtyard, she squeezed her books as her eyes lit with joy, seeing the dancers on pointed toes, stretching. She greeted the musicians tuning their instruments and woodworkers sharpening their tools.

As the mouth-watering scents of cakes and fresh hot pies wafted in the air, Sophie couldn't help but stop by the baker's kiosk. It was filled with decorated chocolates, her favorite. She chose one with a pink flower of icing, another with blue, and then finally, a third with yellow. She bowed to the baker in gratitude for the paper-wrapped treats and continued toward the library steps.

Along the walkway, she smiled to the artists prepping their oils and watercolors. She glanced at a kiosk of pottery and baskets that craftsmen were setting out, but what brought Sophie to a standstill, was a canvas of pastel oils. She took a moment to appreciate the brushstrokes of the artist seated on a stool at an easel. He guided his brush with paint-streaked hands across the linen in gentle, fluid strokes. She glanced around his blond hair and tilted her head. It was a scene of a placid blue lake, a beautiful meadow of pink and yellow flowers, and bluebirds perched in pine trees. The painter laid down his brush and took a towel from his knee to wipe his pink and blue fingers with it.

The angel glowed a bright amber aura and Sophie's cheeks were warmed by the emotions she felt from him. She took a breath to compliment the artist, but the bell tower sounded. As it echoed through the courtyard, Sophie took one last glance at the colorful canvas before she left the artisan area and entered the library.

Once in the library's scroll room, Sophie placed the books on the marble table and replaced the scrolls she had borrowed in their rightful places. She slid them with care in each little nook until something in the polished reflection of the wall caught her eyes.

Twirling on her toes, Sophie knocked over the stacked books, finding the back of a blue jacket. Her scrolls tumbled down to the floor, coming to rest next to a pair of black boots. The male in the blue jacket turned at the sound, bending down to pick up the scrolls and made his way in Sophie's direction. Placing them on the table, he glanced at a book Sophie had brought and smiled at the title.

"Creation," he read aloud.

Sophie knelt on the floor, fumbling to keep the scrolls from tumbling again. She rose and gave a polite smile, peering up into the stranger's gray-blue irises. "It's one of my favorites."

Their eyes locked. With a long pause between them, Sophie's heart thudded wildly in her chest. He was so very handsome. His hair was combed back like raven feathers. His brows were thick but nicely trimmed, hooding his greyish blue eyes. His lips quirked up, seemingly amused by Sophie's stare.

He cleared his throat to introduce himself, but before he could speak, horns sounded outside in the courtyard.

"Would you like to join me for the festival?" he asked with a charming smile. At Sophie's nod, he extended his hand to the door. "After you."

With the handsome angel following behind, Sophie walked outside to join the crowd. It was time for the Jubilee; a festival held every thousandth year to celebrate their king and their birth. Hundreds stood in anticipation, waiting for the eldest among them to approach the podium. He waved at the crowd going up the steps and crossed the stage with a dimpled smile. The crowd roared with excitement, as did the blaring trumpets, then expectant silence fell.

The eldest of the lower angels spoke about how he watched each and every soul be born after him. He spoke of the joy it brought Aramis, and how Aramis glowed with each new birth. He spoke of how they sang with joy together after the last soul arrived, how all lived in peace and harmony. Their story of existence was applauded with shouts and cheering.

"Praise be to Aramis!" the eldest shouted, ending his speech. He took a step back, making room for Aramis to approach the podium.

Aramis nodded in thanks and said a few humble words before gesturing to the band to begin the celebration.

After the crowd applauded, the band struck up a lively tune and the square was soon filled with glowing, dancing bodies. Sophie swayed side to side to the music until someone stepped in front of her.

"Shall we?" the handsome stranger asked with a sideways grin.

Sophie took his hand and let him swept her into the crowd. All knew the festive melody. The movements of the people were lively and in sync. The stranger lifted Sophie up in the air in rhythm with the other couples, twirling her around. The vibrations of bodies pulsed through the air, filling the square with the bright golden glow of their auras.

The dancing went on for three more songs before the crowd paused to applaud.

Sophie glanced up at the stranger, feeling his eyes on her.

"What is your name?" he asked, over the commotion. "Sophie, Truth Keeper of the Seventh Circle," she said with a bow of her head.

"Serus," he said with a slight nod. "Truth Keeper of the Eighth Circle."

The crowd stopped clapping and the band began another tune.

"A pleasure to meet you."

Serus took Sophie's hand, raising it to his lips. "I assure you the pleasure is mine."

Sophie's heart skipped at the light kiss on her knuckles, but as the tempo lifted, she was swept away by the dancing crowd.

Serus lifted his head with a smile, sliding his hands into his pockets. He kept his eyes on Sophie and she kept her eyes on him. The dancers rounded a circle, bringing her back to where she had begun. When she twirled on her toes to fall back in Serus' arms, she laughed, but then frowned finding no one to catch her. The handsome angel was gone.

The memory faded from Sophie's mind as she became aware of something hard and cold pressed against her cheek.

Cracking one eye open, she gazed around the rocky ground of her prison. It was dirty, dusty, and made of quartz.

There was only an orange flicker of light dancing on the floor. It was enough light for her to see tiny flecks of gold, scattered through the brown, smooth stones. Sitting up, she groaned and rubbed her cold cheek and stiff neck. She shivered, wrapping her arms around her knees and frowned at the surrounding stone walls. Aalok was a hypocrite. He preached free will but she had been forced into holding. She winced, looking at her bruised elbows, covered in thick smudged fingerprints.

The soldiers.

She recalled them nudging her forward down a golden hallway and past a fountain molded into a golden image. It was Aalok with his wings spread wide, hovering over the water feature with open arms. The trickling sound made Sophie's chest ache as she passed it, thinking of the fountain in the courtyard of Aramis' kingdom. It was the same fountain Serus had asked her to meet him at, the same fountain where he had asked for permission to court her.

She remembered going down innumerable hallways—they all looked the same, lined in gold. A door had opened to a set of stairs, leading into a dark and dank cave.

The prison.

She remembered passing the empty cells, the sound of the door of her cell as it creaked open, then the heat of Caius' glove as she was shoved inside.

She remembered falling on the ground, her muscles twitching as she peered up at Caius, unable to move. Caius had flicked his tongue over his lips and slammed the iron door, locking her inside with a smug smile. Sophie's vision had blurred and her eyes had fluttered closed as she watched the bars fade into darkness.

She wondered how long she had been in that darkness. How long she had dreamed of her life before Serus' exile. She rubbed her hands over her goose bumped-covered arms, trying to warm herself. Her skin was so cold. She had never been cold before. She suddenly understood why the Outcasts had broken the trees and burned them, why they built fires and sat so close to the blaze.

A rhythmic sound of clicking heels echoing down the hall perked Sophie's ears. She gazed at the flickering lights of the fire sconces on the ground as the hem of a red dress came into view. Her eyes traveled up the fabric and to the female that stepped forward. Her body was a halo of a thin waving crimson. It glowed off her smooth skin as she wrapped her slender fingers around her hip, cocking it to the side. Her waist was the shape of an hourglass. Her hips were wide and her breasts full.

"Well, well. Look what we have here," the girl narrowed her almond-shaped eyes. "Aren't Truth Keepers supposed to be protected by Aramis' guards or something?"

"Why am I being held against my will?" Sophie demanded. Her wobbly legs threatened to buckle as she stood and steadied herself with a hand on the frigid wall.

"You're a Truth Keeper," the female cooed. "Aalok can't let you wander the halls trying to counsel,"

Sophie stumbled forward, focusing on the girl's aura. She didn't feel a mix of emotions from the girl as she had expected. She only felt confidence, laced with hate. When Sophie brought her wary gaze to the female's haughty stare, her eyes widened in recognition. "Jazrael?"

"I'm surprised you remember me,"

"I gave you counsel. You said your eyes were open to the truth."

"Oh, my eyes are open, Truth Keeper."

"Then why are you here? Why are you a follower of Aalok?"

"Not only naive, but stupid." Jazrael sneered, crossing her arms. "I didn't have a choice. I was exiled for not obeying your king and his rules. But I wasn't about to live like a filthy beast in that camp."

"You're an Outcast? But I-I thought-"

"Go ahead, spout off your nonsense. I've heard it all before. Let me guess: It's my fault."

"Jazrael-" Sophie's parched throat choked her words.

"What was it you told me moons ago? Ah, yes, I remember now. 'I could only be worthy of forgiveness if I meant it.' Isn't that what you said?"

Sophie's brows knit together. The waves of jealousy she had felt from Jazrael moons ago were much stronger now. Pinpricks of anxiety crawled up Sophie's neck and she scrunched her shoulders as if it would ease the pain.

Jazrael took a step forward and glared. "You say your king loves you, but look at you. Grubby feet and hands, matted hair—and you smell. You're *filthy*. Is this how Aramis treats all his favored servants? Or just his chosen few?"

Sophie glanced at her hands and dress. She *was* filthy. The ash coated her gown in a grey powder, her feet were black with dirt, grim wedged under her toenails. She slid her fingers over her damp, straggly hair, finding ash smeared between her fingers. She recalled the ash falling from the sky as she went across the bridge, how the smoke burned in her nostrils. Her face twisted, and nausea swept over her from her stench.

"If I were you, I would make up my mind before they come for you," Jazrael told her.

"Make up my mind? About what?"

"Taking Aalok up on his offer, of course."

"I will *never* agree to his terms. He's a liar. Whatever he told you—it's—it can't happen. Aramis has already set a plan in motion."

"That's right. The grand plan of destruction," Jazrael scoffed, rolling her eyes. "So, you would rather die? Go to Earth and live like a beast? I hear these new bodies are disgusting. They get dirty, they smell, and they're weak. Just like you are now. Do you really want to live like that? To be weak and pathetic? Powerless?"

"I'll do whatever it takes to help those who are lost."

"How very noble of you. Well, regardless of your hope of self-sacrifice, Aalok will still give you a chance to make a deal."

"I won't take it. I won't betray my king for comfort."

Jazrael sighed, giving Sophie a sympathetic look. "Your king is not what he appears to be. There are always two sides to a story. I doubt your precious Aramis has told you of Aalok's."

Sophie stared at Jazrael but held her tongue.

"Allow me to fill you in," Jazrael wrapped her fingers around the iron bars. "Millions of years ago, there was only Aramis. But he was lonely. He had created the Cosmos, the planets, and the vast galaxies of stars, and Earth.

But after the grand architect was finished with his designs, he sought for another to share the beauty with; someone to talk to, to walk with in the lush green hills and gardens of the third planet. And so, the first Seraph was born. From Aramis' own being, he made a likeness of himself. This likeness was as wise and as beautiful as he, the first and most perfect soul. He named him, Samria. Pleased with his creation, Aramis sought to make more in his likeness, but with variations in colors and personality. They respected, adored him, worshiped him. Then Aramis planned a new set of angels, many more than all the Seraphim he had created. He made billions and billions of souls. They were much like the Seraph, but without wings, and were limited in power. They lived young and beautiful all the days of their lives until-"

"I know the story." Sophie interrupted.

"But do you know why such a perfect Seraph would be cast out?"

Sophie knitted her brows.

"Samria was also adored by the lower angels. He, Michael, and Gabriel stood beside the throne with Aramis. But when the lower angels began bringing Samria gifts and worshiped him, Aramis became jealous. He had created the souls and thought he, alone, should get all the glory. So, Aramis made the Law. The first decree; was he alone would be worshiped."

"That's not how the story goes."

"No?"

"No. Aalok wanted to sit on the throne. He wanted to be Aramis, so he began coaxing the souls to worship him. He found ways to turn the other Seraphim against Aramis. He taught them to do vile things, corrupted them. He wanted to overthrow Aramis because he knew Aramis wouldn't destroy those Aalok confused. That's what started this war. That's how the disease of Confusion began. Aalok is the one that wants all the glory, not Aramis. Our king loves us, all of us, even those that have turned away. He only wants peace."

Jazrael dipped a finger between her breasts, drawing out a set of golden keys. They clinked against one another as she shook them. "I think you'll change your mind about your king when I show you the truth of what's to come."

"What are you doing?"

"Showing you the truth. Aalok has taught me the secret of foretelling the future. Aramis is not the only one with this power. I can show what is to come if you'll let me."

The lock clattered against the iron bars and with a click the door was opened.

Sophie recoiled until her back slapped flush against the frigid walls.

"Give me your hand," Jazrael ordered, offering hers.

When Sophie hesitated, Jazrael snatched up her wrist and squeezed it tight.

At Jazrael's touch, flashes zipped past Sophie's vision as a wave of pain slammed into her.

"This is the future, Truth Keeper. This is the king you serve."

In the vision, Sophie stood on a crystal platform, gazing at billions of souls standing in a large courtyard. She turned, finding Aramis beside her, standing from his crystal throne. He looked at the souls he had created with furrowed brows. There were those with the light and those that were grey with no light in them. Aramis lifted his hands out before him. With one swift motion, he parted the souls, separating the grey ones to the left and those with the light to the right.

There was a rumble of the ground as Aalok appeared in the middle of the grey and dim souls. Aramis lifted his head, and as he did, Aalok glowed brightly. His glow became so bright that it blinded Sophie and she turned away. When the light and the heat dwindled, she found nothing but a lake of burning fire and a cloud of ashes fluttering up into the sky.

Sophie gasped for breath, coming out of the vision with wide eyes, meeting Jazrael's glare.

"Still want to go through with Aramis' plan?" Jazrael asked calmly. "Still want to follow a king of destruction?"

"I believe there is still hope. They don't have to be blotted out of existence. Aalok has made his choice, but those standing with him...their hearts can still be changed."

"Don't be stupid," Jazrael glared, squeezing Sophie's wrist.

Sophie's body lit, boiling with anger, and she took a step forward, jerking her hand away.

The keys to the prison went sailing through the air, clinking against the bars to the ground.

"At least I care about others," Sophie spat, "unlike you, You're too selfish to think of anyone but yourself!"

"My, my, Truth Keeper. If I were you, I would watch my tone. You're acting more like an Outcast than a priestly saint."

Sophie covered her mouth at Jazrael's words. She didn't know what had come over her.

Has Jazrael's touch infected me? Was it the shock of Caius's glove?

She thought back to the shock and the change in her temperament that followed. The darkness had not only clouded her judgment, it was also changing her. She was a hurricane of resentment. It swirled inside her and she prayed to avoid another outburst, clutching her chest, but it was bare. Her necklace was gone. Sophie peered at Jazrael cautiously as her light faded away.

"I'm sorry, I didn't mean to-"

"Open your eyes, Truth Keeper. Your king will be ruthless. Aalok wishes to spare us. If you join us, you can stop this. You can save everyone and avoid the pain and sorrow of the next life."

Sophie shook her head and leaned back against the cold wall. She was burning up. Her head throbbed to the rhythm of her heart as it thumped in her chest. With shallow breaths, she pressed her cold, nimble fingers to her flaming cheeks and stared at the ground.

The flash of the vision swirled in her mind, torturing her. Her stomach knotted into a tight ball. She was going to be sick. She hunched over, watching the vision over and over in her mind.

How could Aramis blot out all those souls? How could he burn them out of existence?

The room blurred and Sophie watched Jazrael's dress trail like fading light. Her focus went to the glinting keys. She wanted to run to them, to trap Jazrael inside her prison and flee, but she was too weak to try.

Sophie kept her focus on the keys, until a pair of black shoes came into view, and then a hand taking them up. The keys jingled and then silenced as the black shoes walked to the cell door.

"Aalok has requested I get the Truth Keeper ready," a familiar voice spoke.

Sophie lifted her gaze to Jazrael, who had returned to her side. "Did you see who was among the souls burned to ashes?" She whispered. She wrapped her fingers around Sophie's neck and as she did, a searing heat burned as another vision filled Sophie's mind.

Sophie stood beside her king as the masses of lower angels lit into flames in a field. Aalok stood among them in the center with a smug smile. The bodies around him burned bright like the sun and she squinted her eyes to scan the faces of her fallen brethren. Their skin flaked away and flitted into the air. Then, as their ashes rose to the sky, Sophie's heart stopped, seeing a familiar face among the twirling cinders.

Serus.

He frowned, gazing up at her, pleading with his eyes. There was no saving him, not now. Sophie watched in horror as the flames kissed his face. First, his cheeks flaked away, then his forehead and chin. With each piece of tiny ash, Serus turned into a pillar of grey before he too was caught in the wind and was gone.

A gasp escaped Sophie's lips as Jazrael slid her hand down her chest. She pressed Sophie hard against the wall and leaned to her ear. "You serve a king of death."

"Now, Jazrael," the familiar voice said sternly.

Jazrael turned swiftly and went to the barred door. She leaned against it casually, tracing her fingers across the iron. "She won't believe a word you say. Even with the truth before her very eyes."

Sophie leaned her head against the stone and squinted at the hidden figure, trying to force it into focus. She first registered his red suit jacket, then at a round golden badge upon on his chest that glimmered in the fire of the sconces. As the male flipped the key ring around his finger, Sophie moved forward, inspecting the pin more closely.

The gold engraved pin barred a perplexing emblem. At first glance, it looked like an owl. The wings' tips were down and the crown was pointed, hovering over the 'A.' Sophie tilted her head, realizing it was her king's emblem, but upside down. This was a symbol of the rebellion, a symbol of treachery. Aalok's signet.

The male with the keys stepped into the light and Sophie's eyes drifted from the medallion to his stormy blue-gray eyes.

"Hello, gorgeous," Serus said with a charming smile.

"Serus..." Sophie exhaled, her shoulders slumping.

Serus slid his hands into his pockets, giving a smirk. His gaze traveled from her bloodshot eyes to the hem of her sooty dress and then back up to her confused stare.

"She's still yapping about dying as if it's a privilege." Jazrael rolled her eyes in disgust, crossing her arms.

"Is she now?" Serus asked, keeping his eyes locked on Sophie's.

"She doesn't look very happy to see you," Jazrael observed with interest. She glanced over her shoulder at Sophie then back at Serus. "I thought for sure from what you said that she would have rushed into your arms at the sight of you. Maybe she doesn't love you as much as you thought." Jazrael pursed her lips, sliding a hand over Serus' shoulder. She glared back at Sophie with a taunting grin and left the cell.

As Jazrael's heels clattered down the hall, Serus relaxed offering a hand. "Let's get you cleaned up, shall we?"

"No,"

"Please?" Serus frowned, taking a step forward.

Sophie stared at Serus a long moment. In those pleading gray eyes were a mix of relief and sadness, pain and longing. The flash of his face in the vision filled her mind. His eyes had been pleading with her, just as they were pleading now. She couldn't stand the thought of watching him burn. She couldn't lose him. There was still hope. There had to be.

19

ROSES ARE
RED

SERUS led Sophie through arching golden corridors, filled with hanging tapestries. Gold and crimson threaded Aalok as King. His faithful subjects stood with him. Their faces glowed with pride, raising their hands to praise him. He held a scepter and a scroll, and wore a crown of glory, shining upon his head.

Sophie's stomach knotted as she took in the careful artisanship that had gone into the statues lining the walls. They were idols, and her fallen peers had sculpted them.

Serus led Sophie up several staircases and into a tower. He was silent but held a pleasant smile as they turned another corner and paused at a door in a long hallway.

"My quarters," he informed Sophie, turning the golden doorknob.

As Serus pushed the door open, the scent of something sweet filled Sophie's nose. Roses. Hundreds of them lined the walls, packed snugly in black vases. Their fragrance lured her past the threshold to the onyx stone bed, carved with beautiful Seraph wings and draped with velvet red curtains.

"Aalok would like you to be bathed and dressed before I present you to him."

"I'm not meeting with him," Sophie stated, glancing over her shoulder. She paused as her hand gripped the onyx bed frame. She grimaced at the touch of the cold, smooth stone. "You can put me back in the prison...but I'm not..." Sophie shifted her gaze to the red curtains and then paused as a glint on the nightstand caught her eye.

Her favorite book, Creation, sat lonely as if calling to her to come read its pages. Sophie closed her eyes as a memory of the day before Serus' secret proposal trickled into her mind.

In the memory, Sophie leaned her head against Serus' chest, soaking in his soft waving halo of white. He was warm and his voice was soft and mild as he read passages about how the Infinite Realm and Earth were made. He emphasized the lines about the details of why Aramis chose the colors and fragrance of the flowers, why Aramis made the stars and the patterns of the constellations. He read of the darkness of night, how there was quiet, how there was stillness, how the moon only reflected the light of the sun. Serus paused and brushed Sophie's hair from her face, his halo dimming.

Sophie glanced up to meet Serus' torn expression. Her forehead wrinkled but smoothed as he caressed his knuckles softly down her cheek.

He gazed into her eyes for a long space of silence, tracing her lips, and then, he kissed her. The kiss was soft like a feather, gentle, light. He put his forehead to hers and held her.

"Promise you'll never leave me in the still of darkness. Promise you'll always be my light—my sun."

Sophie parted her lips to speak but before she could answer, Serus pressed his lips to hers once more.

Coming out of her memory, Sophie's breath left her. She pressed her palm to her tight chest, holding back her tears. "You kept it."

"Of course I did," Serus said softly.

"I'm surprised Aalok let you."

"Aalok doesn't tell anyone what to do here."

"So, he didn't tell that soldier to throw me in a cell?"

"Caius made a mistake. You were to be brought to me, not taken to the prison."

Sophie crossed her arms. "A mistake." She stared at Serus a long moment, trying to sort through his aura. There was a hint of guilt, but it faded quickly. "How did you know I was here?"

"I was informed the moment you arrived. I'm sorry I didn't come sooner. I was—preoccupied."

Serus slid his hands into his pockets, his eyes shifting to the ground. He thought back to why he had been delayed after finding out she had been captured.

Instead of going straight to her, he had stood, staring at himself in the oval mirror in his room. He had been coaching himself on how to be suave, how to go to the prison and be her savior. He didn't want to show his guilt. He didn't want to appear weak. He wasn't naturally confident, but he had watched Aalok long enough to know how to fake it. Once he was sure he could keep up the mask of confidence, he went to the prison, careful not to break the facade.

"I was surprised to hear about your capture. I thought for sure your Guardian would have been right by your side for every *single* moment." Serus' mouth drew to one side. "Seems I was wrong."

Sophie frowned. It had been her fault. If she hadn't pushed Alexander away, she wouldn't have been home alone; she wouldn't have been shocked by Caius' glove.

She rubbed her neck and rolled her shoulders with a wince.

"You shouldn't have fought them—does it still hurt?" Serus asked.

"You know what he did to me? That he shocked me into unconsciousness?"

"I'm sure you're tired. You can rest for a moment if you like, but you need to get out of those rags before I can take you to Aalok."

"What if I choose to leave? If I have free will, I can, can't I?"

"Do you want to leave?"

Sophie stared at Serus for a long moment. There was so much history between them, but he was different now. The Serus she loved would have never let anyone harm her, but he shrugged it off as if her injury had been justified. She took careful steps to him, swallowing hard. He emanated no halo, no color of aura, but she could feel his heartache. She reached out and rested a hand on his sleeve.

He tensed at first but then relaxed as she squeezed his arm, sending the comfort of her aura through him.

"Please, Serus...you *must* repent," she implored. "Come back with me. I know Aramis would allow you to if you were truly sorry. I can feel your battling with the guilt, you feel some kind of shame for what you have done."

Serus clenched his jaw, heat pulsing off his aura as it lit pink. "Shame? I have *never* been ashamed of the love I have for you. Although—it seems that you are."

"Secretly trying to bond with me can't be the only reason for your demotion." Sophie looked deep into Serus' eyes, but the mask he held kept her from seeing his intentions clearly.

"Come back with me to the Infinite Realm. Ask Aramis for forgiveness."

Serus let out a laugh. "And leave all this?" he asked, spreading his arms to indicate his things.

"But you didn't earn any of this. Aalok is bribing you with luxuries that won't even matter after the end. It will all be gone. Why are you so caught up in his charade?"

"The only charade I see is you pretending that you don't still love me."

Sophie held her breath as Serus took a step forward. He was so close, close enough to touch her, but he didn't.

"We could be together again, just like before. Don't you want that? Don't you miss how it used to be?"

"Of course I do, but we can't change the past."

"I can feel how conflicted you are. You're fighting against what you truly want. Why not just make it easy on yourself and choose what is in your heart?"

"Please don't make me choose between you and my King. I can't..." Sophie's eyes stung as she fought back tears, shifting her gaze to the ground. "I can't bear the thought of not having you in my life, but..."

"But?"

Sophie's eyes darted around the room, gazing at all the black, all the red, then it hit her. The words he had spoken in the meadow replayed in her mind and she repeated them aloud. "Promise you'll never leave me in the still of darkness. Promise you'll always be my light—my sun," she whispered, bringing her gaze back up to Serus. "You chose to be the moon...you were admitting you had already trespassed that day in the meadow...you were confessing you had chosen Aalok."

Serus was silent as he stared at Sophie's back to him. It was true. He had made his choice. She was the sun and he was only reflecting her light. He was a distant rock, cold and out of reach. He wished to tell her how he had longed for her during those weeks of separation. How he had lain awake, staring at the star-lit sky, waiting for morning, waiting for the warmth of the sun to remind him of her touch. If only he could touch her now, take her in his arms...but he couldn't, not yet.

Sophie turned, finding Serus' face a mask of stone. If only she could make him take it off, make him remember who he was, that he was good. "Serus, please. You know this is wrong."

As Sophie reached for him, Serus took a step to the side. He was doing what Aalok had instructed him to do. He would act smooth and calm, unaffected. He could persuade souls, just as Aalok had. If only he would follow his example. He knew if he wanted to persuade Sophie now, he would have to follow that advice. Serus was instructed to keep his distance, to make Sophie want him more. Seeing her confused expression, he had confirmed Aalok's advice to be true.

"I'll inform Aalok of your arrival," Serus made his way to the door, glancing over his shoulder as Sophie picked up

Creation and held it to her chest. Serus winced at her sentiment, but only for a moment, quickly bringing back the confident smile as he pointed to the bathroom.

"Everything you need is in the lavatory. Make yourself at home. I'll be back as soon as Aalok is ready for you."

Sophie kept her eyes on the book as the door shut gently with a click. There was only the sound of her tight breaths and the blood rushing through her ears, thumping in rhythm with her aching heart. As her knees gave way, she fell back on the bed, clinging to Creation. She prayed for Aramis to help her be strong, prayed that Serus' heart could be changed. The only hope now was her faith. Out of everything she had lost, she was thankful she still had that.

SERVANT

READING the passages of the book, Creation, Sophie's mind was flooded with memories. The lines highlighted were the same words Serus had read to her in the meadow; the same passages he had once respected. Those days in the meadow seemed so long ago. Serus had changed so much since that time. It had been so perfect before, but now, that part of her life was gone.

Blinking back her tears, Sophie returned from her memories. She looked around the red-drenched room; the fabrics and roses, thought of Serus' uniform, then to the velvet blanket in his tent.

How had he attained a room filled with so many fine things so quickly?

A knot rose in Sophie's throat, thinking of what treacherous deeds he must have done to acquire his luxuries. Soon, she was suffocating, looking at the four walls she was trapped in.

Rushing to the veranda doors, she flung them open. A wind blew through the suite, lifting her frazzled hair, and her tattered dress as she took a deep breath of the salty sea air. She leaned over the balcony, peering into the darkness below, wondering how far the drop would take her if she were to escape.

The ocean roared, slamming against the rocky foundation of Aalok's fortress. The surge reflected the pounding against her chest. It was a relentless barrage over and over, shouting of Serus' betrayal.

He's right. I am stupid. Stupid for not sensing it before.

She vividly remembered the moment they shared in the tent, how she had been swept away by the music. If Alexander had not been there...

Alexander.

Was he coming for her? Was he captured, sitting in a dark and dank cell, as she had been?

Sophie glanced down at her hands gripping the rail. Soot. Her arms were also covered with ashy handprints of the Outcast soldiers. They were marks of hate and envy, but most of all, pride. She rubbed her palm hard against her skin, but the ash wouldn't move. She had been tainted, again.

Pushing away from the railing, she walked back through Serus' room, making her way to the lavatory, and gently pushed open the door.

In the middle of the room sat a gold tub filled with steaming water, rose petals, and sweet perfume oils. Sophie waved her hand through the rising vapor, aching to be immersed in the bath. She rubbed her stiff neck and winced. Her body was sore. She was weak and dirty.

Filthy.

She stared at the steam again and then gazed at the twirling rose petals, hypnotized. The water called to her, whispering for her to get in, to be clean.

As if in a daze, Sophie leaned down and dipped her fingers in the water. Her shoulders relaxed and she sighed. There was no second thought, no question that she needed to get in. She untied the bow of her bodice and slipped out of her dress. She gripped the side of the tub, stifling a moan as she stepped in. She relished the sensation before dipping further into the sweet-smelling rose petals and herbs.

She welcomed the tingling heat on the crown of her head, the weightlessness of her limbs. Drunk with dizziness from the heat, she rose and rested her head against the tub. She let her mind wander; and the moment she did, a slithery voice whispered in her mind.

"You are too beautiful, too perfect, to endure a life full of pain and misery. Stay..."

As the voice trailed off, a vivid vision drifted into Sophie's head.

She was in a silk gown, walking down the beach hand in hand with Serus; then at a feast with wine. She was dancing after desserts of chocolates and raspberry tarts. The wine was flowing and she drank glass after glass.

She laughed, twirling in her dress, floating into the sky like a feather as Serus flew them above the clouds. Then a tickle came from her back and she unfurled her white wings. Her and Serus flew across the cosmos, soaring over the moon. When Sophie came back down to Earth, Serus kissed her gently. Then Sophie was walking on a red carpet to a throne, ready to be wed, a thin veil over her face, her wings tucked tight against a red wedding gown. All of her brethren gathered at the feet of Aalok as he rose and they bowed. Sophie paused at the altar and took Serus' hand. He smiled at her, and then at Aalok. Serus bowed, pulling on Sophie's hand. Sophie looked behind her at all the heads bowed, and then she looked at Aalok as he grinned. Her eyes grew wide, and she jerked away from Serus' grasp.

Sophie pushed off from the tub, shooting up. The water spilled over the side, splashing the rose petals and herbs to the ground as she came to her feet. She jerked a towel from a nearby chair and wrapped it around her trembling body. The water felt suddenly cold, and she stared at her wary reflection.

"It's an illusion," she told herself. "It's not real."

A knock startled her.

"Milady?" a female voice called from the other side of the door. "May I come in?"

"Just-just a moment please," Sophie answered, surprised by the quiver in her voice. She tucked the towel more tightly around herself and glanced down at her feet. There was sediment at the bottom of the tub. She assumed it was dirt and ash; but when she glanced back at her arms, she rose her brows. The handprints from the soldiers were gone.

"May I enter?" the voice asked.

"I'm sorry, yes, yes of course," Sophie replied, climbing out of the tub.

A petite angel with a sweet face entered, smiling sheepishly. Her big sapphire eyes looked as if they should sparkle, but they didn't. Instead, they were dim with sadness. She swept her long blond hair over her shoulder and went to the onyx vanity.

As the girl set a black sequin handbag on the vanity, Sophie glanced back at the bath. The water. There was some kind of magic in it. It had not only renewed her strength and cleansed her from the soot, but it had also given her an illusion of an impossible future. She knew that now. Suspicion filled her mind, wondering what part this girl was playing, but the silent question was quickly answered.

"Serus has requested I prepare you to be presented to Aalok." She said, gesturing for Sophie to sit at the vanity.

Sophie hesitated, but when the girl raised her brows in waiting, she sat and asked.

"What is your name?"

"Aerith,"

"Aerith...that's a beautiful name."

"Thank you," Aerith smiled faintly, and reached around Sophie for some red glittering hairpins on the vanity.

"Your name...it means breath, rest." Sophie noted. "It's a peaceful name."

Aerith grimaced and placed the brush carefully back on the vanity. Sophie watched her in the mirror, sensing sadness instead of joy for the compliment. Aerith took a vial of red liquid from her pocket and dabbed the rose perfume behind Sophie's ears.

Sensing that Aerith was uncomfortable, Sophie bit her lip and set her eyes on herself, only to find something she didn't expect. She smoothed a hand over her radiant face. It was bright and supple. She then looked at her soft clean arms, and then back at herself in the mirror, remembering rumors that had spread moons ago.

Aalok's magic was hidden in the water. It was said, that it had the ability to imitate Aramis' natural power, through water, that he used technology to infuse it with darkness. Plasma was the very thing in which all life was created. Somehow this magic, this change in Aramis' design, had altered the natural way the plasma worked in the water.

Looking closer into Aerith's eyes in the mirror Sophie searched for what was in her soul. She could see fear and sadness that swirled around her. She didn't understand why she couldn't feel it. It was there and yet, this girl was void of an aura.

While Aerith brushed her hair, Sophie wondered why she had come to Aalok. She appeared thoughtful and sweet, by the way she took careful, even brush strokes, how she was gentle with the hairpins and hummed a little tune.

It was a sweet and gentle lullaby. The chords were steady; rose and fell gently. Sophie knew the song all too well, and could not help but close her eyes. She drew in a deep breath through her nostrils as her soul sparked with the light of Aramis.

"I love that hymn." Sophie admitted, "I would sing it every day on my way up to the meadow,"

When the girl fell silent and turned away, Sophie realized Aerith had been unaware she was humming the tune. Sophie watched as she put the drying tool in her bag, and reached into her pocket. Aerith removed a buzzing glass screen and tapped it a few times, turning off the notification. Sophie studied the plate of glass, wondering who she was messaging, but didn't ask.

Instead, Sophie ran her fingers through her hair. It was silky and clean now. She couldn't help but be relieved to be free of the soot and dirt. She faced her reflection in awe of her radiant skin and bouncing chestnut waves. She then watched Aerith put the screen in her pocket, and continue to wrap half of Sophie's hair up into a beautiful chignon.

"Did Aalok request that this be done?" Sophie inquired, watching Aerith take out a crimson stick of wax from her pocket.

Aerith glanced up and then continued to paint Sophie's lips. "Serus did."

Sophie grimaced.

"Although, I know he thinks you are beautiful without any of this." Aerith let out a breath and shrugged. "I have to agree. You have exquisite natural beauty. You were designed well." Aerith lifted her chin, drawing black paint to the outer corners of Sophie's eyes.

Sophie studied Aerith's makeup. Her eyelids were shadowed and lined in the same deep crimson as hers, but Aerith's lips were painted cherry red, along with her fingernails. Sophie could tell she was just as lovely as she and was a bit saddened by Aerith's desire to cover the way Aramis had created her.

"You're beautiful too," Sophie complimented. "You have such a sweet smile, and your eyes," Sophie continued, looking into them. "Soft blue with a bright yellow starburst around your pupils. It's as if Aramis wanted to mirror the sky on a sunny day. I am sure you've captivated many hearts with just one look. It's a wonderful gift to be able to give joy to those who look upon your beauty."

Sophie caught the twitch in Aerith's lips, but she didn't smile. She went back to concentrating on painting Sophie's lips crimson red without a word. As Aerith rose, Sophie saw the sadness cross Aerith's face and frowned; now feeling her aura. She had somehow hurt the girl's feelings with her words. Sophie didn't understand it and cringed as pinpricks of uneasiness crept up her neck.

"Did...did Aramis exile you?" Sophie asked, looking down at her fidgeting hands. "Is that why you are here?"

Aerith paused as she took the lash tint from the black bag. "No. I came of my own free will."

"Why would you leave the Infinite Realm to come here?"

"I fell in love with someone," Aerith replied, putting the makeup away. "He was exiled."

Sophie followed her eyes as she stared at roses in the vase next to the sink.

"I followed him here," Aerith explained, taking out a vial from her pocket. She pulled the cork top and poured a small amount into her palm, rubbing the waxy liquid in her hands. She came to Sophie's side and turned her toward the mirror, pulling a few strands of hair. They framed Sophie's heart-shaped face, gracing her high cheekbones.

Sophie watched Aerith go into the bedroom and come back with a black box.

When Aerith opened it, Sophie's eyes were filled with the sparkle from a head adornment that rested inside. It was round with winding gold leaves and ruby stones. Diamonds winked around the rose shaped jewels and they glinted in the light from the hanging chandelier.

"A gift from Aalok," Aerith explained, dryly.

Sophie ran her fingers across the sparkling headband and pressed her lips into a hard line. Jewels and crystals had their own frequency. They conducted energy, harnessed it. This particular adornment had a jewel that was meant to lie in the center of the forehead. That was the place closest to the mind. Chills ran down Sophie's spine, knowing she would be treading on dangerous ground if she put it on.

"I don't want to wear this."

"You don't like it?" Aerith asked, tilting her head in confusion.

"It's beautiful. It's just..." Sophie frowned. "I can't accept gifts from Aalok."

"Serus asked that I make sure you wear it."

Sophie's shoulders slumped forward.

Aerith sighed. "Come. There's another gift waiting for you."

Aerith led Sophie to Serus' bedroom door and smoothed her fingers over a silky crimson dress hanging beside it.

The dress was much like the gowns Sophie had worn to banquets. It was covered in lace, beading along the bodice in a pattern down to the hem. Sophie's shoulders tensed as she looked at the back. It was bare, with only lace along the shoulders. As she pulled the dress to the side she found a long slit up the side to expose her thigh.

"This dress is...revealing," Sophie laughed nervously, shaking her head.

"Serus had it custom made for you as soon as he was promoted to Ambassador."

"Ambassador?"

"Such a thoughtful gesture," Aerith smiled, tracing the intricate beading along the neckline. "You will look stunning,"

Sophie's jaw hurt from gnashing her teeth, but she couldn't help it. She was filled with anger. This was Aalok's doing. He had arranged all of this. He had promoted Serus and convinced him to do these things. There was only one way to show Serus the truth. She had to face the Seraph that had caused all this to happen. He was the reason all would perish. She would confront him. She would call him out on all of his lies.

"I'll wear the dress, if I must, but you can take Aalok's gift back to him," Sophie decided firmly.

She watched Aerith give an uneasy smile as she retrieved the box to replace the headpiece.

She knew Serus would be disappointed, but she didn't care. Wearing the color of the enemy was torturous enough, but the only other option was her dirty gown on the floor. She thought to put it back on but her gaze lingered on the dress.

"Can I get you anything else? Some wine perhaps?"

Sophie blinked away from the gown.

"No, but thank you. What you have done is more than enough. I wish there was a way to repay you."

"My service to Serus is payment enough. You should get dressed. I'm sure he will be back any minute now."

As Aerith went to the door, Sophie had a thought. "Aerith?"

Aerith turned with raised brows.

"I can see that you are unhappy here...that you wish to return to the Infinite Realm. If I escape, will you come with me?"

"Sophie, you can't-"

"You don't belong here," Sophie pressed. "This isn't your home. Whoever it is that you followed here—if he truly cared for you, then he wouldn't have asked you to come here with him."

"He didn't ask me,"

"Then why? Why would you stay if you are unhappy here?"

Aerith's face twisted as she frowned.

"Surely, if he loved you, he would understand-"

"He's in love with another," Aerith whispered, blinking back tears.

"Then why stay here? Why serve a false king I can clearly see you do not worship? You still believe in Aramis, don't you?"

Aerith closed in the space and lowered her voice. "It is forbidden for me to speak about such things."

"Aerith, you have someone that loves you more than any soul in existence."

"No one has ever favored me the way you have been favored, Truth Keeper."

"But you *are* favored. You are loved more deeply than you could ever imagine."

"What you speak of is something I have never known,"

"Maybe not from another, but think of the one who created you," Sophie reminded Aerith, taking her arms gently. "Aramis loves you and he wants you to come home. He never wanted you to leave. I saw in his eyes how much it pains him to have lost the souls that went with Aalok."

Aerith wiped her eyes. "He won't forgive me."

"Yes, he will. You didn't leave because you hate the Law. You left as an act of passion. He won't punish you for that. Please, come with me. Look," Sophie pointed to the balcony, "if we hurry, we can gather those curtains and tie them to the railing and-"

"I can't leave,"

"But-"

"I can't go back to the Infinite Realm. Not without him."

"But you're in pain. Why would you stay if he-"

Aerith's glass screen vibrated in her pocket. She pulled it out and tapped it.

"I have to go. Please don't escape. Serus would be furious with me if you're not here when he gets back."

"Aerith,"

"Please? I don't want to get in trouble."

Sophie nodded her head in acknowledgment. "You have my word."

"Thank you," Aerith said, and opened the door.

"Farewell...until we meet again," Sophie said formally, reaching out a hand.

Aerith looked over her shoulder into the hall. Finding it empty, she grasped Sophie's forearm.

"Farewell." Aerith smiled, but soon it was replaced with a frown, as she left.

After Aerith shut the door, Sophie stared at the dress for a long moment. She held it, knowing she was about to do something that her king would see, something she was ashamed of. She cringed, but lifted the dress off the hook, hoping when Serus returned, she could convince him to leave with her.

The dress whispered against the floor as Sophie made her way to the mirror. She gazed at herself a long moment before glancing over her shoulder to her dirty dress in the bathroom.

She could put it back on. She could yank down the curtains, climb down from the balcony, and run from the fortress. Sophie's shoulders fell in defeat. No. She couldn't leave. Not now. She had made a promise to Aerith, and a Truth Keeper always kept their word.

Sophie sat on the bed and leafed through Creation again. She flipped page after page as minutes turned into hours. Halfway through the highlighted script, Sophie's eyes grew heavy and she drifted into a deep sleep, dreaming of her younger years.

21

A DEVIOUS
PLAN

SOPHIE was in the garden, at the fountain, with Serus, dancing to the hymn that Aerith had sung. He twirled her around as the music paused for a barrage of fireworks, lighting up the night sky. The radiant colors lit their faces as Sophie laid her head on Serus' chest.

"If you could make one wish, what would it be?" Sophie asked.

"That you would say yes to my proposal."

Sophie pulled away and stared up Serus. His eyes were soft. He was the same Serus she remembered. The same vulnerability, spread across his face, but also the same hope.

"Only with Aramis' permission," Sophie stated.

Serus took the request from his pocket and handed it to her. "But he has given permission."

Sophie took the paper and unfolded it, finding the waxy blue signet of Aramis' ring. Serus took a silky white ribbon from his pocket and wrapped it around Sophie's arm gently. He tilted Sophie's chin up to meet his eyes and began the bonding vows.

"I am yours," Serus smiled.

"And you are mine,"

"By this tether, our souls are intertwined, and by this blessing, it will never unwind. We have found the soul we sought to find, and with this binding, we are forever, you and I," Sophie and Serus recited in unison.

Serus squeezed Sophie's arm and leaned in. "For I am yours."

"And you are-." Sophie paused in her vows as Serus' gray eyes glowed red, elongating. Fangs shot forth from his mouth and Sophie backed away as the ribbon unraveled, turning red and dripped from her arm in crimson like blood. Serus rose up in the form of a serpent. He hissed at her, coiling back, ready to strike. Sophie turned to run from the garden, but a dark cloud formed above her. The cloud took the shape of a mouth with sharp teeth as it molded into a wolf and swooped down, ready to devour her.

Sophie gripped the sheets of Serus' bed to catch her fall, gasping for breath.

It was only a nightmare.

Clutching her chest, she shuddered, trying to slow her sharp breaths, but the dream still haunted her. Being in the fortress was giving her these visions, messing with her head. She hated it. She hated the tricks and illusions. There was a battle within her own mind between what was real and what was fantasy.

When a knock came at the door, Sophie sat up. She hoped it was Aerith, but her shoulders slumped in dismay as Serus entered, closing the door quietly behind him.

Serus' cocked a brow. "Comfortable?"

Sophie stood, smoothing her dress, and ran her hands through her sweat-dampened hair.

Serus' eyes darted to Creation as she laid it on the bed. "How do you feel?" he asked.

Sophie tried to organize her thoughts, dropping her gaze to the floor. If she told him she felt like she was in a dark and hopeless place, that she felt trapped, he would assume she didn't want to be with him. He would assume she didn't care for him at all. She couldn't lie to herself. She still cared deeply for Serus. A part of her still loved him. She wanted him to be the angel she had fallen in love with, before the Confusion. She wanted to go back in time, so they could start over.

Maybe we can in the new life.

She wondered how she would find him, if it were possible, that she could help him come back to the truth. She scrunched her shoulders, anguished that she might not get the chance. She knew she had to act now.

"I feel like everything I have ever known and loved will be gone forever."

"Oh, Sophie, you know that isn't true," Serus tried to assure her. He glanced at the book again. Emotion washed over him as he recalled the first time he saw her. He never would have met her if he hadn't betrayed Aramis. Every choice he had made in the past had led him to her. There were no regrets.

"Do you remember the day we met?" He asked.

"Yes," Sophie whispered.

"Remember how you felt?" Serus picked up Creation and ran his fingers along the golden lettering of the title. "Because I do. It's so clear in my mind with you here."

Sophie turned away, her heart burning as the past tortured her, memories of him holding her in the meadow, their picnics, dancing in the garden. She rubbed her aching chest, staring at the floor until a thought occurred. A truth.

He's never once embraced me.

She could feel his desire for her and the fight within himself, but he was holding back.

Why? Was it one of Aalok's rules? Can he not touch me until I'm one of them?

"All I want is for us to be together again." He told her. "We could have everything we ever wanted, everything we ever worked for."

"It's emptiness, Serus. Nothing but vanity. It's an illusion."

"It's a new start."

Sophie stared at Serus in disbelief. "It's a death sentence."

"Then so be it," Serus glared, " because I would rather be blotted out of existence than go one more moment without you."

Sophie let out a controlled breath, crumpling into herself. Serus might as well have ripped her heart out. Tears welled in her eyes as she struggled to speak. "But you had me. We were to be bonded, but your choices drove us apart."

"Had?" Serus tilted his head and narrowed his eyes. "Are you saying that I've lost you?"

Sophie didn't know the answer. She was filled with so many confusing emotions. They swirled in her like a raging storm, but it wasn't only her emotions. She could sense Serus' conflict too, and to make things worse, she could feel everyone else in the fortress, beyond the walls, in every room. The auras of pride, anger, and resentment surrounded her, choking her. Her lungs tightened until she could hardly breathe.

"You dismiss everything that was," Sophie said, her voice cracking. "You act as if what Aramis gave you was not enough.

How could you be so unsatisfied?" Sophie shook her head. "I just don't understand. Surely, you do not believe Aalok is the wiser choice."

"So, you didn't enjoy your bath? Don't appreciate the clean gown? When I saw you, you were a mess. Is that how your king treats his Truth Keepers? Leaving them on Earth while he prepares his plan of destruction?"

"You sound just like Aalok. You're twisting everything."

"You don't have to go through with Aramis' plan." Serus fought back the urge to touch her, leaning in, mere inches from her face. "Stay with me and live."

Sophie felt something silky in her hand that wasn't there before. The sweet scent relaxed her shoulders as it filled her nose. A rose. She ran her fingers along the silky red petals before lifting her head to meet Serus' eyes with disbelief. "How did you-"

"I can teach you things you never dreamed you could do, Sophie. There is magic that Aramis won't allow you to practice. A magic that can give you so many wonderful things."

"I know you think Aalok can give you knowledge, but it's not real. He holds no true power, he only imitates it."

"Are you imagining that rose?"

No. It's real. But how-

"Open your eyes, Sophie."

"Open yours. Everything is about to change, but you still have a chance to make things right. You still have a choice."

"I've made my choice. It is you who must decide...me or death."

"You know it's not that simple."

A a knock came from the door.

"Come in," Serus said, his eyes still locked on Sophie.

Aerith opened the door and made her way in with a dining cart, loaded with a bountiful meal; wine, a plate full of fruit, and another covered in roasted vegetables and meats. Sophie's mouth watered as she watched Aerith park it beside the bed.

"As requested." Aerith bowed.

Sophie glanced up from the food and smiled with a nod of thanks.

Aerith averted her gaze, clasping her hands in front of her.

"Thank you, Aerith. That will be all," Serus replied, waving his hand in dismissal.

Pinpricks crawled up Sophie's neck and she wrapped an arm around her waist. It wasn't the pain of her empty stomach, but guilt that hallowed it. She let out a controlled breath as if exhaling for Aerith, to release her heartache. She frowned, watching the girl take one last wistful look at Serus and close the door without another word.

Realization hit Sophie with a punch in the gut. Serus. He was the one she had come here for, he was the one she was in love with.

"Why didn't you ask her to dine with us?"

"Because I want you all to myself," Serus lifted the plate of hot food from the cart, wafting the fragrant steam under Sophie's nose.

"I'm not hungry." Sophie pushed the plate away, although her stomach cried out for substance.

"A Truth Keeper trying to lie." Serus tsked with a grin and offered the plate again. "I can hear your stomach grumbling."

Serus was right. She was starving and she wasn't good at hiding the truth, not like he was. She gazed at him and then the plate, before taking a bright red raspberry. She hesitated to place it in her mouth and thought back to their picnics. The raspberry tarts, the chocolates, he had always brought her treats. He was trying to remind her of the past, of all the times they were together.

Mindlessly placing the berry in her mouth, Sophie closed her eyes, savoring the flavor. Every tart seed burst with flavor on her tongue. She picked up another, and then another, filling her empty stomach.

Serus poured Sophie a glass of white wine and smiled as Sophie accepted it. He raised a brow, pleased as Sophie mirrored his actions as he took a sip. He enjoyed the moment of having her to himself. There were no eyes watching them, no all-knowing king judging his actions, and no brute of a soldier to interrupt their private moment. He could see she was remembering what it was like to be with him. She was remembering his gifts of treats, the time he brought her a bouquet of red roses, and the mornings she had spent in his arms.

He watched Sophie intently as she satisfied her hunger. He had done all he could to impress her, to give her all she could ever want, and he was convinced that she would agree to their bonding now. He didn't need Aramis' approval. Aalok was waiting for them; soon, it would be official. But as he watched Sophie and drank his wine, his brows knitted as a troubling thought crossed his mind.

Caius had passed him in the hallway earlier, informed him of Alexander's capture. He had made a snide remark about Serus having competition. At the time, Serus shrugged it off, but when he made it to his room, he paused at the door. He wondered what Caius had meant. It ate at him. Instead of entering his chambers, he went to Aalok. Aalok informed Serus of the birth of Sophie's soul, and that she had a soulmate. Serus sneered; determined Alexander wouldn't stand in the way. He rushed back up the tower, sending a message to Aerith to bring a hot meal.

With the thought of Sophie having affections for another still haunting him, Serus stood and casually made his way to the middle of the room. He looked out the open doors to his balcony, coming up with a plan to test Sophie. As a Truth Keeper, she couldn't lie. If she held any affection for her Guardian, Serus would know by her reactions.

"By the way, you may be interested to know that your so-called Guardian is here."

"What did you say?"

Serus kept his back to Sophie and watched the ash dancing in the wind. "Yes, your friend, Alexander? You didn't forget about him, did you?"

"He's here, in the fortress?"

Serus glared at the darkening clouds and the blood-red ocean waves as jealousy boiled in his veins. He gripped the stem of the wine glass, pressing it so hard that it fractured with a quiet crack.

"Serus?"

Serus pivoted on his heels, sliding a hand in his pocket. He was hiding his true emotions again. He was fighting the urge to cross his arms and hide his fueled jealousy. Aalok had told him crossing his arms gave away the fact that he felt defensive, that he had done something wrong. It was a clear giveaway of guilt.

Serus swirled his wine and glanced around the room, his lips quirking to the side. "This room is quite lovely, isn't it? Much better than that cold, damp prison the soldiers threw you in."

"So, he's in the prison?" Sophie remembered the shock of Caius's glove. If Alexander had been subdued as she had been, he was in agony. "Is he all right?"

"Your caring demeanor has not changed a bit, I see," Serus smiled and came to stand beside the bed. He placed the wine glass on the nightstand and slid his other hand in his pocket, tilting his head. "However, I am curious why you're so worried about one of Aramis' soldiers?"

Sophie was stung by the aura of Serus' jealousy. "Serus," she whispered. She got up from the bed and reached for his arm, but he took a step back and leaned against the bedpost.

Sophie swallowed, careful of her next words. "Can I see him?"

Serus narrowed his eyes. "If that is what you want."

Sophie nodded and went toward the door. She reached for the knob but paused at Serus' words.

"Or we could stay up here," Serus said, coming up behind her, "catch up on the time we lost."

"I need to apologize," Sophie insisted. "It's my fault he's down there."

Serus swept Sophie's hair to the side and kissed her neck. "Are you sure?" He purred.

Sophie shivered as Serus kissed her again. Her breath was shallow and she struggled to keep her mind clear. As Serus traced her neck with his finger, a voice whispered in Sophie's ear. It slithered like a snake into her mind. It told her how beautiful she was again, that she should stay with Serus, that she loved him. Sophie exhaled, trembling, but managed to answer.

"Yes."

Serus smirked and let Sophie's hair fall over his ashen kiss, hiding any evidence that he had touched her. He reminded himself that soon enough he could take her to his bed. Aalok would wed them, and she would finally be his bride. Until then, he would enjoy the burning desire. He leaned forward; being careful not to let his lips touch her ear and whispered.

"As you wish, Princess."

22

A PRISION OF

PAIN

WRAPPING her arms around herself, Sophie glanced at the cell she had been in not long ago. She followed Serus to a dark corner down the dim hallway and covered her mouth in shock at the sight of her Guardian.

Alexander's wrists were bound in chains, buzzing with the same crimson electricity that Caius had used to subdue her. Sophie's neck tingled, remembering the pain. She took slow steps, approaching the limp soldier with his head hanging on his chest.

When Alexander heard the footsteps, he gathered enough strength to raise his head, but let it fall at the sight of Sophie dressed in red. "No," he murmured.

"Alexander," Sophie whispered in horror, looking down at her colorless Guardian. His aura was gone, no longer the familiar amber glow. Instead, he was a gray silhouette before her. She knelt in front of him, ignoring the chill that ran through her.

Serus watched from the doorway, smirking. He wanted Sophie close to Alexander so he could get a good look at her, to be close enough to touch her, but just out of reach. The pain in Alexander's eyes said all Serus needed to know. Sophie had chosen. Sophie was still his.

"I'll give you two some time to talk." Serus nodded to the guard who closed the door and locked it. Sophie waited until Serus was up the steps and out of sight before she leaned in closer.

"I'm so sorry," Sophie said softly. She reached to brush his hair from his face, but he flinched away with gritted teeth.

"To think, I fought my way in here to rescue you. How long did it take before Serus convinced you to turn?"

"I didn't. I'm still loyal to Aramis."

"Are you? If you were the enemy, they wouldn't treat you so kindly, now would they?"

Sophie looked down at her dress. "It's not what you think."

"I should have known better."

"I'm not-"

"A traitor?" Alexander snapped, glaring at her soft clean hands, pressing to the ground.

Sophie swallowed hard. "I would never betray Aramis."

"Your appearance says otherwise." Alexander glanced significantly at Sophie's dress.

Sophie tugged the dress over her exposed thigh. "I didn't want to wear this, but I-."

"Then why did you?"

A valid question.

Sophie didn't have an answer. She realized she had done it for selfish reasons. The warm bath, the clean clothes; she could have refused.

Serus' voice echoed down the hall into Alexander's cell. "I just spoke with Aalok and he is overjoyed that you have agreed to meet with him."

"You agreed?" Alexander growled.

Sophie tried to touch Alexander's chin, to bring his face up to hers. She knew if he would look at her, truly look at her, he would see in her eyes she was telling the truth. Surely then he could see the light in them, that she still carried Aramis' love inside her.

"Alexander please, just look at me," Sophie pleaded, cupping his face.

Alexander lifted his eyes to meet Sophie's but a shock stung his neck at his movement. His body went rigid and he growled in pain before his head slumped forward again. His body throbbed as the shackles burned through his skin. It was unrelenting torture, and the harder he tried to look upon Sophie's face, the deeper the fire of his bonds cut into him.

The knot in Alexander's gut tightened. He was going to be sick, not just from the searing shocks of his shackles, but from the fear of Sophie choosing the enemy.

Has she turned?

He concentrated on her aura, but there was nothing but a cold draft that soothed his hot cheeks. There was no warmth, no light from Sophie. Alexander was convinced if she had lost her light, she had chosen to stay with Serus. She had chosen to betray her king.

"If this is what you choose, then go." He growled.

"Alexander…" Sophie's voice trailed off as tears welled in her eyes.

"You are no longer a Truth Keeper, and therefore, you are no longer my responsibility. You have chosen your path." Alexander gritted through the pain.

Serus opened the cell door and lifted his chin. "Time to go, my love." He shot Alexander a knowing grin, as Sophie let her hands fall from her Guardian's face. "Aalok is waiting."

Sophie pressed a hand to the frigid floor and one to her chest. "Please Serus…just…just let him go."

At a nod from Serus, two guards grabbed Sophie by her arms and pulled her away from her Guardian.

"Please, you must let him go!" Sophie screamed, but the brute soldiers dragged her up the staircase. Anxiety spiked through her, fearing her Guardian would suffer until the very end of the world. She couldn't leave him. Not like this.

As Sophie fought the soldiers, Serus locked the cell door with an arrogant grin. He leaned in inches from the steel bars and glared down at Alexander. "Aramis may have predestined you two to be bonded, but as you can see, Aramis is not in control of our fate—enjoy yours."

Alexander's eyes opened at the word 'bonded' and he frowned thoughtfully at the floor as the lock clicked. As Serus' footsteps faded away, Alexander repeated words of hope in his mind.

Predestined. Bonded.

His shoulders relaxed and he blinked back tears. There was hope. If Sophie was his other half, his mate, she couldn't have turned, not yet. There was still light in her, even if he couldn't feel it. He vowed to Aramis he would protect her and protect her he would. Strength filled his limbs and he clenched his teeth as he lifted his arms. Enduring the searing burn in his wrists and neck, he jerked at his chains until the stone holding them in the wall clattered to the ground.

Serus hid a grin within a calm facade, making his way to the top of the stairway, but as he met Sophie's teary eyes, guilt shot through him.

"Where is your mercy?" Sophie shouted, struggling to break free of the soldiers' grip. "He has done nothing wrong! He has only done what Aramis asked of him!"

"Mercy?" Serus sneered. "You mean like the mercy the council granted me?"

Sophie bucked against the soldiers, but their grip only tightened. She winced at their fingernails stabbing her skin.

How could he be so cold, so heartless?

Serus took a step forward, narrowing his eyes at Sophie.

He held his stare for a long moment. When Sophie didn't speak, he headed toward Aalok's chamber but turned on his heel when Sophie shouted from behind.

"If you had just followed the rules, you wouldn't have been demoted!"

"The rules," Serus scoffed in disgust. "Don't be so naive. What you believe is what you have been indoctrinated to accept. Look around you. We don't have to follow the Law of Aramis. We can do whatever we please and not be persecuted for it. What do I have to do to make you understand that?"

"Let me go!" Sophie shouted at the soldiers.

At a nod from Serus, the guards released her.

Sophie stumbled forward, gripping Serus' arm as he caught her fall. Her breaths were heavy, uneven. She was trembling, her body aching. Whatever sorcery had been in the water of the tub was waning. She was as weak as she had been before her bath. The room blurred and she clutched Serus' arm tighter as he gently took her by the waist.

Serus drew Sophie close. He could touch her now that Alexander had seen her clean. The illusion of the magic water had worked. Sophie had appeared faithful to Aalok, that she had accepted a new king. Because of the water, the Outcasts appeared faithful to Aalok, as if *he* had washed away of their iniquity. In reality, the soot of a trespass could only be dissolved by the touch of one pure, by light, or by the acknowledgment and admittance of a trespass, by forgiveness. Only then could the marks be removed.

Serus wrapped his arms around her waist and kissed her damp hair at her temple. He was relieved he no longer had to hold back his affections. Aalok had instructed him to comfort her when she was weak; when she was on the edge of losing all hope, all faith. It was now the perfect opportunity to be her savior, her rescuer. Serus smiled. Alexander had turned on her, accused her and not him. Aalok's plan was working, or so Serus thought until Sophie spoke.

"Please, Serus," Sophie implored, peering up at him, "let me take Alexander and leave. You can do as you wish, and I will do as I wish. If you won't come back with me, at least let me go home. I know there is some good left in you. Please just let us go."

Serus' forehead creased.

Us. So, it's true. She does care for her Guardian.

Serus could sense her worry about him, chained in a cold, dark cell, writhing in pain. He didn't want her to see him so affected by his anger. He hid his jealousy behind a mask of confidence and smiled as he traced his fingers along Sophie's jawline. He took a step back and then took a box from his jacket pocket. As the soldiers took Sophie's arms to support her, Serus removed the lid and took out the ruby head adornment.

"I am *not* wearing that." Sophie objected.

"Meet with Aalok and then—you can go free if that is what you wish," Serus said, looking at the adornment. He lifted his gaze to meet Sophie's, offering the headpiece.

"And Alexander?"

"I'll arrange his release."

Sophie stared at the headpiece and swallowed. "Do I have your word?

"I promise."

Sophie closed her eyes and stopped struggling.

Serus smiled and placed the adornment on Sophie's head, situating the hanging ruby jewel in the center of her forehead. This was where Aalok had instructed the jewel to be placed. This was the way to calm Sophie's fears.

A trickle, like the first sip of hot tea, wove its way through Sophie's body. It slithered down to the tips of her fingers and into her toes until she felt nothing. There was no ache in her chest from worry, no fear causing her body to tremble uncontrollably. There was nothing but the tingle of numbness. The raging flame inside her, fueled by her indignation, had been snuffed out with a single motion.

When Sophie's pupils widened and then shrank, Serus lifted his chin and gave a sideways smile. The jewel had worked just as Aalok had said it would. Sophie's mind was now a blank space, a blank page to fill with new thoughts, new words.

"Come," Serus said with confidence. "We have made Aalok wait long enough."

23

AALOK

THE doors shut with a thud as Sophie was led into the grand throne room. She gazed around, finding the walls plated in gold. Red velvet curtains hung on every window. The curtains also hung above the golden throne at the top of an onyx stairway. There were great golden wings above the golden seat, spread wide with the symbol of Aalok in their center.

Sophie lifted her gaze to the candle-lit chandeliers. There were at least twenty flickering lights in each of the candelabras. The gold ceiling curved into a dome and was carved in geometrical shapes and symbolic patterns of power. Statues of gold had been modeled into the form Aalok as if he were a great king. His arms were open wide, and a humble smile had been plastered on his face.

There were also paintings of him covering the walls, depicting scenes of creation and the time before Sophie's existence. In these paintings, Aalok was the creator of all souls; his aura was more glorious and magnificent than any who bowed at his feet in worship. When Sophie spied Aramis kneeling before Aalok, offering a crown and scepter, her heart struggled to burn. Her anger couldn't be kindled. Not with the headpiece controlling her emotions.

Applause reverberated off the walls and Sophie's attention snapped to Aalok. He paraded toward her with a gleaming, tooth-filled grin. His long white hair seemed to float as he took graceful steps to her. His eyes were as blue as the ocean and his face was as smooth and white as porcelain. He wore a crimson robe, threaded in gold, and his raven wings were tucked tight behind him, peeking over his shoulders.

"My dear, sweet Sophie, such a pleasure!" Aalok clasped his hands together, his eyes shifting to Serus with a nod as if to say, well done.

Serus gave a humble smile in return.

"Please! Join us!" Aalok urged, gesturing to the table. "We were just about to dine."

Aalok signaled for one of his servants to pour Sophie a glass of wine.

Sophie hesitated but went to the chair pulled out for her. Tucking her gown beneath her, she sat, and glanced around at the Seraphim sitting at the table. They paused from their conversation, scowling over their cups as her chair squeaked across the floor. She glanced at one of the Seraph at the other end of the table. His hair was white, dipped in red. He levitated a knife, twirling it in the air. Locking eyes with Sophie, he stopped rotating his fingers, and let the knife clatter to the table.

Sophie flinched, her eyes darting to her cup. She could feel his glare. His aura was curious. She dared to look up to find him tilting his head as if searching her emotions, waiting for a reaction.

Sophie's spirit rose up, ragged against the fog in her mind. It tugged at her as if telling her to look around, to realize the danger she was in. No matter the fog the headpiece caused, her soul screamed the truth. A wave of heat spread from her chest as her heart begged for her to focus.

Shifting her gaze across the table, Sophie found another Seraph with bright long blond hair and a pointy nose. He cocked a brow as if asking if she liked what she saw. Sophie rolled her shoulders, her lips twisting in disgust. She gazed around to the rest of the Seraphim at the table. All the Seraphs were blonde and pale skinned. All of them...except the one sitting next to Serus. He looked so much like him. He had the same eyes, same skin, but as the Seraph combed back his hair in his fingers, Sophie noted a defined widow's peak. His black onyx hair hung over his shoulders, a small braid dangling beside his left temple. The tip of it and the rest of the ends of his hair were as white as Bevol's mane. Bevol. The thought of her beloved horse sent a sharp pain into Sophie's chest.

The dark-haired Seraph met Sophie's eyes. He stared at her for a few heartbeats before flashing a grin and turning back to Serus. Sophie's shoulders tensed as Serus laughed at the fallen angel. She listened to her heart and focused hard, listening to their words. She thought for sure she heard her name.

Are they making fun of me? Is Serus gloating?

She leaned closer, trying to overhear their conversation but her attention was drawn to the thumping of her heart. She could feel the presence beside her, the presence that made the hair on the back her neck stand up. Sickness swept over her as she felt Aalok's eyes on her. She didn't want to look at him, didn't dare to try. It was impossible to sort through his aura. She could feel nothing but a swirl of pleasure and a hint of pain. The harder she tried to make sense of the emotions; the harder her head pounded. She rubbed her temples but lifted her head to the servant who stood beside her. Another meek servant laid a napkin over Sophie's lap, and another poured a glass of water.

Aalok eyed the jewel on Sophie's head and grinned. He had the Truth Keeper right where he wanted her. This had worked on others in the past, and it would work on her too. All he had to do was make her see that it was Serus she desired, that a life with him was all she wanted.

"It has become unbearable out there, has it not?" Aalok asked, his tone shifting from cheerful to concerned. "Aramis and his grand plan of destruction. Such a shame. You have been informed of his decision?"

Sophie nodded in acknowledgment as her head began to ache. The more she tried to clear her head, the harder it was to fight the waves of confusion. She focused on her plate as a servant placed a steaming bowl of soup in front of her. She gazed at the steam, remembering the bath.

"So then, you know what will happen to you—to *all* the lower angels?" Aalok asked, resting his elbows on the table with clasped hands.

Sophie gripped the wine goblet in her hand and frowned. She squinted at herself in the reflection of the chalice. Her eyes. They were glazed over with a milky veil, reflecting the fog in her mind. Uneasiness crept into her chest, pressing against her heart and her breaths grew shallow.

Run! Her heart screamed. Run away, before it's too late!

"He must have kept the details from you." Aalok continued, feigning concern. "So like him; everything a mystery, complex, when really, it all could be so very simple. He could have plainly told you what was going to happen; not riddle it with parables and prophecies.

"That way, you could make the choice whether you wanted to go through with his plan or not, but he likes to conceal matters, for control." Aalok leaned back in his chair. "I propose a new idea, one that involves you being able to stay in the Infinite Realm, to be a part of the New Order, even take part in its creation. Do I speak the truth?" he asked his confidants.

The Seraphim at the table nodded in agreement as he gestured toward them.

"Aramis' plan is cruel. He knows many will still choose to follow me and yet he would have them suffer a whole lifetime in vain. Do you know why so many follow me, Sophie?"

Serus eyed Sophie from behind his goblet, taking another sip of wine. He regretted using the jewel. She was so pale, so weak. He wished there could have been another way to bring her to Aalok, but there wasn't. This was the only way to make her see, make her listen. He managed a smile and leaned back in his chair. He had to act as if nothing bothered him. He had to be smooth, calm.

"For the same reason, Serus has chosen to follow me." Aalok smiled at Serus. "Look at him. Before his exile, he came to me and told me of the loyalty and service he had provided Aramis. I was impressed by his works and simply wanted to reward him for all that Aramis had not.

"What pained me most, however, was when he told me he was denied your hand. I took pity on him. Gave him all the luxury he deserved, provided him with all that was taken from him. It's such a shame. Your brethren were cast out for doing nothing wrong. Poor Serus simply wanted to live his life as he saw fit. Is that such a crime? To love with a burning passion? To long to hold the one he loves in his arms?"

Sophie held back the urge to vomit. She couldn't concentrate, she couldn't think. All she could do was sit and listen with no objections.

"All he wanted, all he has ever wanted," Aalok explained, looking upon Sophie with pity, "was to be with you."

Sophie dropped her head and squeezed her eyes. She had to get out of there. She had to escape, relieve the pressure in her head. Then something touched her. A draft. It was icy but soft like the wind. The pressure in her head eased as a gentle whisper cooed in her ear. Then another in her other ear whispered, and another. It was as if there were several cold waves of air around her, huddled around her chair. They coaxed her to listen, to trust. They were soft at first, but as Sophie shook her head to shake away their presence, they grew louder.

Aalok studied Sophie as she sat. She hunched, staring at the table, scrunching her shoulders. It was working. His spirit was affecting her. It wouldn't be long before she would comply. He glanced at Serus, asking with his eyes if he was ready.

Serus nodded and rose from his seat. He placed a hand on Sophie's back and took her hand to help her stand.

"Would you like to see why Serus was banished from the Infinite Realm? Why he was sent away from you, the very soul whom he cherishes so deeply?" Aalok asked.

Sophie rose; ready to escape the voices, and followed Serus to the middle of the room to stand across from Aalok.

Aalok waved his hand in the air and a liquid like substance appeared between him and the Truth Keeper. He grinned at

Sophie on the other side, as her waving face becoming clear when the liquid solidified. At a tap of his finger the screen filled with files, marked with names and places.

As Aalok searched through the names on the files, Serus kept his hopeful gaze on Sophie. He knew Aalok was about to show her something that would convince her. She would be shown that it was not his choice to leave her, but her King, who had sent him away. This would be the truth. This would give her a reason to stay with him.

"No doubt Aramis has concealed these matters from you," Aalok informed, "I simply want to show you the truth. No secrets." He slid his fingers across the screen of glass, enlarging a holographic image as footage of the past played.

In the image, Sophie saw Aalok doing marvelous works for Aramis. She saw time shift forward, to the great Seraph standing next to Aramis' throne, side by side with Michael and Gabriel. Then Aalok tapped on Serus' name, bringing forth his file. He skipped the beginnings of his birth to the first meeting with Sophie and then another of him with her in the gardens of the kingdom.

Then, she saw herself and Serus walking hand in hand in the meadow. Then she saw all the times Serus brought her gifts. She could taste the chocolate on her tongue, smell the roses, and feel the tickle of the falling blossoms as they caressed her cheek. Then, there was the image of their first kiss. Sophie could feel the touch of Serus' lips again; the sweet and salty taste of his mouth. She was lost in the past; exhaling at the same time she exhaled in the images before her.

Serus took her hand in hers, weaving their fingers together. As he squeezed her hand, Sophie glanced back up at the images of their first kiss. He had been so gentle back then, almost as gentle as his touch was now.

As if a switch had clicked, the fog in Sophie's mind cleared. She was back in time in the meadow, back to when she was happy. And then, the images appeared to lose color, fade. They grew dim as Aalok paused at the pivotal point of Serus' exile.

Whispers wove their way back into Sophie's mind. They pressed her to take a step closer to the screen, to not turn away from the scene before her.

Serus dipped his quill in ink, gliding it across a parchment. Sophie read along, mouthing the last sentence, recognizing it as the request to Aramis to bond with her. Serus melted a wax stick and stamped his Truth Keeper signet, and headed for the castle, brimming with light.

Sophie pressed a hand to her flushed cheek as time skipped forward to Serus standing before the council.

Aramis stood from the seat of his throne, then, the scene jumped past the words Aramis had said as well as Serus' answer to him. Then, the images went to Serus, escorted out of the gates of the Infinite Realm. Then the images showed him in the campsite. The flames danced in his eyes as he played his violin.

Then a halo of a silhouetted white appeared. It was her. The image shifted back to Serus and the hope in his eyes when he saw her, standing before him.

"Now you know that Aramis did not see fit to bond you to Serus. At Serus' second request for your hand, he was cast out of the Infinite Realm, separated from you, unable to return."

Sophie stared at the ground for a long moment, trying to focus her thoughts. She closed her eyes, mentally shouting at the whispering voices to leave her, that in the name of Aramis they flee.

At her words in her mind, the fog lifted and she glanced up at Serus, remembering the truth. "No," she whispered. "He wouldn't have exiled you without cause."

Aalok frowned. Sophie was stronger than he had assumed. It was now clear why Aramis chose her. The unseen demons of his spirit were no match for her strength, her faith. He concentrated on the jewel, drawing back the clawing demons of his spirit, and focused all of his energy on the head adornment. He lifted his chin with a façade of fake pity. "Poor Serus, separated from his love, never to be reunited. Until now, that is. Thanks to me."

The screen became liquid again and disappeared.

Serus grimaced, squeezing Sophie's hand in hopes she would return his affections, but Sophie pulled away.

She was sorting through the images, trying to connect them, trying to read Aramis' words. The footage had gone by too fast, there was no finding the truth now. She would have to concentrate; she would have to fight the Confusion.

"Sophie, I have seen your life as well," Aalok said, catching Sophie's attention. "And I know you have always wanted to do well, to please Aramis, and you have, but dear, sweet Sophie, you must know the truth. Your king has hidden so many things from you. I only wish to bring what was in the dark to the light."

Aalok came to Sophie and waved his hand.

Out of thin air, a golden chalice appeared.

"Hold out your hand, my dear," Aalok requested and Sophie's body complied. "I can give you living water so that you will not die. You will not have to suffer this new age the way your king intends," Aalok explained; making the cup, pour on its own. The pristine water trickled from the goblet and onto Sophie's palm. It absorbed into her skin, spreading up her arm, rejuvenating her body like the water from her bath had, but this particular water was different. This water was much like the trickling feeling she felt from her head adornment, but it wasn't. It was stronger. It sent warmth through her veins, a comfort much like she had felt in the presence of Aramis. She exhaled and relaxed her shoulders as all thoughts melted from her mind.

Aalok discarded the cup with another wave of his hand. "There is another way. I only wish to show you that way. If you trust in me, I can give you all that you desire. I can teach you how to obtain anything and everything you wish. You will want for nothing, my dear. As you can see, I have taken very good care of Serus. He has all he has ever dreamed of. All but the one thing he has been denied."

Sophie turned to Serus. He was hazy, like a dream, but beautiful. He was more handsome than she remembered. His eyes were bluer, soft and hopeful. His smile was sweet and trusting. His hair was shiny and his skin was smooth. A desire to touch his face rose up in her. This was the Serus she had fallen for, the Serus she had loved.

Serus lit to a waving white flame and took Sophie's hand. He warmed her icy fingertips and drew her close to him. "It is your choice to make, Sophie." He leaned to her ear and whispered. "I only hope that choice is me."

Sophie melted in Serus' arms as he exhaled a warm breath on her neck. All the emotions from her past came flooding back to her, reminding her of how it used to feel to be with him. Heat flushed her body and she embraced him as he took her into his arms.

Aalok smiled in victory. He hovered beside the Truth Keeper, licking his lips like a hungry lion, ready to pounce on its prey. With his power, he created an illusion of a grand arbor filled with red, winding rose vines. Their scent filled the room with their sweet smell.

Sophie's nose filled with the familiar scent and she opened her eyes to discover the beauty around her. She was in the kingdom gardens again and before her, was Serus, dressed in his royal attire as a Truth Keeper.

For that one short moment, Sophie forgot about Aramis. She forgot about the aeon's impending destruction. She forgot she would have to face death to enter a new life, to help her lost peers. There was only Serus and the illusion surrounding them. There were only the deepest desires of her heart.

Serus smoothed Sophie's hair from her face, smiling as she shivered at his touch. She was in his arms again; she was his. He leaned forward, gazing into her eyes until they closed. He swallowed his fears of her rejection and closed his eyes, pausing to savor the moment. He traced her lips with his thumb and glowed. "Sophie—I have loved you with a passion beyond measure. Say yes to my proposal, say you'll stay."

Serus drew Sophie close, wrapping his arms around her waist. But as he pressed his lips to hers, his eyes opened wide at Alexander's angry voice.

FALLEN

"HE'S nothing but a liar, Sophie!" Alexander snarled as he fought against the guards that struggled to gain a grip on him.

Aalok dropped his hands at the disruption and the illusion of the garden melted away.

Caius stomped in. His face was red with wrath as he reared back and punched Alexander in the gut with a shock of energy from his glove.

Alexander doubled over with a pain filled gasp.

"Alexander!" Aalok announced joyfully, signaling Caius to bring Alexander to the center of the room. "So nice of you to join us."

Aalok circled Alexander, before raising his brows to Caius in disappointment.

"Release his bonds," Aalok ordered.

"But, my Lord-"

"I said," Aalok glared, "release him."

Caius gritted his teeth but did as instructed. He jerked the electric rope from Alexander's wrists painfully and shoved him forward.

Sophie covered her mouth in horror, seeing the lashes on Alexander's body. He wasn't healing and she could feel his pain. As if she had been bound in the dungeon by the same electric current, her face twisted as her skin burned. As Caius tugged on Alexander's chains, her wrists pinched with unbearable pain.

"You say I am a liar, Alexander, and yet you, it is you who do not hold to the truth," Aalok pointed out. "You have kept secrets from Sophie. How shameful. Did you tell her about the agreement between Aramis and myself?"

Alexander held his tongue and glared at Aalok.

"You hid the truth." Aalok continued. "The truth, that she can avoid death. She did not know she could avoid living like the beasts of the field, made of flesh and blood, a filthy animal, roaming the Earth," Aalok circled Alexander, arrogantly. "That there will be unbearable pain, sorrow. That the new life will only end in a sad and horrible death, and for what? For all to choose as they already do now? Aramis has told you everything, the future, and the ending result. Which is, that no matter what he does, I still win.

"You didn't tell Sophie this, did you, Alexander? Why, oh why would you keep this from her— I wonder? Is it because she could stay here with Serus, living a full and happy life, eternally, just as she and Serus have always wanted?"

"You twist the truth," Alexander spat.

"Do I?" Aalok raised a brow. "Perhaps we should see what truth is, reveal everything about you and your past." A mischievous grin played on Aalok's lips. "What might we find there?"

Sophie's face contorted as her eyes darted back and forth between Alexander and Aalok. Their conflicting auras overwhelmed her. Anger, malice, guilt, and doubt thickened the air. She realized Serus still embraced her. Sophie took a step away from him, feeling and seeing the crimson aura he now emanated. It burned in her chest with more pain than she had felt at the rejection of his first proposal.

Aalok brought the liquid screen forth again with a wave of his hand. He tapped a file, enlarging it, showing Alexander approaching Aramis' castle, then enter the throne room.

Aalok looked over his shoulder and grinned at Alexander. "I know of your little meeting with Aramis, Alexander. What did you talk about in secret? We all want to know." Aalok asked, glancing at the Seraphim at the table. They smiled at him, leaning back casually in their chairs.

At a tap of Aalok's fingers images filled the screen: Alexander and Aramis dining, the keys to the Library of Souls, and Alexander looking through Sophie's book.

Sophie knew that Aramis had asked Alexander to watch over her, but now she saw that Aramis had allowed him to read about her life, about Serus, about anything and everything that was documented in her history.

He cheeks burned with heat as she watched Alexander reach for Serus' book, reading through the pages. The images on the screen skipped, and then slowed, showing Alexander and Sophie on the beach after leaving the Outcast camp. The images moved forward again, displaying the entrance into the secret spring, Sophie staring at the waterfalls, and looking to the ashen kiss from Serus. But it also showed what she had not noticed. It showed Alexander glowing bright amber in the realization of his love for her.

Sophie pressed a trembling hand to her chest. Her heart raced, watching Alexander's face on the screen, seeing the conflict in his eyes. Knowing he had hidden his feelings from her, she looked to her Guardian, but he averted his eyes.

As Sophie wrapped her arms around herself and winced, Aalok smiled. The time was right. He had cunningly and underhandedly placed a thought in The Truth Keeper's mind, a clever lie based on facts. The lie, that her Guardian had kept her away from Serus because of his jealousy.

Now caught up in the deception, Sophie was sure that Alexander didn't care about Serus at all, that he felt as if Serus' soul was not worthy to be saved. Sophie knew, even through the confusion, that Serus' soul was just as valuable as hers, or anyone else's, for that matter. There was no one she could trust, not even her Guardian. Knowing he had kept this from her, she began to question everything about her protector and his intentions. The fog seeped in again, clouding her mind, her reasoning. She put her hands to her head and squeezed her eyes shut, rubbing her pounding temples. There was no relief.

Aalok smiled deviously and waved his hand.

The room went black.

As her own voice echoed from above, Sophie lifted her gaze to the domed ceiling, filled with twinkling lights. Her heart thumped against her ribcage, realizing what was about to be revealed to everyone, especially Serus.

Aalok watched Sophie and Serus' faces for a moment before glowering at Alexander with a sly grin and eerie eyes. They glowed from the light of the screen in a milky yellow, and his pupils' slit into diamonds.

"Will you stay with me to the end, Alexander? I mean, is that what is required of you? To watch over me until this aeon ends?" Sophie's words repeated verbatim, as did Alexander's reply.

"Yes, those are Aramis' orders." As his projection responded, Alexander opened his eyes. He glared at Aalok, who gave a cunning grin.

The hologram skipped forward, to the water droplets vibrating in the air. The footage then slowed.

Serus peered up at the screen, painfully. His aura rose in crimson with his jealousy, expanding outward, engulfing him in the flames. But the moment Sophie and Alexander's lips touched, his aura dissipated all at once as a stab pierced his chest with grief.

Sophie bowed her head in shame, unable to look at Serus. She too was tortured by the pain and jealousy he felt. It stabbed at her over and over as the footage of her and Alexander's kiss rewound and then played, again, and again.

Finally, the footage paused as Aalok turned to her Guardian.

"You can hide your feelings from her and yourself," he taunted, clasping his hands behind his back, "but not from me. You took her by surprise, leading her into that enchanting cavern to seduce her."

"Stop twisting the truth!" Alexander barked. "You know that is not how it happened!"

"I think we can *all* see," Aalok chuckled cruelly, glancing at the Seraphim. They shook their heads, shaming the Guardian, clearly holding back their grins.

Alexander clenched his jaw, but Aalok's attention shifted to Serus, who was shaking. He was sick with disgust. His aura was full of crimson again, and his eyes reflected its glow.

Sophie dared to glance at him, fearing the flames of red flickering in his glossy eyes. She lifted a foot, ready to take cautious steps toward him, but before she could, he lunged at her Guardian, and struck a blow to Alexander's face.

At the deafening smack, Sophie froze.

The room fell silent.

Alexander rolled his jaw, letting out a throaty groan. He then licked the fluid from the cut at his lip but made no attempt to retaliate. He knew he had done wrong by Serus, by Sophie, and took the assault gracefully, lifting his head.

Serus spat at Alexander's feet and made his way to the chamber doors without looking back.

"Serus! Wait!" Sophie ran to him, desperately gripping his sleeve.

Serus glared down at her and slowly pried her fingers away. He took her by the wrist and squeezed it tight.

Sophie shrunk back, cringing, but not from the pain, it was from the maddening look in his eyes.

"Serus, please. Let me explain."

"I thought spending thousands of years without you would be unbearable," he croaked, holding back his tears. "But this..." He couldn't finish his sentence. His throat had closed up. With nothing more he could say, he stomped to out the doors of the throne room without another word.

Sophie crumbled to the ground.

There would be no saving Serus now.

"Well," Aalok said jovially, clapping his hands together, "now that everything's out in the open, I think we should get on with it." He waved a hand, lighting up the room, and then sauntered to Sophie. Her arms were wrapped around herself and her blank stare was set to the floor.

"None of you are perfect, my dear. In time, you can make things right with Serus. You know as well as I do, that love covers a multitude of trespasses. We all make mistakes, well, everyone but me, that is." Aalok grinned a crooked smile as his wings rustled beneath his red robe. "I can forgive your transgressions." He said offering a hand to Sophie. "All can be made right again, but, only if you follow me. You don't have to play by Aramis' rules." He glanced at Alexander. "My offer still stands for you as well, Guardian. Care to join us? We can talk over a hot meal. I'm sure you're hungry."

At a snap of Aalok's fingers, a servant came forth and set a place for the warrior. Another servant brought a goblet, filled it with wine as another sat a steaming bowl of soup down on a golden plate.

The scent of vegetable broth wafted into Alexander's nose. His stomach tightened. He was starving, but he wouldn't let his body control him, nor Aalok.

"A game?" Alexander asked, fixing his stare on Aalok. "So, you see us as pawns."

Alexander glared at the Seraph for a few thudding heartbeats before shifting his gaze to Sophie. His eyes softened at the sight of her. She was so weak. So confused.

What have they done to you?

He tugged away from Caius, who gave a few inches, but watched his every move.

"You know Aramis loves us," Alexander told her gently. "He would never use us. Not like this. What our king does, he does out of love. Not manipulation, not like this prince of darkness would have you believe. Whatever he said, whatever he promised—you know it cannot be. Your purpose is far greater than this life."

Aalok's feathers threatened to rise, but he drew them back. He couldn't lose control, not when he was so close to winning over the Truth Keeper. He had seen the future. He had seen himself as king. Sophie would be the last Truth Keeper to stand against him in the next aeon. If he didn't convince her now, she would be pure, without fault. This was his only chance to corrupt her faith. This was his only chance to make her doubt Aramis and his plan of redemption.

"He doesn't care about Serus' soul," Alexander continued. "He's corrupt, tainted by his own lustful desires. He followed his, but you don't have to follow yours. You can take the other path. I know you want more than anything to help change the fate of all those who fell away, but you can't...not if you give in. Not if you give up now."

Sophie didn't look up.

"Your soup is getting cold, my dear," Aalok noted. "Come. Sit. Warm your weary soul with comfort."

Aalok's words were a distant echo in Sophie's ears. She stared with blurry vision at her reflection in the fallen Seraphs' emblem. She saw the ugliness in her heart. It showed itself in her distorted face. The illusion of the miracle water was passing. Every inch of her body hurt, but worse, was the relentless aching in her chest.

I have to explain. I have to make Serus understand.

Is it for your own relief or his? a voice whispered.

Tears fell to the floor as Sophie stood.

His. She tried to tell the voice.

Liar. It snickered. You are unworthy.

At the words of the whisper, Sophie stumbled to the ground. The crack of her knee's echoed in the room, but she couldn't feel the pain in them. She could only feel hopelessness as a cold darkness closed in.

Alexander reached out to comfort her, but at the shock of Caius's glove on his shoulder, he went rigid with a groan.

"Oh, you poor dear. Here, let me help you," Aalok gushed with fake concern. He bent down, reaching a hand for Sophie to take.

"Don't. Touch her." Alexander growled through his teeth.

"I think Alexander is ready to return to his quarters now."

"I can't." Sophie choked out. Tears rolled down her face and neck. Throbbing spread from her knees down her shins as the knot in her stomach tightened. Pain. It was there now and it was relentless in every way. She was bound by her regret, her guilt. She wept, bracing herself with her palms and prayed.

Faith... a peaceful voice whispered. It wasn't the one that called her unworthy. It was one she recognized; one she knew to be of her king.

Sophie tried to stand again, and as she leaned forward, her head adornment slid off her forehead and fell with a clink on the floor.

Breath that had once been unattainable came in swift, deep drawls through her nostrils. She stared at the headpiece, then at herself reflection again, praying to Aramis to aid her. At her plea, she found Armais' humble face replace her reflection.

"Can't what, my dear?" Aalok asked, reaching out again to take her arm.

"Stop!" Alexander spat, lighting with a spark. "You know the agreement."

Aalok turned to face Alexander, seeing the color coming back into the Guardian's face. "I'm afraid I do not know of this *agreement*," Aalok lied smoothly. "Another ploy of Aramis is it?"

"You know *exactly* what I speak of. Do you really want to take the chance of losing? To void the contract?"

Aalok's lips twitched. He hadn't forgotten the agreement concerning what he could and could not do to sway souls to his side. The touch of a Seraph was a very powerful thing. From Seraphs of Aramis, there was given peace and comfort, from the touch of Aalok's followers, darkness and confusion. The touch from Aalok himself would mean full and utter submission.

If Sophie had allowed Aalok's help, it would have been her choice. However. If the fallen Seraph *was* to touch her against her will, he would be put in chains, awaiting his chance to rule at the proposed time; the end of the next aeon. There was one way, and one way only to guarantee the corruption the first human that Aramis would make. He would need the freedom to do so. If he bothered with this Truth Keeper now, he would risk losing that opportunity.

Drawing back casually, Aalok gestured a servant to help Sophie to the table.

"How about we discuss this further over some wine?" he offered, signaling a servant to pour her a fresh glass. "Your nerves must be frazzled from all this excitement."

"She's done discussing." Alexander contended. "Let her go."

"Caius," Aalok said, taking a seat next to Sophie.

Caius shoved Alexander toward the chamber doors, but Alexander bucked back. He looked over his shoulder at the Truth Keeper he had vowed to protect. She was faithful. He had seen a glint of it in her eyes, had seen the faint hue of white when she had stood. She needed her Guardian, she needed Aramis, and if didn't she have the strength to stand against the wiles of their adversary, he would do it for her.

Serus' final words to Sophie reverberated in her mind. She had wronged him, betrayed his trust by falling for another. It was clear to her now what she felt. She had ignored the truth all along. But the illusion of what had happened in the twinkling cave was her proof. She was completely and undeniably in love with her Guardian.

Seeing Aalok whispering in Sophie's ear, fueled Alexander's anger. No matter his bounds, he wrestled the soldiers, gritting his teeth against the searing pain from Caius's gloved hand. There was only one thing he could do now. There was only one hope that could aid him.

"I have failed you," Alexander prayed aloud. "But I ask that you strengthen me now. Not for my sake, but for hers. So long as you stand with me, none can defeat me."

"Go ahead and pray to your king," Caius sneered. "He's forsaken you, just as he has forsaken us."

As Caius mocked, a rush of power flowed into Alexander's being. It washed over him like a warm wave, and as it tingled through him, his aura lit into flames of amber. At a deep breath drawn and then exhaled, Alexander opened his eyes.

Caius stood in disbelief, but soon, his shocked expression was squashed as his ex-ally, elbowed him in the nose.

Soldier's flocked to the fight.

Caius retaliated with a swift blow.

The Seraphim at the table clapped and shouted. They whistled through their teeth and laughed as if the tussle was solely for their entertainment.

Caius caught hold of Alexander's chains, jerking him to the floor. He clutched the Guardian by the neck, ready to ignite his glove, but a shout made him freeze in place.

"That enough!" Aalok narrowed his eyes at his General. "Caius,"

Caius let his red glowing fist fall to his side, but jerked Alexander's chains, waiting for further commands.

"Come now, Alexander," Aalok scolded. "I only wish to give you the forgiveness and understanding that your king does not allow. Can't you see that? Can't you see that Aramis is cruel? What just king sends his faithful subjects to a world full of pain and suffering? Let me give you a way out. Let me be your salvation."

"You were raised in wisdom, Samria," Alexander quoted Aramis' words, "but you have fallen from pride. You are only a shadow of who you once were, and your light is only the reflection of your maker."

"Fallen? Ha!" Aalok scoffed, strutting to the steps to his throne. "I have not fallen, nor will I falter."

Aalok climbed gracefully to his throne and then turned swiftly, throwing back his red robe. "I will ascend above you." Aalok pointed to Alexander, and then the room full of his followers. "Above all, I shall rise," he shouted, chin lifted, hands out before him, "above the clouds of the heavens, above the stars of your king." His wings unfurled, casting off his robe, revealing his military uniform. "I shall be the highest and you will kneel to worship me!"

As the soldiers and the Seraphim roared, Sophie and Alexander prayed. At their petition, a white pure light filtered through the windows and into the room. It was merely a vapor, merely a wisp upon the wind, but it was there, and Aalok's face-hardened at the sight of it.

He watched it swirl around the Truth Keeper as she prayed, and then her Guardian. The light dissipated into their chests and lit their faint auras into pillars of white flames. An image took form in the flames, stepped forward, making the double image combine into one.

Aalok narrowed his eyes as the image of Aramis.

The apparition of Aramis smiled and placed a comforting hand on Alexander's shoulder.

Before Aalok could take a step toward the Guardian, he exploded into a brilliant blue flame. It permeated so fully, that it blinded everyone in the room but him, Sophie, and Aalok.

The shockwave of power overturned chairs and tables. It cracked the inlaid tiles, breaking Aalok's emblem in half.

Aalok let out a growl, spreading his wings, and took to the air. He swooped down, aiming at Alexander, but the power of Aramis blasted him back.

The floor shook, splitting across the tiles. The crack grew, traveling between Sophie's feet, shaking her chair. Glasses of wine burst on the table. Plates clattered. The windows flew open, bringing a wind that roared, forming into a wisp in the image of a lion. It thinned, circling around Alexander and the image of his king. The blazing fires from them became pillars of blue twisters. They rose to the ceiling, churning like raging whirlwinds, combining into one force of power.

Sophie lifted her head, filled with strength, and gazed in astonishment. She gripped the table, her mouth gaping as she took a step toward the blue tornado, and whispered Aramis' name.

At his name, the earth erupted beneath the fortress. It shook its foundation, splitting up its side, cracking open the dome of Aalok's throne room. The golden sculptures of his images broke into pieces to the ground, his paintings clattered to splinters onto the floor.

The shaking of the fortress eased.

The show of Aramis' power had been recognized.

Caius, blurry eyed, staggered to regain his balance and took his chance to make his attack on Alexander, but the Guardian ducked his blow. He avoided each feeble attempt, spying Caius' prize on his wrist. Alexander ducked under Caius' fist again, and snatched his wristband from his arm as a soldier came barreling toward him.

As the Seraph, servents, and soldiers tried to regroup from the commotion, Aalok floated down the staircase, landing gracefully on the pads of his feet. He walked up to the image of the king and snickered at his spirit. "Bide your time, Aramis. This isn't over."

Aramis narrowed his eyes and lifted his chin with a smile. "Oh, but it is."

ESCAPE

AALOK glared at Aramis, clenching his teeth and fists, rising above him. At the flap of his raven wings, the king's apparition dissipated into swirls of white smoke. Aalok glided to his fake throne and sat calmly, swirling the wine in his golden chalice. He was calculating another plan, and as he did, he watched the show below him. His lips quirked to one side, watching in amusement as Alexander took down every one of his soldiers that rushed through the door. The Guardian was far too faithful to turn. But as Aalok had observed, Serus was his best chance at corrupting the Truth Keeper in the next aeon.

After knocking the last soldier out cold, Alexander turned and ran to Sophie. He led her out a door in the back of the room, leading to a kitchen, and then through another door that led to the hall.

Caius stumbled to kneel at Aalok's throne staircase, rubbing his eyes as if it would clear the white dots in his vision. "My Lord, please."

Aalok rolled his eyes, before waving his hand in the air. A cup appeared with his magic water. He flung it over Caius and the soldiers that knelt beside him.

"This will be your last chance, Caius," Aalok warned, restoring their sight. "Do not disappoint me."

"Yes, my Lord." Caius rose to his feet and signaled the soldiers to follow him, hoping to cut Sophie and Alexander off in the hall.

Alexander bolted down a hallway a few corridors away from Aalok's throne room, tugging Sophie behind him. She slammed into his back when he froze mid-step. After gathering his bearings, he reclaimed her hand and rushed down another hallway.

Sophie stumbled over the hem of her gown as they made their way through the warmly lit hallway.

Alexander curled his lip, flashing glances at the walls lined with framed paintings and statues in Aalok's image.

At the sound of clanging armor and hasty footsteps, Alexander slid to a stop by one of the supporting pillars of a corridor. He then glanced at his hand. Aramis' strength was still inside him. It pulsed through his veins and he could feel its power.

Gently pushing Sophie to the side, he reared back and struck the pillar with his knuckles. The stone cracked a straight line down from his fits to the base, toppling it over. It rolled end over end, barricading the corridor. Snatching up Sophie's wrist again, Alexander sprinted down the hallway, grinning at the sound of Caius cursing at him from behind the blockade.

Painful jolts shot up through Sophie's shoulder as they ran. She scrunched her face as her lungs burned for breath. The muscles in her legs ached with each step as she tripped over her dress time and time again.

They ran past the carved gold and onyx pillars standing in each hallway, descended a winding stairway, and burst through the dungeon door. Alexander didn't stop. When his feet hit the dungeon floor, he all but dragged Sophie behind him, rushing past the empty cells.

Sophie couldn't bear the pain in her shoulder any longer and let out a cry as she wrenched her wrist away.

"We have to keep moving or they will catch us." He told her.

"Let me run on my own," Sophie panted. She took a step back, favoring her shoulder. "You're pulling my arm from its socket."

"I almost lost you once. I won't let it happen again."

Sophie opened her mouth to object, but the thunder of footsteps above them urged her to pick up the pace. She followed Alexander through a wooden door and into a rocky tunnel. It was a dark and gloomy cave maze, but Alexander rest assured that his aura would stay bright enough to navigate the damp labyrinth.

With slow cautious steps, Alexander listened to Caius and the soldiers from above. He knew they would first check the upper rooms; assume that Alexander wouldn't dare go back to the place of his torture.

But Caius was wrong.

Although the Guardian had been in and out of consciousness, Alexander remembered this place. He remembered how his boots dragged against the rocky floor, the musky smell of the damp walls, and the sounds of the droplets falling from the stalactites to the ground. He remembered the way through the winding underground maze. He knew it was the only way to an unguarded exit, the only path to their freedom.

Tunnel after tunnel, turn after turn, Alexander could hear Sophie grunting every time she tripped over her dress. She was a little more than five feet behind him, a little too far away for his liking, but not far enough away to ignore her melancholy. He could sense the weight of her grief had been lifted, but her internal struggle was still there. Her emotions were a mix of guilt and relief, even sadness. He would have to keep his distance from her to stay focused. He would let her fall behind, for now.

When they came to a crossroad, Alexander paused, considering the three options before them. He huffed, looking down the dark tunnels. There was no light, no indication of which way to turn. He pressed a beacon on his wristband, searching for a signal. There was none.

Lifting his gaze, he looked Sophie over. She had propped herself against a wall. Her eyes were closed, her breaths labored. Sensing her body's exhaustion, he frowned. There were still many more turns to take, still much further to go. His eyes traveled to the slit in her dress and scrunched his nose as it revealed the skin of her thigh.

"That needs to come off."

Sophie's head snapped up. "What?"

"Your dress. Some of the fabric needs to come off the bottom."

Alexander bent down beside Sophie and used a rock to break another, making a sharp edge like a blade. He placed a foot on the hem of the Truth Keeper's dress, trying to keep his eyes off her exposed skin.

"What are you doing?"

"What does it look like?"

Sophie snatched the rock from his hand and pushed her Guardian back. "I can do it myself. Turn around."

Alexander bit his bottom lip, holding back a grin as he threw up his hands. He then crossed his arms, turned his back, and faced the wall.

Sophie let out a frustrated breath and bent down to cut her dress, but she couldn't. The angle was too awkward. She grunted as she pressed her foot on the fabric as Alexander had, but still, she couldn't split the hem.

"Okay," she huffed, giving up. "I need your help."

"No, you said you could do it yourself." Alexander grinned at the rocky wall.

Sophie swept the hair from her face and wiped the sweat from her brow. She hated asking for help, and after the scene she made, her cheeks warmed with embarrassment. "Please?"

At the word please, Alexander looked over his shoulder. Sophie was holding the rock out to him, pleading with her eyes for him to take it.

Taking the rock, he stepped on the hem again, gripping the fabric with his fingers. As his knuckles grazed her leg, she flinched, and his cheeks flushed. "Ready?"

Sophie nodded, holding very still as the sound of thread popping echoed down the tunnel. She turned in a circle, aiding Alexander as he tugged, until she froze, finding the alarming length just above her fingertips.

"Thank you," she said, although heat pulsed in her face. She pinched the tattered hem and held it against her thighs to regain some sense of modesty. But it was no use.

Alexander nodded, tossing the rock to the side. He would have told Sophie she was welcome, but his throat was tight and his cheeks were burning with his own embarrassment. No one ever saw that much skin. Not unless they had been bonded.

Avoiding the uncomfortable silence, he glanced down the tunnels and picked one, unsure if it was the right way to go.

After several turns and more tunnels, Sophie thought back to meeting with Aramis. She thought of the kiss in the secret spring her and Alexander had shared. Her heart fluttered at his tenderness, but that flutter quickly slowed, remembering how he had treated Serus in the camp of the Outcasts. The memory of Serus' rage formed an ache in her chest the more she thought of him, the more his fiery eyes glared back at her. She feared any hope of him coming back to the light was gone. She wondered where he went after stomping out of Aalok's chambers. She imagined he was in his room reading Creation in tears, or ripping it apart in a rage. She shivered, and rubbed her arms, grieving the choices she had made. Perhaps if she had listened to her Guardian, to Aramis, things could have been different.

Smoothing her hair to the side, Sophie pulled the hairpins, poking at her skull. She thought of her new friend. Aerith was an Outcast, too.

She wondered if Aramis thought she herself was unfaithful now but quickly reminded herself that her king had helped Alexander save her from Aalok. He had answered her prayers. She reached for her necklace to find comfort in Aramis' gift, but it was gone. Sophie let her hand fall to her side, following Alexander a few steps behind.

"Keep up, Truth Keeper,"

Sophie stopped in her tracks at his words. Truth Keeper. He was always calling her that, acting as if she was nothing more than an assignment. Why? What had changed since the secret spring?

"Is that all I am to you?"

"What?" Alexander asked flatly, pausing at the next fork in their path.

"Am I just Aramis' asset to you?" Sophie asked, refusing to take another step.

"Do you want to get caught?" Alexander glared over his shoulder.

"Well?"

Alexander ignored her and went down the tunnel.

"If I am such burden and you think me so disloyal, then why did you save me?"

Alexander turned down the next tunnel and kept marching forward. He didn't want to be reminded of what he saw when he came through Aalok's doors. Yes, she was an asset, but she was also more. He had been trying to not think about his affections for her, or how he felt in the cave. The images of their kiss flashed in his mind. Then his mind drifted to what might have happened in Serus' chambers.

Did he kiss her? Had she kissed him back? What did he do to convince her to meet with Aalok?

His glow burned brighter with a tinge of orange at his thoughts. Sophie and Serus had been courting for some time. He knew a love like that didn't just fade away in a day. Although he fought his feelings for her, they hadn't changed. Even if she had turned out to be a traitor, Alexander couldn't help but be in love with her.

And then something hit him like a punch in the gut from Caius' glove.

She couldn't help caring for Serus. No matter how hard she had tried, she loved him. That part of her would always love him, because no matter what happened, Alexander knew he would always love Sophie.

He paused in the cave, listening for the footsteps of his enemy, then glanced back over his shoulder at Sophie. He thought about what Serus had said, wondering if it was true.

Is she my soulmate? Did Aramis create us to be as one?

He shook his head.

It doesn't matter. Not now.

The aeon would be over soon and they would be strangers in a new world. Not even his love, his possible bond to her could change what was coming.

Aramis' plan would be fulfilled.

A burning question went over and over in Sophie's mind as she followed Alexander left and right. After a few more turns, she couldn't take the silence any longer and spoke.

"Do you think I am that weak? That I would choose Aalok over my king? My creator?"

Alexander swung around. "Be quiet or they'll hear you," he warned, looking around the corner to another path.

"Is that what you think of me, Alexander?" Sophie prodded, "That I care so much for Serus that I would vow allegiance to Aalok?"

Alexander turned to face her again. He let out a breath, placing his hands on his hips. He searched her eyes for a long moment, wondering if she had indeed been blinded by her love for the traitor, believed somehow that Serus could change, that she could save him.

Would I have done the same? Would I have risked the future for her?

"Why is it so hard to tell me how you feel?" Sophie shouted in frustration.

Before Alexander could shout back, a rumble came from the cave ceiling. Pebbles fell at his feet and dust filled the air. He set his hard gaze to Sophie and pressed a finger to his lips, warning her to be silent again.

Sophie froze and waited for several pounding heartbeats until her Guardian gave a cue to move.

"Not another word," he ordered sharply.

Anger fueled Sophie's steps as she brushed past him. She didn't care if she was going down a wrong tunnel. She had to get away from the pulsing waves of her Guardian's suspicions.

FREEDOM

LIGHT. It glinted in Sophie's eyes like a beacon as she turned the corner. Tears of joy flew from her eyes as she rushed to the glittering wall. But at its arrival, she frowned. She lifted a hand in the moonlight and closed her eyes, pretending it was the sun. But this source of light couldn't warm her stiff fingers. The moon was only a reflection of the great star.

Sophie dearly missed the sunshine. She missed the bright blue sky, the way the beach breeze blew over her skin during a morning ride with Bevol. Most of all, she missed her freedom.

Peering up at the tiny square window where the moonlight filtered in, Sophie lost hope again. Her knees gave way, and she slid down the damp quartz wall to the ground. She held back a whimper, clenching her teeth as she pounded her fists against the cold wall.

"So that's the way out," Alexander huffed. He had heard the hum before he turned the corner, but still scowled at the electrified door as he ran his fingers through his hair.

"We came all this way and now..."

"Sophie," Alexander reached out to touch her shoulder, but she flinched away.

"Leave me alone."

Alexander sighed and turned away.

"Where are you going?"

"To find another way out."

"There is no other way out! We have gone through all these tunnels."

"We need to go back the way we came."

"But Caius will be coming that way."

"We have no choice. If we turn around now, maybe we can find a way to get out before-" Alexander paused, sensing a presence.

"What? What is it?"

"I don't know," Alexander admitted, looking around the cave. The aura wasn't threatening, but he didn't want to take any chances. "Let's go,"

Sophie stood, but couldn't bear to leave the door. Their freedom was just a few steps away. She felt around the cave walls for a lever, or button, anything that would turn off the buzzing barrier.

"Sophie, stop," Alexander insisted, taking her arm, but she ignored him.

"There has to be something..."

"We have to go,"

"Leave me be!"

"Maybe I can be of some assistance?" a soft voice asked from the shadows.

Sophie spun around, "Aerith!"

Realizing that this was the presence he had sensed, Alexander examined the stranger. Aerith's blue eyes were dim but there was still some light in them. She wore the red vestment of Aalok's followers, but her aura was meek and lit in pink. Alexander could feel she was troubled as sadness rolled off her in waves. Still, he tilted his head, unsure why Sophie's face brightened at the sight of her.

"Aerith, what are you doing down here?" Sophie asked.

"The servants in the kitchen were clamoring about the great power of your Guardian after the fortress shook. I knew it wasn't an earthquake, because I could feel his power and see his light shine from under the kitchen door. Others that were in the hallways spoke of him evading Caius with one blow to a pillar. How he hurled it into the air, knocking all of them down at once!"

"Well, I don't know about that last part," Alexander admitted, rubbing the back of his neck.

"Where do you draw this power?" Aerith asked with big round eyes.

"It's was not my of own power. King Aramis aided us," Alexander assured her.

"He must favor you highly to grant you such strength," Aerith observed.

"I am no more favored than you are, Aerith," Alexander said with a sweet smile.

"Hearing of your escape, I wanted to help you," Aerith continued. "So, I went to Caius's chamber while he sought to capture you and found this." Aerith offered a small gold key.

"You have endangered yourself," Alexander said, graciously accepting it. "Why did you do this?"

Aerith shrugged. "I guess...I wanted to atone for my trespasses before it was too late, seeing as I won't be able to make it back to the Infinite Realm. There are rumors that the king is very close to destroying the realms." She looked down to the ground, pushing a pebble with her shoe.

Alexander put the key in the lock and at a click, the hum of the barrier ceased.

Sophie sighed with relief as Alexander handed the key back to Aerith, who wrapped her fingers tightly around it. "Now you're free," she said in almost a whisper.

"Come with us,"

Aerith glanced down at Sophie's offered hand but didn't take it. "I can't."

"I understand," Sophie nodded. She knew now who Aerith loved, who she had stayed for. She wouldn't ask her to choose. Perhaps, Aerith could be the one to save Serus. Maybe that's why the king had let her go.

"Thank you, Aerith," Alexander said, taking her forearm in a farewell.

"Sophie is blessed to have you as her Guardian."

"May Aramis' grace be with you," Alexander added in parting.

"And with you both," Aerith replied, glancing at Sophie. Her brows pinched together. "Will you tell Aramis that I never wanted to disobey him? Tell him that I'm sorry that I left him that night at the Ball."

"He knows your heart, Aerith. If you are truly sorry, then you have already been forgiven." Sophie reassured.

"Praise be to Aramis for his mercy," Aerith said, proudly. Her glow emanated from her body in a thin milky hue.

"Yes. Praise be to Aramis," Sophie agreed.

"Well, I guess this is goodbye then," Aerith sighed, fighting back her tears.

"No," Sophie assured her. "Until we meet again."

"Then, until we meet again, Sophie of the Seventh Circle," Aerith said, holding out her arm for Sophie to grasp it.

Sophie looked down at Aerith's arm, then back up, before wrapping her arms around Aerith's neck and hugging her tight.

Aerith's eyes widened at first, but then she closed them, accepting Sophie's warm embrace. She squeezed her eyes tight letting the tears she had been holding back roll down her cheek.

"I do hope to see you again," Sophie whispered.

"As do I," Aerith whispered back, squeezing Sophie tighter.

"Sophie, we have to go," Alexander reminded softly.

The two souls parted.

Moving to Alexander's side, Sophie waved. She prayed her friend would not be caught on the way back to find the one she loved, and exited through the door.

Aerith shielded her eyes from the light that encompassed them. They glowed with hope, with the joy of their freedom. And then they were gone, leaving Aerith alone in the dark.

Blinking to readjust her sight, Aerith gazed around the damp cave and then stared at the door for a moment before locking it and shifting the lever up.

With a click, the beams turned on with a quiet hum.

She looked at the key once more before tucking it in her pocket. She would have to find a way to get it back in Caius' room. Wrapping her arms around herself, Aerith took a step forward and looked at the small window in the door. She remembered how the sun had once warmed her.

Pain ached in her chest with regret. She bowed her head, believing what Sophie had said about forgiveness, but took the opportunity to say a prayer out loud. In the dark, cold cave, she asked for her king's forgiveness, pleading with him to lift her burdens, to forgive her trespasses. As she prayed, her light began to shine brighter, ever expanding, no longer a vapor of what it once was. Her shoulders relaxed as her heart swelled with joy. Warmth spread from her chest through her body, bringing back her white waving aura.

When Aerith opened her eyes, she looked down at her glow and smiled. She now knew she was strong enough to face anyone or anything if Aramis was with her, even the end of the aeon.

With her newfound confidence, she made her way back through the tunnels, and up the stairs. She would go declare her love with a sliver of hope that Serus, in return, would accept her, and they could go back to the Infinite Realm before it was too late.

SENTIMENT

SERUS leaned back in his chair, watching the world burn. The sky was darkening with ash fall. The mountains wept in tears of red. The waves crested over themselves, sloshing the toxic tide, filled with dead floating fish.

A strong wind blew the curtains against the veranda doors to Serus' room. It whipped his hair as stars fell from the heavens into the boiling green sea. Serus placed the wine glass on the marble table beside him, and without a care, folded his hands together in his lap. He was drunk and glad to be.

Resting his heavy head back against his chair, the illusion he had seen in Aalok's chamber came into his mind. His stomach twisted as image after image of Sophie in the cave in Alexander's arms taunted him.

He wrung his hands and sucked in a sharp breath as his thoughts fled to a shake at his balcony. His bottle of wine danced on the table at the convulsions, and he, as if it was nothing, placed a finger to its mouth to silence it.

It was the book beside the bottle that caught his attention. It slid at another rattle of the fortress. Serus caught it with one hand, placing it in his lap, letting the wine bottle shatter. Paying no mind to his drink leaking onto the marble tile at his feet, he ran his fingers across the title of Creation.

His heart softened, reliving his courtship. Memories of him and Sophie and days spent in the sunshine, warmed him. Words from his own mouth filled his ears with the passages of the book. It was as if he could feel Sophie beside him, feel her glow. He let his mind take him back in time.

They were lying in the meadow again. She was in his arms under the pink-blossomed tree. A flower fell in her hair. He picked it up and leaned down, kissing her soft lips.

The memory faded as he ran his thumb along his lower lip. He had been so close to kissing her. She had been so close to accepting his proposal. The change had been all too much for her. If he had proceeded differently, she would have been in his arms now, watching as the world fell away. He shouldn't have been so hateful to her. He had lost his temper again. He had let his emotions get the best of him. But he didn't blame his temper; he blamed Aramis.

It's his fault we were separated. Not to mention that so-called 'protector'. He was always getting in the way. If he hadn't been there, I could have kissed her in the tent. If only I

had been myself. If only I had confessed everything I had done.
All she wanted was the truth.

He clenched his teeth as regret made him all the more bitter. He looked at the blood moon and crimson waves lapping in the distance. Three bottles down with no word of Sophie's alliance, Serus grew anxious.

Give it time.

No matter the hurt from Sophie's betrayal, he still loved her. No matter what he saw on that screen, he held onto what had been. He had to. She was his, no matter the universal bond getting in the way. He needed her. She was, after all, the good in his life, the only good. Everything else surrounding him was cold and dark. He peered down at the book, letting a small smile tug at his lips.

"No reason to get all sentimental," a velvety voice purred from behind him.

Serus rolled his eyes.

"Why hold on to the past when you can make your future so much more?" "Bree cooed, sauntering over to him. She took the book from his lap, but Serus snatched it back without hesitation. "What do you want?"

"I came to see how you were doing after that *dreadful* scene I heard about in Aaloks throne room." She faked a pouty lip. "The Seraphim said you were crying,"

"Of course they did,"

"I thought you could use a distraction."

Jazrael slid her fingers up Serus' chest and unbuttoned his collar. A devilish grin spread across her lips. Seeing Serus reaction at her touch, Jazrael smirked, before letting her palms slide to his hips, over his pants pockets.

Serus tensed again, knowing not only she was trying to get a certain reaction from his body, but that she was also checking him over for more sentiments. A slimy thickness crept over his shoulders and he rolled them as if it would roll away his repulsion. Seduction. It was the very thing that made him despise her; her sickening sweet, oozing aura of manipulation.

Jazrael was incredibly beautiful, but her spirit was ugly, and he was tired of looking at it. He snatched Jazrael's hand from his crotch and shoved her away. "No. No telling where these hands have been."

Jazrael grinned, unaffected by his harsh tone. In fact, she took pleasure in his anger; she fed on it, just as the girl with violin in the Outcast camp did. "Nehia has requested you visit her bedchamber. After what happened in Aalok's throne room, it would do you well to find a release from all that frustration."

"I have no desire to play more than strings with her."

"What about the both of us? You could serenade us a little beforehand."

Serus scoffed. "To any other sad sack, that would be quite tempting. For the last time, the answer is no."

Jazrael let out a sigh. Her plan didn't work. Nehia was her closest friend and had begged Jazrael to convince Serus to visit her. She had wanted him ever since she had seen him with Sophie. Nehia thrived, as Jazrael did, on pain and distress. She admitted to Jazrael that she wanted Serus more now than she had in the Outcast camp. He was full of jealousy, envy, and sorrow. She could feel it as he passed by her door when he had rushed past her in the hall with blazing heat earlier.

Serus tilted back his head, guzzling the remaining contents of his spilled wine bottle as he walked into his room. He was trying to ignore the thoughts of what could happen in Nehia's chamber, but the wine wasn't helping. His body was insisting he needed the release, but his mind fought against the desire.

His heart didn't want Nehia or Jazrael. It wanted Sophie. He rubbed his eyes and hissed as the tender skin around them burned. They were sore from crying, sagging from lack of sleep.

No. He didn't want a release. He wanted to rest. He wanted his mind to fade into nothing but a black void of silence. He wouldn't trespass against Sophie, the way she had trespassed against him. If they were going to be bonded, he would make sure she would be the first he would lie with. Even if he weren't innocent, he would, at least, have saved himself for the one he truly loved. He would be able to tell Sophie truthfully that he had waited for her, and her alone.

Laying Creation on his bed, he nudged it up and down, placing it exactly where Sophie left it before he had taken her to Aalok.

Jazrael watched in amusement before she came to lounge on Serus' bed, letting out a sigh.

Serus ignored her, shuffling through the items inside his nightstand drawer. He sifted through the letters Sophie had written him, through sheets of music he had composed for her, and broken strings from his violin.

"Could you be any more obsessed?" Jazrael sneered. She rolled her eyes and picked up her glass screen. She typed in a message, informing Nehia of Serus' rejection. She would have to find another way to get him to forget about the Truth Keeper.

"You haven't slept in this bed once since you arrived, have you?" Jazrael asked. She laid down the screen and traced her fingers along the red silk pillow.

Serus ignored her attempt to seduce him and reached into the back of the drawer. Finding the dainty item, he carefully withdrew the gold chain. He studied the jewel pendant as it spun slowly in a circle, remembering the moment Aalok had offered him Sophie's necklace. It sparkled while he recalled Aalok explaining how to woo the Truth Keeper, how he told him to act as if she was nothing and yet everything to him. Serus had never understood that way of courting but had followed Aalok's instructions. He regretted doing so now. He should have just been the Serus that Sophie knew, the Serus she trusted.

He stared into the crystal as if it was a window into the past and drifted back to the memory of dancing with Sophie in his tent at the Outcast camp. He could still smell her sweet, soft skin, and could feel her thick, wavy brown hair through his fingertips. The warmth of her glow warmed his heart and he was comforted for a short moment until Jazrael spoke.

"Is that for me?" Jazrael reached for Sophie's necklace, but Serus pulled it away.

"No," Serus told her flatly. He let the necklace fall into his palm, gripping the jewel tightly. He could still get Sophie back, he could still show her how much she meant to him.

"Why don't message that servant girl? Tell her to fetch another bottle of wine and cheese. I could keep you company for a while."

Serus huffed a laugh and tucked the necklace into the small inner pocket of his uniform. "Never satisfied, are we? Haven't you already had a few rounds with the Seraphim?" He smirked.

Jazrael narrowed her eyes and sat up. "Jealous?"

Serus patted the lump the necklace made in his chest, sure to keep it securely snug at his heart. He would bring the necklace to Sophie, maybe play a game, as they used to when he wanted to steal a kiss in the meadow.

A kiss. Maybe that was all that was needed to remind her of our love.

Still thinking of how he would approach Sophie, he closed the nightstand drawer hard.

"Message Nehia. Tell her I decline. To both of your offers."

"That's not the only reason I came."

"Is there something else you want? Because I can assure you the answer will still be no."

"The question is...what do you want? Hm? You sit here, moping over one little incident when you should be focused on converting souls to help Aalok win this war. I'm starting to think you care more about your feelings than power."

"Did you come here just to gloat or do you serve a purpose?" Serus demanded. He went back out to the balcony and fell into his chair. He glared at his half-empty wine bottle on the ground until a crack came from the sky. Wailing followed the neon lights in the sky as a rumbled beneath the fortress shook it again.

"Poor, poor Serus," Jazrael cooed, running her fingers along Serus' arm. "I hate seeing you so upset."

"Were you ever pure in any way or have you always been this revolting?"

"What would you know about a pure heart?"

"I know you don't have one," Serus smirked.

The earth trembled again as the tide slapped the jagged rocks below the fortress. Jazrael leaned over the railing, glaring at the raging sea.

Serus bit his bottom lip as the thought of shoving her over crossed his mind. The sound of her scream and the clap of impact would be music to his ears.

He didn't act on the impulse. Instead, he drank wine, pondering the possibilities of how he would approach Sophie in the prison. If it were true what Aramis said, the Earth would soon be destroyed. He wouldn't let her stay down there during the end. He would hold her and await their doom.

"All great change," a male said from Serus' bedroom in a poetic voice "proceeds after an upheaval. A beautiful chaos."

"Mal," Jazrael grinned, turning on her toes. She leaned back against the balcony railing, watching Malphas approach. "What a pleasant surprise."

The same dark-haired Seraph Serus had been talking to at dinner, walked through to the threshold of the balcony doors and leaned against them, seemingly pleased by the view.

"I'm not interrupting am I?" he asked with knowing eyes.

"No, Jazrael was just leaving," Serus informed.

Mal tilted his head slightly, keeping his eyes locked on Jazrael. "I won't take too much of his time."

Jazrael kept her fixed stare and brushed past him. She walked out of Serus' bedroom, swaying her hips, putting emphasis on the way her heels clacked against the glossy onyx floor.

As Jazrael closed Serus' bedroom door, Mal walked out on the balcony. He ruffled his black wings and leaned on the railing clasping his hands. "Such a sight," he said, gazing at the ocean as dark clouds veiled the moon.

"What can I do for you, Mal?"

"You never gave me an answer to my proposal." Mal leaned his back against the railing and crossed his arms. "As you can see," he looked over the arch of his silky black wings, and then back to Serus. "You don't have much time to decide."

Serus didn't believe Aalok, not fully. Aramis was the Creator. He gave life and he could take it away. Aalok was just his creation, just a Seraph, not a god. The worlds were coming to an end and there was no stopping it.

"So how about it?" Mal grinned, lifting a brow. "Are you ready to damn your soul for the one you love?"

THE FIELD

ALEXANDER stood in an inch of ash fall, holding out his hand. As the soft substance fill his palm, he wrinkled his nose at the smell of smoke that filled his nostrils. He wiped the ash off on his chest and turned his gaze at the blood-red sea. He watched the moonlight ripple in the choppy waves until his wristband buzzed against his skin.

He tapped on the screen sending his coordinates with a numeric code and let out a breath, relieved. It was a request that he and Sophie return to the kingdom.

Finally.

A crack from the sky jerked Alexander's head up and he watched as lightning sparked from the dark purple clouds. Urgency swept over him as his gaze darted to Sophie, who was walking toward the beach. The clouds above her flashed and grumbled. They circled, swirling like a whirlwind, rotating to form a column on the sea.

"Sophie!" Alexander ran after her, but the Truth Keeper didn't acknowledge his call.

Sophie couldn't take her eyes off the swirling cone forming less than a mile out at sea. Her hair whipped in the wind as she stared in awe at the crackling storm. The purple and black clouds swirled down into a twisting horn, roaring louder than the crashing waves on the shore. Her heart pounded against her ribcage as the clouds swirled down and split into two. The noise of the twisting clouds reminded her of her spaceship taking off, but its force was like nothing she had ever experienced in nature.

The funnels leaned left to right, dancing around one another until they suddenly dissipated. Like a vapor, they lifted to the black and blue blanket above as if they had never been there at all.

"Sophie!"

Thunder rolled as Alexander ran down the hill and grasped her shoulder tight. "We have to go! The ship is on its way."

Alexander's words fell on deaf ears. All Sophie could focus on was her trembling body and the stab in her chest as her anxiety soared. Bevol and his terrified eyes entered her mind. She couldn't be there to soothe him, couldn't hold him as everything came to an end. She wondered if he had hidden in the forest or if he was shaking, staring at the chaos as she was. Her breath hitched, but she managed to whisper her horse's name.

Another deafening clap of thunder echoed from above. Alexander watched the dark clouds sail away. The danger was passing, heading to the fortress as if drawn to its own darkness like a magnetic force. The wind died down, no longer rustling the palm trees. There was only the sound of the waves rolling over Alexander's boots as he brought his gaze back to the frightened Truth Keeper.

"I don't want him to suffer," she said, her voice cracking. "I don't want anyone to suffer."

"Aramis will be merciful. Do you doubt him? Do you not think he will do everything in his power to set things right?"

Tears rolled down the Truth Keeper's cheeks. She couldn't answer his questions. She looked into the distance with thoughts of all the confused souls at Aalok's fortress. She looked down the beach wishing Bevol would come galloping up to meet her, but there was nothing but a deserted inlet. There was nothing but the crimson waves leaving brown kelp as they broke and drew back. Tears rolled down her cheeks, recognizing the emotions she thought she had escaped. They were full of fear...of doubt in Aramis.

"We need to get to the summit," Alexander said, and made his way up the ashy knoll,

Sophie waited a moment, gazing down the shore. The waves poured across the sandy beach like spoiled wine.

Bevol wouldn't be here. He would be deep in the forest, hiding in a thicket. There was no reason to wait any longer.

Sophie whispered 'goodbye' before she followed a few steps behind Alexander. She trudged up the hill, but paused, sensing a familiar aura. She glanced at the exit of the cave, waiting for Serus to exit, but he didn't. Still, somehow she could feel him nearby. She looked at the top of the fortress where she had planned her escape from his balcony only hours earlier.

Picking up her pace, Sophie followed Alexander, knowing she couldn't go back to the fortress. She had tried to help Serus and had failed. She remembered the look on his face when he saw Alexander kissing her in the illusion of the cave. She clutched a fist to her chest, wincing from the dull pain in her heart. She went over and over what she had seen in the images, and paused at the vision of Alexander in the Library of Souls. She had to know what he had read, why he was so angry with Serus, and what her suitor had done to be banished.

"What did you read in Serus' book?" Sophie called out to her Guardian.

Alexander kept marching forward, paying no mind to the Truth Keeper's question.

"What was his crime, I mean? You read his history, so surely you know."

"That's something you should have asked him while you were in his chambers. It's not my place to say."

"I found it strange that Aalok skipped past what was spoken between Serus and the council. It all went by much too quickly to read anyone's lips. Aramis wasn't angry. He was disappointed. Aalok was hiding something, hiding the truth."

"Oh, you picked up on that too?" Alexander grinned, but there was no humor in his smile.

"Aalok made it appear as if Serus was exiled for trying to bond with me without permission, but I know that can't be the reason."

"*Now* you realize it wasn't about your bonding?" Alexander huffed a laugh.

"I never assumed that was the reason."

"You did in Aalok's throne room."

Sophie gritted her teeth. "I was under a spell. It was the Confusion."

Alexander didn't admit he knew that the headpiece had affected her. The moment it had fallen off, he had felt her aura change.

"What was his crime? What was so terrible that he was banished from the Infinite Realm?"

Alexander turned on his heels to face her and studied her confused expression.

Had she loved Serus so much that she had been blinded by his treachery?

"You really don't know, do you?" He asked.

"No, I don't."

Alexander rested his hands on his hips, thinking he should tell her the truth. Then again, it wasn't his business to get involved. He was only her Guardian.

"Please,"

The word please, the way her eyes pleaded. It made the words tumble out of his mouth before he could revoke them.

"He was a spy for Aalok."

"A spy?"

"Yes, for as long as you two were together."

"But that can't be. He was a Truth Keeper."

"He was a spy—and you were his cover."

"No, he wouldn't-" She shook her head. "He may have been a spy for Aalok, but he would've never used me—not like that. He wasn't always like this. Aalok deceived him."

"He still chose to follow his own selfish desires. You were under Aalok's illusion, and yet, you fought it, did you not?"

Sophie pressed her lips into a thin line.

"He could have done the same. The point is, he chose not to."

"Why didn't Aramis tell me? Why didn't he put a stop to it?"

Alexander sighed. "I don't know. Maybe Aramis thought your goodness would bring Serus back. Maybe it was to see if the lower angels could be corrupted by the infiltration."

"That's why he allowed Aalok's spies into the kingdom—it was a test." Her gaze turned inward, wondering who else among the Truth Keepers could have been working for Aalok.

The Eighth Circle. Were all of them spies?

"Aalok gave them offers they couldn't refuse. Why work when you can be given everything you have ever wanted if only you betray your maker? Why follow the Law when you can do whatever suits you, be rewarded although you did nothing to earn it?"

"Why didn't I see this sooner?" Sophie whispered to herself. "I should have known. I should have seen past the deception."

"It seems Serus has a way with you." Alexander took a moment and looked Sophie over. "Tell me, did he help you into that thing they call a dress or did you put it on by yourself?"

Sophie jerked her head up at Alexander's accusation. "How dare you ask such a thing,"

"It's just a question."

"Is that why you were so angry with me when I came to see you in the prison?"

"Must be a trend among Aalok's followers," Alexander shrugged, rubbing his chin. He looked over her shoulder as in deep thought. "No modesty." He brought his gaze back to Sophie's dress with a raised brow. "Do all the gowns have slits up the side like that?"

With a glare as Sophie's only reply, Alexander scoffed and then turned, heading toward the cliff.

"I can't believe you would be angry over a dress. It's just a garment, nothing more. It has nothing to do with my loyalty to Aramis," Sophie tried to explain.

"Sure had me fooled." Alexander sneered. "I assume you took a bath as well. Did Serus join you?"

"How dare you suggest such things?" Sophie huffed, tripping over a patch of thick grass.

"Well, did he?"

Alexander's throat was knotting up. He didn't want to ask Sophie these questions, but he couldn't stop thinking about what could have happened when they were alone. He needed to put his mind at ease, but every time Sophie answered his question with a question, his stomach tightened.

"What is this, Alexander?" Sophie crossed her arms and held her ground.

Alexander turned and mirrored her. "What do you mean?"

"Is this about our kiss?"

"No, of course not."

"No? You stand there and practically accuse me, assume all these things happened, but you don't know. You act as if we have been courting and I have betrayed your trust. This isn't about my loyalty to Aramis, is it?"

"I'm just curious if that headpiece was on your head the whole time or if at some point you thought to betray Aramis because of the one you loved."

"You can't presume to know what happened."

"Then perhaps you should fill me in? Your actions were fairly questionable. For all I know, you could be pretending to still be loyal. Should I risk taking you to the kingdom so you can convince souls to believe Aalok's lies?"

"Do you really think I was convinced?" Sophie's face crumpled and she pressed a hand to her middle as if she had been punched in the gut.

In his heart, Alexander knew Sophie wouldn't betray her king, but his jealousy told him otherwise. Aramis' holy aid may have healed the burns and lashes from his torture, but the deep wounds of seeing Sophie in Serus' arms still stung. Thoughts of them together in Serus' bedroom still lingered, still tormented him.

What if she has turned? What if she was fooling me, just as Serus had fooled her?

"Look at me, Alexander," Sophie pleaded, tugging at his shirt sleeve. "Look into my eyes and tell me if I am the enemy."

Alexander's eyes shifted past Sophie to the summit. There was a long pause between them.

"Well, am I?" Sophie asked desperately.

Alexander locked eyes with Sophie. He was afraid he would see a sliver of disloyalty in her, but to his relief, he didn't. His shoulders relaxed as he saw a flickering light behind her heartache. The heartache was not because of Serus, but because of him. His words had hurt her, assuming she had never given a second thought to what happened in the twinkling cave, but she had. He thought to tell her what Serus had said about them being soulmates. The tug he felt between him and her—it meant something. There was more than just his attraction to her. He couldn't deny it, but he couldn't bring himself to tell her.

"When I saw you in Serus' arms I thought..." Alexander sighed. "I thought you turned. I thought you had traded your new life, a life meant to save others. But then I could feel you strengthen with Aramis. I felt your loyalty. "

"Then why do you keep asking me all these questions? Why do you keep pushing me away?"

Alexander's wristband buzzed with an alert. He lifted it and looked at the numeric code, letting him know the ship was close. "We need to hurry."

"You said we would talk about this when we were out of the fortress." Sophie insisted. "I can feel your struggle to conceal how you feel. Why are you holding back?"

Alexander let out a laugh, taking a few steps forward. "You're not going to let it go, are you?"

"No. I'll keep asking until you admit the truth."

Alexander turned, letting out a groan. "You are the most zealous and stubborn Truth Keeper the cosmos has ever-"

The ground rumbled, stopping Alexander short. The roar filled his ears as the earth cracked beneath his feet. Sophie stumbled and Alexander grabbed her elbow, drawing her to his chest. He braced her against him as the convulsions shook them for a long moment. After watching the earth split, sending a crack up the mountainside, he closed his eyes and held Sophie tight. It was only minutes of convulsions but to Alexander and Sophie, it felt like it went on forever.

When the shaking trailed off to only a quiet rumble, Alexander loosed his grip and opened his eyes. He glanced down at his quivering chest, but it wasn't from the aftershocks, it was from Sophie. He cupped her face gently. "The sooner we get to the summit, the sooner we can get on the ship, and get away from here."

"Why couldn't Aramis have chosen a different plan? Why must it end this way?"

"I don't have the answer to that. Perhaps it is far beyond our understanding. Have you ever asked Aramis why he made the Earth in the first place? Why he made us?"

"No,"

"Then why doubt?" Alexander asked, placing comforting hands on her shoulders. "You have never questioned Aramis before, why do so now?"

Sophie didn't answer. Instead, she stared at her Guardian, biting her quivering lip as she fought back tears that threatened to fall.

"It all comes down to a choice. We may not understand the reason Aramis has chosen to end the aeon in this way, but we can understand he chose those that turned away from him."

"You're speaking of the third that followed Aalok. This is the only way that they can be saved."

"Yes, he must cleanse this aeon so we can start over. It's a blank page, a new canvas. If the third doesn't get that second chance, to be born innocent from the memory of all this, they will be blotted out of existence. Imagine what it must feel like to have that heavy burden upon your shoulders. To have to kill something you love. If you loved something that much, something you nurtured; would you be able to destroy it if it betrayed you or would you give it a chance at redemption?"

Sophie's mind went to Bevol. She loved him. She had nurtured him and taught him when the colt didn't have a mother. She had been his mother. She could never turn her back on Bevol, even if he had turned away from her. She understood how Aramis must feel now.

Sophie pulled away from Alexander and turned her back to him. "I can't do this, Alexander. I'm not capable of helping anyone. I keep doubting Aramis' plan." Sophie confessed with tears streaming down her face. "Why would he choose me to help them? How can I show them how to have faith when I keep losing hope?"

Alexander took her hands in his before fixing his gaze.

"If the world wasn't ending, but you were asked to give your life for a soul who was lost, who was to be blotted out for their trespasses, would you choose your life or would you choose to take their place?"

"I would die for them."

Alexander smiled and squeezed her hands gently. "If that's not faith, I don't know what is. Aramis believes in you, and so do I. You should believe in yourself."

Sophie forced a smile, but her forehead wrinkled at a thought. "In the new aeon, you won't be there to remind me to believe. I won't even remember this conversation. I won't remember you."

Alexander stared at the clover green starburst around Sophie's pupils. The light in her eyes was dimming, the spark of hope dwindling. He slid a hand from her shoulder and cupped her chin. "Light seeks light. You remember I told you there would be a spark?"

Sophie nodded. For her, Alexander was that spark. He was a light she could follow, that she would search for. She vowed in her heart to find Serus, to bring him back to the truth. But she knew her feelings for Serus could never compare to what she felt for Alexander.

"I have no doubt that I'll be looking for that spark, searching for your light. I promised to protect you to the end, but even thereafter, I'll seek to find you again, Sophie. I promise you now, I'll never stop looking."

Sophie lost a breath at Alexander's words. Her aura lit and that light reflected her hope. It was hope that Alexander would be there to protect her in the next life, hope that they would someday meet again. He hadn't admitted his affections, not straight out, but *this*...this was his definition of love, this was his truth.

THE DEAL

"HOW can I be sure your plan will work?" Serus asked Mal.

"As I said before, the Seraph and I have it all figured out. It's true what Aalok said. Aramis plans to make the lower angels human. There will be daughters of man, a womb. Humans will be birthed, just like the beasts of the field. We will, I guess you could say, *intercede*. Procreate our own species."

"And this species will be half human, half Seraph?"

"We're still working out the details, but yes."

"And this will give me an advantage?"

"Your genetic connection will allow access, yes, but it will also give us access to you as well."

"And what does that entail?" Serus asked, going to his telescope.

"You won't be able to turn off the ability to see past the veil Aramis will create. You will see everything others won't, even when you don't want to."

"Access to the other dimension? I don't see the disadvantage of that."

"Yes, with some limitations. The flesh you will be in will limit your ability."

"I'm sure I can manage," Serus smirked, leaning his face back on the eyepiece to view the blood moon.

"There is *one* thing I must make very clear."

"And what's that?"

"Your innocence will be completely void. Your soul will be damned by association, by the corruption of your genetics."

Serus drew away from the telescope. He straightened; crossing his arms and ran his tongue over the edge of his teeth. "Then, how is this a good bargain? What would be the point of me finding Sophie and getting her to fall for me all over again, only to be separated from her in the afterlife?"

Mal's black wings rose and fell as he arched his back. "We have a plan for that. It will take millions of years after the creation of man, but when the time comes and the cycle run its course, and the stars will align. When the planet crosses, we will be able to come and show our prodigies the right technology, the way to live like an immortal. If we can accomplish this, there will *be* no afterlife."

"That still doesn't answer my question."

"Free will. Just as we can choose now, you can choose there. During your life, you can still choose light. If you do, Aramis may show you mercy, forgive you for your trespasses, but there is no guarantee. The damnation of your soul can still be...debatable. Especially if Aramis places you with a family that is pure, that will fight for you. There are loopholes in his plan, plans for all to find redemption." Mal gazed at the stars. "It's very thoughtful."

"Thoughtful? You sound as if you respect Aramis and his plan of destruction."

"I may no longer follow the commands of Aramis, but I don't doubt his abilities or his wisdom. He is, after all, my creator."

Serus contemplated why the fallen Seraph had chosen his path, what had happened to make him take Aalok's side. Was it because he wanted freedom, as Serus did? Perhaps they were much more alike than he had realized.

"Loopholes that allow my existence, despite my faults. Sounds like I'll come out just fine either way. I agree to your terms, to as you call it, intercede for my soul." Serus held out his hand to take Malphas' forearm, but Mal only grinned.

Reaching over the arch of his wings, he plucked one of his feathers. Taking the tip of it, he cut his wrist. Clear blue plasma dripped onto the stone floor of the balcony.

He handed the feather to Serus, waiting for him to follow suit.

Serus drew back his sleeve, glanced at Mal, and then sliced open his skin. The clear plasma bled from his cut and trickled down his wrist into his palm.

Mal took Serus' arm and gripped it tight. "A deal to live lifetimes, a promise of immortality with the one you love."

As their plasmas seeped through into one another's wounds, Serus felt Mal's aura stronger than ever before. It burned as his blood drew up his arm like black ink seeping up the wick of a quill.

When Serus' arm was fully tainted, Mal withdrew his hand and rolled down his sleeve. He climbed to stand on top of the balcony and glanced down at Serus. "I'll be seeing you on the other side."

"Where are you off to?"

"Aalok is taking a little joy ride to the Infinite Realm. I'd offer to take you, but no lower angels allowed." Mal looked up at the sky. "Enjoy the show. Knowing Aramis, I'm sure the end is going to be *absolutely spectacular*."

With that, Mal took a step off the balcony. He fell to the rocks below and then shot up with his wings spread wide, lifting him into the sky.

Serus gazed at the horizon, watching Mal soar to the stars. He nodded to himself, knowing now there was nothing that could separate him and Sophie. With a smile, he walked into his room, tracing his fingers along the black line marking the evidence of his deal.

A crack paused his footsteps and he gripped the doorframe, waiting for the earthquake to pass. He laughed to himself, knowing it didn't matter if this world fell. He had his tether to the other dimension, to Sophie. As the trembling eased, Serus turned but paused lifting his head. A frown replaced his grin, seeing a dark-haired beauty on his bed.

"Aalok should know that you are more concerned with that girl than making sure we win this war," Jazrael pointed out in mock concern. She sat up, holding the wrinkled sheets of music Serus had written for Sophie. "These chords are so sweet and soothing they're sickening."

"Shouldn't you be in Caius' chamber?"

"Why do you say that?"

"Because I know you have visited his room many times since you arrived here," Serus replied, getting a new shirt from his closet. He undressed, tossing his inky stained one on the bed.

"Caius doesn't have much to offer,"

"Oh, I see. You prefer the Seraph, now."

"Its only business." Jazrael took her glance from the tight lines of Serus' stomach and picked up the stained shirt. "Much like yours with Mal. What was your deal?"

"You have your secrets and I have mine," Serus smirked. He folded his collar over his jacket and headed to the mirror standing in the corner. He smoothed down his suit, looking at himself in the oblong glass.

"I made a deal as well, with Zarak." Jazrael stood, grabbing her glass screen from the pillow beside her. She followed Serus as he headed back out to his balcony.

"Ah, Zarak," Serus said, taking up his bottle of wine. "Is it true the tips of his hair are stained with the blood of flesh?"

"Part of his spells. It takes the sacrifice of innocent creatures to make his magic work."

"Seems a bit drastic," Serus noted, pouring a glass of wine. "Why can't he do it the same way Aalok does?"

Jazrael shrugged. "It's more creative."

"It's dark."

"That's why I like it."

"I thought you trusted in Aalok's plan?"

"I do. I only agreed to sign with Zarak for fun. He was so intent on me being on his *list*."

"I can't imagine why."

Jazrael glanced at the glass screen in her hand as it vibrated. "Oh, and speaking of Caius, you'll be pleased to know he is advancing toward his former ally as we speak. Alexander escaped his bonds and fled."

"Good riddance," Serus sneered, sitting in his chair.

Jazrael lowered the glass screen and turned it toward Serus to show him the message from Caius. "He took her with him."

Seeing the words 'Truth Keeper' Serus snatched the screen from Jazrael and read the text.

```
J: Where are you?
C: Underground. The Truth Keeper is
on foot with her Guardian.
```

"Oh, you didn't know?" Jazrael asked with fake concern. She took back her glass screen and tapped the side. The light went off, making the glass look as if it was invisible.

Serus turned slowly with shallow breaths. "Sophie is with him?"

"Poor thing. I thought for sure Mal would have given you such information." Jazrael taunted. She couldn't help but hold a grin of pleasure at the sight of Serus' clenched fist.

She sauntered to the telescope and scanned the beach and then the field until a glint lit the lens.

How convenient.

She sent a message to Caius and then glanced back at Serus, licking her lips.

"Would you like to know where they are?" She tilted her head toward the telescope and smiled.

Serus stood and pressed his brow against the eyepiece, focusing on a light, glinting through the lens. There, in the middle of the valley, a few hundred feet from the exit of the cave, Serus saw two illuminated bodies.

"See? She's forgotten all about you."

Serus sucked in a sharp breath, squinting to see past the glow. He quivered with jealousy as he watched his worst fear. Sophie was embraced in her Guardians arms. Swallowing hard, Serus pulled back and glared at the telescope, before he lifted it over his head, and heaved it over the balcony with a primal roar.

It tumbled end over end through the air and shattered into pieces on the jagged rocks below, but the sound of it breaking wasn't enough to relieve Serus' rage.

He stumbled back, picking up the marble table. With a groan, he slammed it into one of the veranda doors with trembling hands. Glass flew everywhere. Adrenaline coursed through him as his aura flamed crimson like the raging waves.

"So, now you know for sure where her loyalty lies and from what I heard of you and Mal's little deal, I know where yours are. I wonder what Aalok will say about that?"

"Shut up!" Serus snapped, twisting around.

"My, my, she really got to you didn't she?"

"If you don't shut up, I'll throw you off this balcony! Don't think for a second I wouldn't enjoy doing so,"

"Awe. It hurts, doesn't it? Your sweet, innocent Sophie isn't so innocent, is she?"

"Don't say her name." His eyes were like daggers and if he could have, Serus would have run her through with one. He shoved her out of his way, ignoring the crunch of the glass crunched beneath his boots, and hurried out the door, slamming it behind him.

A WEAPON OF

DARKNESS

CAIUS held his fist in the air to halt his soldiers. "Alexander!" His shout echoed through the field.

Sophie and Alexander's heads jerked up as Caius and his army came to a standstill on the hill. There were more than fifty men behind the traitorous warrior.

"Run to the cliff." Alexander ordered Sophie. "I'll hold them off."

"What? No!" Sophie held him tight. "I won't leave you behind!"

"Do as I say!" Alexander pried her grip from his uniform and shoved her away.

As Sophie protested with her Guardian, Caius gave the silent command to take the shot from his bow. The flickering arrow of polarized energy zipped through the air toward the Truth Keeper.

Alexander jumped in front of her, taking the direct hit. It slammed into his shoulder with a thud and he gritted his teeth as the painful shocks brought him to his knees.

"Go!" He growled at Sophie as she bent down to help him.

Thoughts of Alexander chained up again, swirled in Sophie's mind, but she did as requested, and ran.

Caius halted his army again. They stood ready to take action, weapons drawn, only twenty feet from Alexander.

"Give me the Truth Keeper and I will spare you further pain," Caius called.

Alexander stumbled to his feet, breaking the arrow in half. "I can handle a little pain." He gnashed his teeth as the last few shocks sent spikes coursing through his body but then lifted his chin, drawing out the lodged spine of the arrow.

"So you think," Caius sneered.

Caius took a step, drawing his battle-ax, but stopped as the ground beneath him roared.

The eyes of his soldiers' widened, watching the earth split beneath there feet. They backed away, shouting at one another and Caius.

Caius didn't move, he only watched, soldier after soldier, cry out to one another as the earth swallowed them whole.

Sophie clung to the rocks to keep her balance, shielding her head and face from the falling debris of the slope.

Alexander glanced down at his wrist as an alarm alerted him the ship was close, then took one look at Caius and the few soldiers that were thrown left to right behind him.

Caius yelling at his men to hold their positions, to fire their weapons, but when he looked behind him, only ten men stood as the rest fled back to the fortress.

"Cowards!" Caius bellowed.

The earth calmed to a quiver as Caius jumped the wounded soil, paying no mind to the men that pleaded with him. He crushed one's fingers with his boot, stepped over another, ignoring their wailing as they fell to their doom. His focus was on one man, and one man only.

"Alexander!" he shouted, lighting his ax in crimson to match his aura. "You have your chance to best me, and yet you flee like the cowardice painter that you are!"

Alexander froze from climbing the cliff. He knew the ship would not be there for a few more minutes. He knew he had to stall Caius long enough for Sophie to make it back to the Infinite Realm. No telling what Aramis would say to her, what knowledge he would bestow before the end came.

"What are you doing?" Sophie cried as he climbed down the cliff.

"I gave my word to keep you safe."

"No! Alexander, don't!"

Alexander ignored her pleas and met Caius face to face on the second tier of the rocky plateau.

"Let's finish this," he said, balling up his fists. He had no weapon, but he still had the strength of Aramis and it lit his aura in a light blue hue.

The remaining bowmen stood ready for Caius' signal to attack. The others climbed up the cliff.

Sophie held her breath, watching for few heartbeats as Caius and Alexander glared.

With a bellow, Caius attacked first.

Alexander ducked under his blow. He elbowed one of Caius's soldiers in the throat, taking his sword from him.

Caius swung again but was blocked by Alexander's sword. "Now!" he ordered.

Energy arrows flew past, missing Alexander's face by inches. Another soldier swung, just missing the Guardian, who leaped backward, out of the path of the glowing beams. He dropped to his knee, swinging his foot behind the soldier's calves and brought him to the ground. Alexander's glow grew brighter as he triumphed over his enemies and former brothers. He twirled, wielding his sword, bringing yet another soldier down on his knees.

Caius lunged forward to attack and Alexander met him with a clash. Their weapons hummed and sparked above their heads as Caius spat his words.

"You should have just given her up, Alexander. You know I have bested you before. Save yourself the embarrassment and kneel."

Alexander let out a deep growl, thrusting himself off of Caius's weapon and took a few steps to the side. "Pride before the fall," he replied, flatly.

"It is pride alone that got me this far. The humble are weak. Your king is weak, and under Aalok's rule, we will triumph over you. You will be my slave, and your high priestess, my footstool."

Alexander's aura intensified and his sword roared into a fiery blaze at the thought.

Caius spun around behind him as two soldiers charged at once, weapons raised.

The first soldier came with a loud bellow. Alexander clutched the uniform at his chest, jerking him down to face the ground, and rolled over his back. He elbowed the other soldier running at him, backhanding another with his fist and spun, slashing him across his middle.

Sophie watched from above in sheer panic. She clenched her teeth and tensed her shoulders as the soldiers rushed her faithful Guardian. She watched his feet closely, fascinated by his graceful steps. The fight was like a dance. Each movement was a pivot, a twirl. It was a waltz with weapons.

As Alexander head-butted a swordsman, he plunged his flaming sword into his last opponent's chest.

"Shoot her!" Caius yelled.

The bowmen pulled back and at their release, energy arrows flew through the air, like lightning, bolting across the sky.

Alexander's gaze shifted from Caius to the direction of the arrow. "Sophie!"

Sophie heeded his warning and crouched behind the rocks. As she dodged the electrically charged bolts, light burst into fireworks, smashing the boulders of her hiding place into rubble. Those same rocks fell on the steep below where Alexander and Caius fought.

Caius dodged them, countering, but a moment too late as Alexander's sword slashed his wrist.

The crimson flames of Caius' ax went out all at once, as did his aura. He watched his blood drip to the ground, seething at the wound until it healed. He then smiled and threw his fist into the air.

The bowmen waited at his command.

"I think I will take her back to my room before delivering her to Aalok," Caius taunted, drawing his sword. "She should know what it's like to be embraced by a real warrior."

That remark was all it took to enrage Alexander. He gritted his teeth, blazing brighter than ever before. He wouldn't let Caius or Aalok lay another hand on her. He swung his sword in fury, but Caius caught the blade against his. They were face to face again, their swords humming like a tapped tuning fork.

Alexander spun around, breaking their hold. He drew all his strength, all of Aramis', raising his sword again with a growl. He was ready to give a final blow, but Caius gripped him by his shirt and pulled him close.

"You could be like me, Alexander. You could have knowledge and power like never before. Choose Aalok, and you can keep your precious Truth Keeper."

"I'd rather die," Alexander grunted, struggling to free himself from Caius' hold.

"So be it," Caius glared, holding his gloved hand to the sky. Sparks ignited Caius' fingertips and he closed his eyes. He drew all the negative energy from his soul, along with that of the Outcasts, into his glove. Once satisfied with the power, his eyes flew open. He took Alexander by the throat, and squeezed, sending waves of negative energy into him.

Alexander choked, convulsing at the painful shocks. Worse than the pain was the fear accompanied by a hellish darkness consuming his soul.

"My parting gift to you, old friend."

"Stop it!" Sophie cried out from above them.

Caius glanced up, delighted by her face draining of color, how her aura lowered.

He squeezed Alexander tighter, taunting her to come quickly to her Guardian's aid.

"Please, stop!" Sophie cried out in tears.

Caius ran his tongue along the edge of his teeth and narrowed eyes. "As you wish, oh high priestess."

Alexander thudded to the ground at the release of Caius' hold. He was overcome by pain, but even worse was the unimaginable and incomprehensible evil consuming his heart.

"I told you I would win, Alexander." Caius crowed in his ear. "I always do." Caius kicked him, rolling him over on his side.

Alexander pounded his fist against the ground as his veins boiled. His hatred, anger, and jealousy heightened to such extremes, that his aura dissipated, and then rose again in red. The bright turquoise of his irises thinned as his pupils widened until there was nothing but a black void in his eyes.

A roar in the sky startled everyone and they looked up to see Aramis' airship descending over the top of the plateau.

"Enjoy your torment," Caius said, turning casually back towards the fortress.

"Run, you coward! Run back to your master!" Alexander yelled.

Sophie stood watching as Aramis' airship hovered, waiting for them to board.

"Alexander!"

Alexander's aura crackled as hate, Caius' hate, churned inside him.

Sophie shrank back in fear as Alexander stood. For every step he took toward her, she took two back, watching his face contort.

The ground convulsed again and gave way between them.

Alexander took a few steps back and broke into a sprint to leap over the chasm, only to slam against the rocky wall. His fingertips gripped the ledge at Sophie's feet. He hung, his feet dangling over the fall there was no coming back from.

Sophie fell to her knees, grasping one of Alexander's forearms to help him up, but as he made it onto the ledge he shoved her away.

"Don't touch me!" He hissed.

Startled by his harsh tone, Sophie let go and fell back. She cowered at the hate burning in her Guardian's aura as he stood, piercing her with his black stare. Her lips quivered as she opened her mouth to speak. She had to say something, anything, to bring him back to himself.

Alexander glared at her for a moment before he turned away, heading for the ship. He shoved soldiers out of his way, making no attempt to move out of their path as they hurried to collect the horrified Truth Keeper.

She stood in shock for a long moment, but quickly regained her senses, and thanked Aramis' soldiers as they escorted her on board.

The ship's door closed as it lifted into the atmosphere before zipping up into the sky. With a double flash of light, it disappeared into the clouds, heading for the stars.

RAGE

AFTER piling into the elevator in the ship, Sophie observed deck after deck through the glass walls as they headed for the floor indicated by a lit icon on the screen. She gazed at hall after hall of lights until they passed deck five, where she saw the helm and the Captain's chair surrounded by screens and boards filled with glowing icons. On deck four, she glanced at the dining area. Chandeliers of fine crystal hung above a large round table, set for more than twenty with a view of the cosmos. When the elevator slowed to a halt, she swallowed hard as the glass doors opened to deck two.

Following the soldiers, she glanced down at Alexander's fists. She could still feel his aura burn with rage as they turned several corners of the brightly lit hall. Finally, they came to a door, and a soldier knocked before a voice answered for the group to enter.

"Captain," one of the soldiers bowed.

"Ah! Yes." The Captain turned quickly from a holographic projection of the Infinite Realm and put down his touch screen. He gleefully made his way across the room to greet his men, seemingly overjoyed by the rescue.

Sophie studied the angel who glowed bright amber. The Captain wore a blue-buttoned down vest resting over a white tunic that was laced loosely up his dark-skinned chest. It was tucked in a pair of fitted black trousers held snuggly at his waist by a belt buckle with Aramis' signet. At his side, there wasn't a sheathed sword as Sophie had expected, but instead, a telescope.

"I knew you would succeed," the Captain grinned triumphantly. He reached out to greet the Guardian, but Alexander did not offer his arm.

The Captain's deep brown eyes faltered at the sight of Alexander's hollow eyes.

"Alexander?" he asked, taking a step back.

"Zeruiah, I have delivered Aramis' asset. My duty in this matter is finished." Alexander answered tonelessly, turning away.

"Yes. Thank you, but-"

"You will personally escort the Truth Keeper to the king." Alexander looked back at him with eyes flaming red, challenging Zeruiah to question his authority.

"What troubles you, my friend?" Zeruiah asked placing a comforting hand on Alexander's shoulder.

"Don't touch me!" Alexander gritted out, shoving Zeruiah away.

"Alexander! What has gotten into you?" Sophie admonished from behind him.

"And you," Alexander spat, turning on the Truth Keeper. "I should have left you in that cave for Aalok, and saved myself the trouble. You are a disgrace to your Circle and are not worthy of being on this ship, or in the presence of Aramis. You will be judged for your trespasses, Truth Keeper."

Sophie's lip quivered as she opened her mouth, but she couldn't speak. It was as if the wind had been knocked out of her from Alexander's harsh words. They were more painful than the shock of negative energy she had felt aboard the enemy ship. She gulped, gathering the courage to take a step forward, but Alexander took a step back in her attempt to touch him.

"What? Is the truth too harsh for you?" he asked. "You hide behind your title, acting as if you keep the truth, but you lied to me, Truth Keeper. You lied to Serus." Alexander seethed. "No wonder he left you. Who would want a companion as fickle as you?"

"You don't mean that!" Sophie looked to Zeruiah over Alexander's shoulder in desperation. "Caius did something to him. Used some kind of weapon of darkness. I have suffered its ill effects too, but not like this. He has lost himself completely."

"I think you should have a seat, my friend." Zeruiah looked to the soldier. They took Alexander's arm to lead him to a chair, but Alexander whipped around, shoving them back.

"Make way." A deep voice came through the open door. The soldiers parted, saluting the Seraph as he entered. Alexander did not salute with the rest of his team. He only glared at Gabriel with hate-filled eyes.

"Alexander," Gabriel greeted, with authority. "Be at peace."

Alexander ignored his request and lit up like a fueled flame.

Although such a stance would be an insult to a Seraph, Gabriel calmly raised his wings and spread them wide.

"Be at peace," Gabriel repeated.

The Seraph's soothing tone only enraged Alexander further, and he lunged towards Gabriel.

"You put no fear in me!" he snarled as the soldiers held him back.

Gabriel noted the voice. It came out not as Alexander's, but Aalok's. Possession. That was the new weapon that Aalok had used.

Alexander swung at Gabriel's face, but Gabriel avoided the blow and gently, but firmly took hold of Alexander's shoulder with one hand. With his other hand, he drew the spirit of Aalok from Alexander's chest. A light formed in his palm, drawing out the darkness with a magnetic force.

It coursed through the air, letting out a shriek, fighting to stay in its host, but gave up, dissipating into the Seraph's closed fist.

Alexander's red glow dimmed and his natural amber color returned. With a harsh breath, he slumped forward, grasping Gabriel's shoulder to steady himself.

The Seraph gently slid Alexander down to the floor as the crowd looked to one another in astonishment.

"Rest now," Gabriel murmured, squeezing Alexander's shoulder gently.

Sophie knelt at her Guardian's side, cradling his head in her lap. She looked up anxiously at the Seraph. "Is he going to be okay?"

Gabriel leaned down and placed a comforting hand on Sophie's shoulder. In seconds, she found relief from the chaos inside her. All of the fear, anxiety, and panic that Caius had shocked into her, vanished.

"Yes," Gabriel assured her. "He shall be restored."

"What evil is this?" she asked.

"This is the work of Aalok," Gabriel announced to the ship and its crew. "He has found a way to harness and magnify negative emotions, to place his own spirit in those who are vulnerable. We have never seen a weapon like this used before today. You would all do well to be on guard."

Sophie peered down at Alexander. She thought of all the horrible things he had said in his rage but stroked his dirty blond hair tenderly.

"Do not be disheartened, Truth Keeper. Your Guardian would not have said such things if he had been of sound mind. This kind of darkness is very powerful. We must all be cautious now."

"You do not know how grateful I am for your assistance." Sophie told him.

Gabriel nodded in acknowledgment. "Be of good courage. The time is drawing near to the end. Peace unto you." He glanced around to address the soldiers and Zeruiah. "Peace be unto you all."

The crowd replied with the known mantra, and then parted for the wise Seraph to go about his way.

Zeruiah knelt down in front of Sophie, shaking his head.

"He is *so* lucky. No one has ever taken on a Seraph before, figures he would be the first to do so." Zeruiah placed his hand on Alexander's shoulder. "Rest well my friend, it is well deserved."

The Captain stood, pointing to the chaise lounge by the window. "Put him over there."

Three soldiers lifted Alexander from Sophie's lap, placing him gently on the couch.

Sophie stood, bowing in greeting to Zeruiah. "Sophie of the Seventh Circle."

"The Seventh? Seven means completeness in Divine Numerics," the Captain noted, wondering why the king had required an Eighth. He guessed because eight in Divine Numerics meant new beginnings. Aramis had been hopeful, but the Captain was aware that Aalok had corrupted the majority of them.

Sophie smiled with a nod. "So it does. Have you studied Divine Numerics long?"

The Captain gave a charming, yet shy white smile. "You could say I've always had a thing for numbers."

"Your gift." Sophie acknowledged.

The Captain nodded with a smile. "Zeruiah,"

Sophie took his arm and squeezed. "It is a pleasure, Zeruiah."

"The pleasure is all mine," Zeruiah assured, squeezing Sophie's arm back. "Please, make yourself at home. I will notify you when we are about to land in the Infinite Realm.

"We're going home?"

Zeruiah smiled, before tapping on the screen of his wristband, giving orders to the crew through the speakers of each deck. "Prepare the portal,"

As Zeruiah and his men left the room, Sophie glanced around it. There was a large desk filled with blueprints and navigation tools. The walls were covered in books with titles of space travel, metaphysics, and mathematics. Sophie then turned to the porthole with a view of the stars, and planets of blue, green, and red. Her gaze followed the sunlight to the lounge chair, where it illuminated her Guardian's peaceful face.

Sitting carefully on the couch, she placed Alexander's head back onto her lap. Sweeping the hair from his brow, she gave thanks to Aramis. Before long, her eyes grew heavy and she fell into a blissful sleep as the ship coasted through a vast galaxy of twinkling stars.

32

ARRIVAL

ALEXANDER woke clutching his chest, before remembering that Gabriel had healed him. He exhaled a breath, relieved that the negativity had been dissolved. Aalok's spirit was gone. He was no longer possessed by the Confusion.

The past day's events came flooding back and Alexander cringed as regret overtook him. He glanced up, finding Sophie sleeping peacefully. She let out a sigh, wrapping her arm more tightly around his chest. He couldn't believe, despite all he had said to her, she was there, holding him.

Wiggling out beneath her, he carefully ducked under her arm and tucked a pillow in his place. Seeing that she was comfortable, he backed away silently, and stood, watching her for a moment.

By the way she was glowing a joyful hue of white, he could tell she was dreaming of something wonderful. He hoped it was of the time she had spent on the beach with Bevol, basking in the sun's warmth. He hoped the smile spreading across her face was a memory of the secret spring, of the comfort he gave her in all her times of despair. No matter what she remembered, he hoped it was not his rage.

He didn't want her to hear the echo of his rigid tone, or his countless orders for her not to poke at him about his true feelings. He had been the warrior sent to protect her, but he wondered if she had seen past that. He had only shown her a glimpse of his soft side; the sentimental artist he truly was.

He longed to wake her, to tell her how much he cared for her, but couldn't bring himself to do so. He couldn't look into those beautiful green eyes. Not after what he had done. He knew he had not been himself, but it didn't matter. He couldn't take back what he had said.

Taking one last look, Alexander locked away one last beautiful memory. In the end, he would picture her like this; the angel glowing brightly with joy and peace. He caressed her cheek with his knuckles, before leaning in. After a light kiss to her forehead, he drew back, mourning what he knew he must do.

"May it be Aramis' will that we meet again, Truth Keeper," he whispered softly.

With that, Alexander departed quickly, pausing at the door to take one last look at the slumbering Sophie. He smiled painfully, pulling his hood over his brows and hurried through the automatic doors.

He made his way through the winding corridor, keeping his gaze to the floor. Once in the glass elevator, he pressed the button for the dining hall. Passing tables and chairs, he grabbed an apple from a cart, making a straight line for the door to the docking station. He kept his head down, never making eye contact with the soldiers he passed. It was not just Sophie he couldn't face, but his fellow brethren.

Closing the door to the docking station, he leaned against the doors with relief. He had completed his mission of retrieving the Truth Keeper, but there was one more matter to take care of before the end of the aeon. He entered one of the smaller ships and punched in the coordinates to the kingdom.

The small craft detached from the flagship with a jolt, and at the touch of his finger, the ship flashed into a portal, heading for the Infinite Realm.

At the arrival announcement, Sophie lazily yawned, but as she stretched her hand across the soft linen fabric of the pillow, she stiffened. She tossed it to the side, looking around the room, before rushing to the window. Pressing her palms against the thick glass, she peered down the ship's cargo area to a mist from a cascading waterfall of the kingdom walls.

"Thanks be to Aramis,"

The doors of the room opened after the whisper of her king's name. Sophie spun on her toes. Her face lit with glee, but it dimmed finding only the Captain entering.

"We have arrived, and right on schedule," Zeruiah announced cheerfully. As he looked up, he came to a standstill.

He glanced at Sophie and then looked at the chaise lounge in dismay. "Where is Alexander?"

"I thought he was with you,"

"No," Zeruiah shook his head. "I suppose it is I who have the honor of escorting you to the king now."

"Is he...is he still angry with me?"

"I believe he is angry with himself."

"Surely he didn't mean what he said. It was the darkness that consumed him."

The Captain seemed to hold back a grin. He understood Alexander better than anyone, besides Aramis. He had been receiving messages about the Truth Keeper, and teasing Alexander about the tough guy act.

Sophie was taken aback by Zeruiah's many conflicting expressions. It appeared as if he was trying to keep from laughing at a joke she was unaware of. She didn't understand why he was taking the matter so lightly.

"Alexander is a complex soul," Zeruiah began, glancing at his screen then back at Sophie. "You have experienced these ill-effects first hand. As you know that particular weapon only intensifies one's adverse emotions. I believe the begrudging Alexander felt was real. I'm uncertain of what you two have been through, but it seems to me, it was something more than just the Confusion."

"He thinks I'm a traitor."

"He wouldn't have brought you on the ship if he believed that. What do you think he was really trying to say in his anger? If you read between the lines, I think you may gather what he meant in his hateful words." Zeruiah couldn't hide another grin. "They were quite telling to me, as his friend."

Sophie battled in her mind with what Alexander had meant and then it hit her all at once. He hadn't been speaking about her. He had been rebuking himself. He had felt guilty for their kiss, guilty for betraying Serus...for failing in the duty Aramis had entrusted him with.

Alexander wanted to be with her. He just couldn't admit it. He couldn't bring himself to say the words. His orders had been clear. He was to keep her from Aalok's grasp. All the while he had been struggling with his affections, but he never let it distract him, not like Sophie had.

"Come," Zeruiah urged. "I must bring you to Aramis immediately. Let us not make him wait, shall we?"

"Yes, of course, Captain," Sophie agreed, blinking from her daze. "Please lead the way."

FORGIVNESS

"MY Lord," Alexander said, bowing his head at steps of Aramis' throne.

"My faithful Guardian. Why did you leave the Truth Keeper in the Captain's care?"

"I couldn't face her. As you see, I can hardly face you, my king. I must ask your forgiveness."

"For?" Aramis inquired, clasping his hands in front of him.

"You know what I have done. You've seen everything."

"Ah, the rage."

"Yes,"

"Possession of one's spirit in a time of weakness. Aalok found yours and used it against you."

"I must also apologize for nearly losing the counselor to Aalok."

"Because of you, she wasn't swayed."

Alexander lifted his head. "Only because you interceded. I don't know what might have happened if you hadn't. I could feel her slipping away. She was so confused. Something about being in the fortress made us lose ourselves. She was so close to forgetting, too blinded by the illusion, by the lies."

"Sophie may have been blinded, but she would have never bowed a knee to Aalok."

"How did you know she wouldn't? Did you foresee it?"

"I know the depths of all hearts. Her heart, no matter her affections for another, still held onto the truth. She will never be swayed by the lies of Aalok, in this life or the one to come. And you, Alexander, have proven to be stronger than you realize. You stood in a den of lions and yet, your faith in me did not waver. Not once did doubt cross your mind."

"But it wasn't me that saved her. It was you, it was your power."

"You fervently requested that I help you, and so I did."

"Aalok didn't seem too disappointed at our escape."

"Aalok is patient. He thinks that he is wiser, stronger, but he forgets, that it is I who gives life, and it is I who can take it away. His day will come to rule, but he forgets that his choices have consequences. Do not fear for what is to come. I will put a shroud of protection over you. But know, in your time of weakness, Aalok will be waiting like a serpent in the grass for the opportunity to strike."

The castle shook, and Aramis' aura grew brighter.

"The time has come," Aramis announced, bringing his gaze from the window to Alexander. "Are you ready for your journey, to stand as one of my soldiers?"

"I'm not a warrior. I'm just a painter you dressed as one."

Aramis lifted a questioning brow. "Is that you speaking or Caius?"

Alexander knitted his brows with no reply.

Aramis rose and stood in front of Alexander. "You are as I say you are, Guardian." He said, placing a gentle hand on the top of Alexander's head. "And you are a noble prince."

A bright blue flame emanated from Aramis. It flowed from his fingertips to the top of Alexander's head, spreading through his clothing, brightening his attire down to his boots. The ash and dirt disappeared, and Alexander felt renewed.

"I chose those who are humble, selfless, and kind. I chose you, a painter, because you see the beauty in what I've created. You see light, despite the darkness. You yourself are a light, Alexander, and you will shine the way when others can not see the path before them."

Aramis removed his hand and Alexander stood.

"Thank you, my Lord."

"You would have made an excellent Truth Keeper."

Alexander thought of how he saw the truth in Sophie's eyes, how he could see Serus' intentions were not bad or good, but something in between. It was his gift. All his life he had thought he was only a painter, but he now realized he was more. "If this is true, why I was I knighted as a Guardian?"

Aramis lifted his chin. "Because your destiny was already written in the stars at the moment of your creation, and destiny leads one exactly where they need to be."

Alexander stood quiet, gathering that Aramis had paired him with Sophie deliberately. It was not only to keep her from falling into confusion, but also for another purpose. A thought tugged at Alexander as Sophie's life history flashed through his mind. He was flipping through the pages of her life book to her birth. She was among the stars, gleaming, and beside her was a soul, glowing with the same steady fire.

He again felt the burning in his soul as Sophie and his eyes met on the beach. The spark. The connection. He felt the anger of seeing the soot on Sophie's body from Serus. But now, seeing it again, the jealousy was just, it was right to feel that way. Sophie was his mate. His. Not Serus'. The realization hit Alexander harder than the moment he knew he had fallen for her. Sophie was his counterpart.

All those times he had gazed upon her beauty, all those times he found himself breathless, wasn't solely his attraction to her. It was because they were destined to be together. Their light called out to one another, crying out to be whole again. His shoulders fell, relieved that everything he felt for Sophie was not infatuation, but a divine and cosmic connection formed the moment of their very existence.

Soulmates.

Aramis read Alexander's thoughts and smiled with a nod. "I hope you spend your last moments wisely, my son. I know you fear this life will be forgotten, but remember—fear is an illusion...but truth and love are absolute."

Truth. Love.

The truth was Alexander loved Sophie. He knew there could still be a chance he would find her in the next life, but what about Serus? He couldn't be sure if it was destiny for Sophie and Serus to ever meet again and he didn't know if he could face the end with that on his conscience.

Serus wouldn't listen to him, no matter if he went to him, no matter if he was a Truth Keeper at heart and had the gift of counsel. Sophie would be the only Truth Keeper he would listen to now. No matter Serus' heartbreak, he still loved her. Alexander knew that love was the only way to dissolve a trespass. Truth was the cure to Confusion, and love was the light that could disperse its dark burden.

The castle shook again and Alexander glanced around the room as thunder rolled.

"The time is drawing near, but it is not yet the end," Aramis smiled faintly and held out his hand. "I believe this belongs to you."

Alexander's sketchbook and a quill appeared, floating in the air.

Alexander took the items and glanced up at Aramis gratefully. "Thank you, my Lord." He tucked them in the inner pocket of his uniform.

Aramis placed his hands on Alexander's shoulder and looked him straight in the eyes.

"I know you think that doing anything now is in vain, that none of this will be remembered...but know that nothing, not even my power, can break a bond as true as the one you feel now. Not in this life, nor the next."

"Can Serus still be saved?"

"All of my children have a choice, right up until their very last breath."

Alexander nodded in understanding and held out his hand. "Farewell, my king,"

The king smiled and squeezed his arm. "Until we meet again."

34

THE LAST
GOODBYE

"THIS is where I leave you," Zeruiah informed, standing at the doors of the throne room.

"Thank you, Captain." Sophie bowed.

Zeruiah mirrored her. "Please, call me Zeruiah."

"I hope to see you again, Zeruiah."

"As do I." Zeruiah smiled and reached for the doors but they opened on their own accord.

Alexander exited, coming face to face with Sophie.

The door thudded behind him, echoing down the hall.

"Feeling better I see," Zeruiah grinned, looking over Alexander's attire.

"Zeruiah, may I speak with you?" Alexander asked, averting his gaze from Sophie. "Alone?"

"Of course," Zeruiah nodded.

Alexander stepped around the Truth Keeper and headed for the courtyard.

"Alexander wait," Sophie ran to him, taking his hand in hers.

Alexander came to a standstill, staring down at their intertwined fingers.

Sophie was his soulmate, but she still had a duty, she still had a choice. He couldn't wait for her, because if he were standing by her side at the end, she wouldn't be standing with the Outcast. Maybe if Serus were with the Truth Keeper in the last moments, knowing he might not see her again, it would change his mind. Maybe then, he would come back to the truth. Maybe he could still be redeemed...before he took his last breath.

The ground shook the hallway, but Sophie's gaze was fixed on her Guardian.

"You should go see Aramis while you still can," Alexander said, and slipped from her grasp.

Sophie didn't understand why Alexander was still keeping his distance. Even as he walked away, she could feel his aura. She could sense his heartache and how much he wanted to hold her, but the emotions trailed away as Alexander walked down the steps and out of the castle doors.

When the hallway quivered again, Zeruiah turned to Sophie with a tender voice.

"Farewell, Sophie. I do hope we meet again. Perhaps in the next life."

"One can only hope," Sophie agreed, forcing a smile.

They took one another's arms in farewell before Zeruiah made haste to catch up to Alexander.

Sophie brushed her fingers along the silky crimson fabric of her gown and cringed. Not only was her dress the color of her enemy, but it was also filthy with ash, with the soot of trespasses.

At another shudder of the hallway, Sophie took in a deep breath, and entered Aramis' throne room, kneeling at her beloved king's feet.

"Father, I must ask your forgiveness."

Aramis tilted his head slightly. "What trespass are you asking forgiveness for?"

Sophie rose but kept her gaze on the ground.

Aramis came to her and lifted her chin gently. "Look at me, my child."

"I betrayed Serus, I never meant to hurt him...I know you saw what happened-that I kissed Alexander in the cave, but I can't help but have feelings for him."

"In your heart, I can feel you are truly sorry for what you have done, but Sophie, your affections for him are innocent."

"But I care for Serus too."

"You have a deeper connection with Alexander. You know this, because your soul whispers it. You love him, don't you?"

"I-I don't know...I'm so confused," Sophie admitted. "How can I love them both?"

"Let me help you see the truth clearly." Aramis reached out and placed his hand on Sophie's head.

Just as Alexander had been restored, Sophie was as well. Her torn, filthy dress had transformed into a gown of white. The smudges of ash upon her cheeks disappeared and her whole body brightened at the touch of Aramis' glowing fingertips. Sophie's fear and anxiety melted away, leaving her emotions clear.

"Thank you," Sophie smoothed her hands down the beautiful white gown. This was no illusion. This was the true power of her creator, her king.

"Now, the question I asked...do you love Alexander?"

Sophie paused to think about the time she had shared with her Guardian. She thought about when they had met, about the secret spring, the cave, and their kiss. She thought about all the times he comforted her, the times he yelled at her because he wanted to keep her safe. She flushed with a warm wave and glanced up at Aramis, sure of her answer.

"Yes."

"And Serus?"

"Yes, but in another way. I don't know how to explain it."

"There are many types of love, dear one. There is no need for explanation."

"I pray that...if I may be so bold to ask; if there can be a way I may aid him in this next life?"

Aramis smiled at Sophie's selflessness. No matter the hurt Serus had caused, she still wanted to make sure he made it through the next test; that he came back to the truth.

"You and Serus were never supposed to meet."

"We weren't?"

"No. He was to be bonded with someone else, but his choices led him to a new path. That path led him to you."

Sophie's forehead wrinkled.

"Having been unsatisfied with his rank, he sought other means to get what he desired. He had heard of Aalok's offers and proved himself by stealing for him. The day you two met, he was stealing a scroll. I watched his heart grew dark, caring for nothing but himself as he took it. But as he picked up that book he held so dear, he was met with a beautiful Truth Keeper. In the same moment he had faltered, he was also given a chance at redemption. I've never seen a soul fall for another that was not predestined."

Sophie wet her lips, gazing at the ground. "Alexander told me he was a spy. I thought I could see through falsehoods. Why was I not able to see the truth?"

"Serus has loved you since the moment he saw you, Sophie. That was never a lie. The time you spent together was real, but he was conflicted between what he desired and what he knew was right. Had he not chosen his selfish desires, you two would have never met. By his choice of courting you, his path diverged. I had hoped he would come back to the truth because of you, being around your purity, your goodness, but he didn't. He became possessive of you and sought to gain more things to impress you, to win your love rather than earn it. Had the path not diverged, you would have been exactly where you were supposed to be after you left the library. "

"Where was I supposed to be?"

"It would have been a perfect meeting at the festival."

Sophie searched her mind for the memory, grasping fistfuls of her dress in her hands.

"Alexander. He was the painter at the festival, the day I met Serus?"

Aramis chuckled. "Yes, and if he had turned around sooner, your eyes would have met. You would have felt the connection spark just as you both did at the beach. If it had gone according to plan, you would have been bonded by now. If he had turned around sooner, you would have complimented his painting and he would have thanked you.

"You two would have talked about your mutual love of horses, and Alexander would have asked you to dance. The two of you would be outside the castle right now, holding onto one another, waiting for the end, just as the other soulmates are now."

Sophie stood in silence for a few heartbeats as every moment she had spent with Alexander went through her mind. The tug she had felt, the magnetic force that had been pushing them together made sense now. At the first sight of him, she knew in her heart there was something calling out to her. Their souls had been reaching out, begging to be one again. Alexander had fought the tug to keep her safe. He was selfless and noble, and Sophie loved him now more than ever. Her voice was almost a whisper as she lifted her head and met Aramis' gaze. "Alexander is my soulmate?"

Aramis nodded. "I make all of my children in pairs. Alexander was your complement, your other half. You have been trying to understand why it felt right to be with him, never realizing he was the missing piece."

Sophie's breaths quickened as her heart raced, not only from her realization but also from the urgent spike that ran through her as the castle shook.

"Does he know?"

"Yes."

"Then why didn't he want to wait for me? Why didn't he say anything?"

"That, my child, is something you should ask him yourself. There's not much time left. Aalok is drawing near. He still thinks he can change what I have already set in motion."

The castle shook furiously and Sophie stumbled into her king's arms.

"You must make haste!"

"I'm not ready for this new life, Aramis!" Sophie cried above the rolling thunder. "Please, I need more time!"

"I'm sorry, my child. There is no more time I can give."

Aramis and Sophie looked out the window to see the kingdom crumbling in the distance. The homes far off had caved into themselves. The ground and all it held above it fell into heaps of rubble. The sky grew darker as ominous black clouds rolled together like a scroll, blanketing the heavens.

"But, Serus! He believes they do not have to pass through this new age."

"I alone hold the fate of the world in my hands and all who dwell within it," Aramis replied, taking Sophie's hands in his. "No matter the distance, or time, or even dimension, love remains. It is imprinted in the depths of our souls and we carry it wherever we go. That love will remind you of what was, but it will only come as a whisper, so listen closely with your heart."

The castle convulsed as a low rumble sounded. The ceiling split down the center and Sophie could feel the power emanating from Aramis, protecting her. "You only need to believe."

Sophie hugged Aramis tight, never wanting to let go.

"This is not goodbye, dear one. It is only farewell for a little while."

Sophie wiped her tears, kissed Aramis on his cheek, and hurried to the doors.

Aramis watched her slip through them, clasping his hands behind his back until she was out of sight. He then went to his window and watched his own power crumble his creation, piece by piece, into oblivion.

35

CONFESSION

SERUS slid his bow across his violin, sending a dark, yet beautiful solo into the smoky sky. It was a melancholy sentiment that would have lumped a souls throat if they had been there to hear it. But he was alone, serenading his own sorrows.

After the last somber stroke, he propped the bow and violin against his chair and stumbled a few steps to the balcony. He took one last drink tossing the empty wine bottle over the balcony. The sound of a clink was its goodbye, but he paid it no mind as he uncorked another bottle, and raised it to the heavens.

"To my end, may it be swift." He toasted.

Lifting the bottle to his lips, he scowled at a ruckus that filled his ears.

"Serus!" Jazrael shouted as she burst through his door.

He grimaced at the wave of noise that continued. "You could at least shut the door. I've heard quite enough of their blathering," he yelled.

"Where is Aalok?"

Serus squinted an eye, looking into the wine bottle.
"Nope, not in there." He tipped it to his mouth and chugged
the wine sloppily. He wiped the dribble on his chin off with his
sleeve, staining the white cuff without care.

"I went to the docking station, but the ship was gone!"

"No." Serus gasped, covering his mouth in mockery.
"Say it isn't so. I thought for sure they would take their most
loyal of whores. I mean-subjects."

"This is not a game!"

"No? I thought we were playing 'Guess where Aalok is,'"
Serus smirked, taking another gulp.

"How can you just sit here and drown yourself?" Jazrael
shrieked, snatching the bottle from his hand. "We'll die if we
don't find the ship!"

Serus leaned his dizzy head against the back of his chair
and sighed. "Must you shout?"

Jazrael pointed to the tumultuous waters pounded by
fireball after fireball. "Do you not see this? Do you not see the
smoke rising from the mountains? Aramis is going to destroy
us all!"

"So dramatic. How am I to enjoy the end with your
annoying voice in my ear?" Serus slouched in his chair and
closed his eyes in aggravation. "Do shut up."

"No, no, we can't die! Aalok promised to spare us!"

Jazrael ranted, pacing back and forth. She was talking to
herself now, as Serus was doing his best to ignore her.

"He promised we would not go through a life of pain and sorrow. He told us that we could choose to stay and live out our lives as we did before Aramis made his grand plan. There must be another ship. Come on! If we hurry, I am sure we can find it."

Serus sighed and sat up. He pulled a cork from a new bottle and tipped it up, taking a long swallow.

"Are you listening to me?" Jazrael demanded, taking hold of his shoulders. "If we don't find Aalok, we will die!"

"You're blocking my view."

The fortress convulsed, crumbling the walls, and they fell to their watery death. Serus let a smile pull at his lips. He was ready for his.

"Fine! Stay here and wallow in self-pity over that self-righteous Truth Keeper,"

Serus had been drinking to forget Sophie and he had been so close to doing so. Now, she was all he could think of. He wondered if she was with Alexander; if she was thinking of him at all. He jumped to his feet, spitting his words in a sudden rage.

"If you're so worried about yourself, then go! Leave me in peace! I've had enough of your incessant whining!" he yelled, thrusting the bottle to the ground. He stumbled back and stared at the glass shards. He wouldn't ask the servant to come sweep it up, not after the other mess he had made earlier.

"At least I care for my life! You sit here weeping over one who clearly doesn't want you. Why do you still love her after all she has done to you, but reject me time and time again?"

"She," Serus glared, taking up his violin, "is not a selfish parasite. You only look after your own well-being. You're nothing but a conniving, self-serving leech."

"And she's a whore! She's in love with that Guardian and you know it!"

"She's a whore?" Serus let out a laugh. "Have you looked at yourself in the mirror lately?"

"I did what I had to do."

Serus tuned his violin before sliding his bow across it. He played the tune he had composed for Sophie, the same sweet melody Jazrael had called sickening.

"I came to save you, you ungrateful wretch!" Jazrael shrieked.

Serus tightened his finger on the strings, making it whine to mock Jazrael. He chuckled as he sat, laying his violin and bow in his lap. "You only came to see if I knew of Aalok's whereabouts. See? This *is* a game. Charades."

Jazrael narrowed her eyes.

"Don't tell me..I've got it!" Serus snapped his fingers and jumped up, placing his violin and bow gently on the ground. He leaned in and bit his lip with a smile." You're pretending to be a saint." He went to the railing and lifted his hands out to the sky. "All hail Saint Jazrael!" he shouted to the sky.

"And what of you, huh?" Jazrael spat. "You act as though you were never a spy for Aalok."

"A spy yes, but my trespasses are nothing in comparison to yours, my dear." Serus stumbled into his chair and leaned his head back against it. The world was spinning, and he was ready for unconsciousness to take him. "You're just a filthy rag, and now—you've been discarded as such."

"I should be on that ship. I sacrificed everything to serve Aalok. All you did was move a few documents here and there and fall for the enemy. I, on the other hand, convinced souls to bow down at the feet of our great king,"

"Now that," Serus said, slightly slurring "is exactly my point. Look, I know this may come as a shock to someone such as yourself, but you deserve to suffer the same fate that awaits us all."

"Fine, stay here and die," Jazrael said, and stomped toward Serus' room.

"Go find Caius. I am sure he would be more than happy to help you look for Aalok,"

Jazrael glared, pausing at the balcony threshold. "And I'll be happy to accept his offer."

"Shut the door on the way out, won't you?" Serus muttered before tipping the wine bottle to take another swig.

"If there is another life to endure after this, I will be sure to make yours as unbearable as possible."

Serus ignored Jazrael and picked up his violin. He played a serenade, slurring the lyrics as another fireball exploded against the mountains. Fire rained down to the ocean and he closed his eyes, hoping one would singe him where he sat.

Jazrael let out another growl, and left, slamming the door behind her. She darted out into the hall, frantically pushing through a river of people. She followed them towards the exit, until a servant girl, going the opposite direction, bumped into her.

"Watch where you're going, you pathetic wench," Jazrael spat, before shoving her out of her way to catch up with the fleeing soldiers.

Aerith continued squeezing through the crowd of the corridor. When she reached the door, she took a deep breath, and then quietly slipped inside.

Smoothing her tunic, she looked around the room but didn't see Serus. Her shoulders slumped in disappointment, assuming he had already fled, but as she turned to leave, she heard him shouting.

She ran to the balcony doors but jumped back at the glass shattering at her feet. She glanced up from the trail of pouring wine, seeing Serus stumble forward on the balcony ledge. "I'm ready for my next life, Creator! Kill me at your leisure!"

"Serus! What are you doing?" Aerith asked, running to the railing.

"Aerith?" Serus whipped around to face her. He slipped on the spilled wine and wobbled.

Aerith lunged forward and grabbed onto his coattail. After giving it a hard jerk, Serus fell backward, and she caught his fall.

"Hey!" he yelled over his shoulder. "I was getting a better view."

"You were about to kill yourself!" Aerith grunted, shoving him off of her.

"Ha! As if it matters. We're all going to die anyway." He laughed, unable to contain himself.

"This is no time to be irrational,"

Thunder rolled in the distance and Serus' laughter turned to sorrow. Aerith wasn't sure the tears pouring out of his eyes were from madness or grief. When his laughter tapered off to silence, she stood by him, allowing the quiet moment. She followed his gaze to the sky as it streaked with veins of pink, listening to the roaring waves, and the screams of the fireballs until they fizzled out into the ocean.

"Everything is coming to an end." Serus sighed. "I have lost the one I love, disgraced myself before Aramis, and been a fool to believe that I could be happy."

She stared at him, wondering how long he had known about Sophie's escape. How could she tell him how she felt when she knew his sorrow was for her and her alone?

"Why aren't you running like everyone else?" he asked.

"I had to see you."

"You *had* to see me?"

"I-I needed to tell you something," she admitted, sheepishly.

"Then say it!" Serus slurred. "We are moments away from destruction!"

Aerith fidgeted with her hands, knowing if she didn't tell him how she felt now, she would never get another chance. "I just wanted to say that...although it may feel like no one cares for you...there are those who still do."

"We care for so many and yet they leave us," Serus sighed, bowing his head.

"Some are still faithful,"

He turned to her and stared for a long moment before he spoke. "Do you think love is eternal, that it transverses time?"

Aerith gulped down a deep breath. "Of course I do."

Serus smiled faintly then looked at the stars through the space between the clouds, sending out a plea.

"My only prayer is that I'll see her again...just one more time, just one more chance to prove how much I love her. I'd take everything back if I could just hold her in my arms one last time."

Aerith's face drained of color and her brightness vanished completely.

"I'm glad you're here, Aerith," Serus said, picking up a half-empty bottle.

A flash of hope lit her eyes but dimmed just as quickly at Serus' next words.

"Seems I'm almost out," he hiccupped. He raised the bottle, shaking it significantly.

"Y-yes, of course," she stammered with tears welling in her eyes.

Without another word, Aerith walked out of Serus' chamber and into the hall. She didn't bother to wipe the tears streaming down her face, and let her peers push her left and right down the hall. As she walked in a daze, she prayed to Aramis. Her request, her one, and only plea, was that she would find Serus in the next life, and have the opportunity to tell him that she loved him.

Serus fell into his chair and turned up his bottle.

"I wonder where you are in these final moments." He said before gulping down the rest of his wine until his body became numb.

He replayed happy memories of him and Sophie, over and over, trying to forget the images of her and Alexander in the field, but it was no use. They would haunt him until his end.

Thrusting the bottle over the balcony with a shout, Serus cursed the wind.

"If this life must end, then end it! Do you hear me?"

36

THE END

THE courtyard cracked beneath Sophie's feet as she quickened her pace, rushing toward the bands of her brethren. She passed by bonded souls that clung to one another with their mouths agape in fear.

Finally, she found a group of warriors dressed in the same attire as Alexander. She apologized for tugging on them when they turned to face her with furrowing brows. She searched the crowd; on tip toes, calling out to her Guardian, until her eyes lit, seeing a familiar face.

"Zeruiah!" Sophie called out to him.

Zeruiah turned from his bonded mate, kissed her temple, and met Sophie in the crowd.

"Sophie, you should be with those dear to you."

"You spoke with Alexander, yes?"

"Yes, but-"

"Did he say where he was going?"

"No, but I saw him heading toward the nearest docking station over there," Zeruiah pointed above a sea of people. "I believe he was heading to Earth, but I can't understand why. Earth will be the first to go."

"Thank you!" Sophie cried out.

"Where are you going?" Zeruiah called after her as she pushed through the huddled masses.

"I must find him!" Sophie shouted. She didn't bother looking back as she ran to the docking station to board a ship.

Zipping through a portal, Sophie shifted her ship to top speed, praying she would not be too late. As she entered Earth's atmosphere, she stared in horror, at the chaos that loomed all around her. The behemoths fled the open fields, scrambling to take cover. The mountains moved, spewing lava and ash as the dark, cloud-filled sky lit up with lightning all around her.

Alexander stood alone on a deserted beach. It was the same place in which he stood days before, ordering Sophie to stay and wait for him. The once calm and serene sea was now angry. It bore little resemblance to the peaceful place Sophie had loved so much.

He played the memory like a song, holding on to what he felt at the sight of her floating in a white halo of peace. He held onto the joy he had felt from her watching from the shore, a shore that was now barren and desolate. There was no angel of light in the water now, only debris and stringy seaweed.

He sketched a drawing of her, reminiscing about their time in the secret spring. His lips curved up tracing her sweet smile, remembering their time together in that place. The memory went on like a calming melody, and for a brief moment, Alexander was happy.

The noise of the meteors that fell was so great that he didn't hear Sophie's ship as she landed nearby. She jumped out, hoping that this, of all places, would be where she would find him. She looked around in horror to see her beloved sanctuary in disarray. Palm trees had broken in half like twigs. The forest behind her was splintered and burning as ash billowed into the black sky.

She ran down the beach, and to her relief, she spotted her Guardian. He sat against a palm tree, a pencil in his hand and a sketchbook on his lap. She paused for a moment, gazing at his hand drifting back and forth. Seeing the drawing from afar, she found him shading in a horse, nudging a girl with a long braid with his nose. A misty waterfall was then being traced, but then Alexander's hand froze.

As if he could hear her fluttering heartbeat, he glanced over his shoulder, hiding the sketchbook in the sand.

"I would have thought you would be spending your last moments with Serus." He said, setting his gaze to the sea.

Sophie shook her head.

"There's still time to convince him, Sophie."

He waited for a few thudding heartbeats, before casting his gaze back out to sea. Her silence had been her answer and it wasn't the one he had expected.

There was silence between them until thunder rolled in the distance. Yes. There was still time, but it was short.

"Serus made his choice and it wasn't me," Sophie began. "I had hoped he would come back to the truth, that we could be together again but he lost me the moment I found out he betrayed Aramis...when I realized he betrayed me. I know now that our souls were never meant to be bonded."

Alexander gave no response.

"Please...just say something."

"Say what?" Alexander demanded, standing. "That I care about you, that I can't stand the thought of not seeing you for another lifetime? Is that what you wanted to hear? When it's all over, I won't know you and you won't know me. We will be two souls, lost in a sea of faces we can't remember. If you're not going back to Serus, then at least go back to the Infinite Realm. Pray with your brethren for the Outcasts while you still have time."

Alexander took strides down the beach to put space between him and Sophie, but what she said next halted his steps.

"You spoke of faith, that you believed, and now you act as if you don't even believe your own words. You promised to be with me until the end, you promised that you'd find me in the next life. You kept your word to Aramis to protect me, and now, here you are, breaking your word to me."

Alexander didn't turn around, didn't speak. He only swallowed the knot in his throat.

"I know Aramis told you...that we're soulmates...that we were meant to be together."

Alexander turned, revealing his tortured expression.

Sophie made her way to him and peered up through her long lashes. "If you love me, Alexander, please, tell me. Give me something that I can hold onto, something I can search for in the next life. If we are soulmates, then I know that bond can't be broken. Don't you believe that?"

Thoughts raced through Alexander's mind. How could he admit how he felt? Surely, Aramis would bring her and Serus back together. She was his only hope. She was his only salvation. She was the only tether Serus would have to this place, to this life, to the truth.

No matter if Aramis originally predestined them to be bonded, Serus needed her. Even if Serus was angry with her, even if he was hurt, Alexander knew it didn't matter. A part of him would remember that love. He couldn't stand in the way of Serus' redemption. Traitor or not, he deserved that chance. He deserved council from a Truth Keeper and he didn't want that Truth Keeper to be searching for him, he wanted her to search for Serus. One soul saved would be worth never knowing her in the next life, never having that selfish satisfaction.

"Please, say something," Sophie begged.

Alexander closed his eyes, wet his lips, and shook his head. To tell her the truth would be a relief, but to hold her as heaven and Earth fell away, would only tear him apart. He could feel her desperation. He could feel her soul reaching for him, crying out for him to hold her. Not only was the salvation of Serus' soul holding him back, but also the fact that Earth was moments from destruction. Aramis had promised the end would be quick, but he couldn't make her stay with him. If she were in the Infinite Realm it would spare her a few moments of pain, of fear. He didn't want to put her through that. Not for him. He wasn't that selfish. He wasn't Serus. He wasn't Aalok. He was her Guardian, and he had vowed to protect her.

Sophie stood trembling before she hung her head in grief. She wrapped her arms around herself, her face twisting at the stab at her chest.

"If you wish me to leave, then I will leave," she whispered mournfully. "But know this, Alexander. As I stand with my brethren, I won't only be praying for the Outcasts. I'll be praying that we meet again, that even if I have to wait a whole lifetime, I'll wait to hear the words."

Staring at the waves rolling over his boots, Alexander frowned. She had made her choice.

He vowed to the heavens, to Aramis, that he would find Serus and remind him of the truth. He would find Sophie too. She was his counterpart, his other half—his soulmate. Nothing could separate them. Not even death. But he knew he had to confess. He had to say the words before it was too late.

Sophie didn't look back at Alexander as she walked away toward her ship, but before she was out of his reach, Alexander grabbed her wrist, jerking her into his arms. In his kiss, he held nothing back. He prayed she would remember this moment, no matter the space of time, that she would hold on to this memory.

The Truth Keeper melted into her Guardian's arms and the two souls glowed against the twilight sky. There was peace and comfort in the looming chaos, a light in the dark, filled with the truest and purest of love.

Alexander withdrew his lips, leaving Sophie breathless, and brushed away a tear that trickled down her cheek.

"I love you, Truth Keeper, and I will love you until the end of time...and thereafter," Alexander vowed.

Tears streamed down Sophie's face as Alexander held her close. She couldn't feel the Earth shaking around her, nor the sand blowing against her legs. Neither of them felt the waves pulling out to the sea. They couldn't hear the fireballs exploding into the forest behind them, blowing trees from their roots.

As the soulmates gazed into one another's eyes, the water receded out toward the horizon, building upon itself into a monstrous wave, heading towards them.

"I'll find you," Alexander vowed. "Even if it takes me a whole lifetime."

"Do you promise?"

"I give you my word."

Sophie's gaze shifted to the towering wave closing in, and her heart stopped, and then sped to a painful gallop.

Alexander couldn't let it end like this, not without their bonding. He knew he had Aramis' permission. He ripped his uniform at the hem, making a tattered ribbon and wrapped Sophie's arm with his. He tied it off with his teeth, securing the ribbon with an infinity knot over their wrapped hands. Taking Sophie's other hand in his, he began reciting the bonding vows.

"I am yours,"

"And you are mine."

"By this tether, our souls are entwined, and by this blessing, it will never unwind. We have found the soul we sought to find, and by this binding, we are forever, you and I." Sophie and Alexander recited in unison.

Alexander smiled, squeezing Sophie's arm. "For I am yours."

"And you are mine." Sophie smiled back.

The Earth rumbled beneath their feet as Alexander wrapped his free arm around Sophie's waist. They watched as the mountains trembled and the gray sky lit to blood red. Sophie closed her eyes, clinging to Alexander, as he watched the meteors careen down. The Earth cracked behind them and still, they clung to one another, never letting go.

Alexander looked up at the wave, but his attention was drawn to the sky. It brightened with a blinding brilliance as the sun's corona expanded outward in a massive supernova.

"Look at me," Alexander pleaded with Sophie, turning her away from the ocean.

The wind grew louder and Sophie couldn't help but stare at the roaring wave.

"Sophie, look into my eyes. What color are they?"

"Blue," Sophie answered with quivering lips.

"Remember the blue of the ocean that day we met," Alexander yelled over the noise of the rushing water. "Remember Bevol, and your days spent in paradise. You will see it again. All perish now, but one day we will live again, with Aramis, with our friends. It will all be just as it was before, and we'll be together. Forever."

"Smite me with your fury, oh great and powerful creator! Let your will be done!" Serus shouted as he stumbled forward on his balcony ledge.

He tilted the wine bottle to his lips as a meteor crashed into the fortress. The wine bottle leaped from his hands and over the railing, and he jolted to his hands and knees.

As the wave came nearer, he crawled to the balcony and climbed to stand on top of it again. He called out to Aramis, holding his arms out wide.

"What are you waiting for?"

The sky grew brighter as the sun expanded toward Earth. It lit Serus' face as he roared over the wave, his final words.

"Finish it! Do you hear me?"

The blinding white filled the sky as the supernova flashed, and Serus took one last look upon the wave that spilled over the top of the fortress. His body was nothing but a vapor and his soul rose to the sky. The flood filled his bedroom, covering Sophie's jewel necklace, still lying upon Creation.

Before being swept under by the water that funneled into the corridors, Aerith and Jazrael were turned to dust. Their souls rose, as did Caius', and all who had fled. They floated, one by one, pulsing in glowing orbs to the heavens.

At the same time, in the instant of the flash, Alexander embraced Sophie and kissed her as the light blinded them. The tattered ribbon from their vows imprinted on their wrists; marking their eternal bond, and then they disintegrated, exhaling their last breath.

The wave crashed to the shore of black dust and the flood covered the whole world. Sophie and Alexander remained together through the chaos, lifting to the heavens like a twinkling star.

There were no birds, nor beasts, or fruitful trees any longer. The cities had been broken down and swallowed up by the waters. The Earth was void and without form and darkness was upon the deep. There was no light; only the souls, rising into the heavens, like millions of paper lanterns.

In the Infinite Realm, the blue flames of Aramis' power dwindled. He gazed at the floating rubble that had once been his kingdom. He eyed the destruction of the Earth below, and the void before him. He was the only light in existence, all but the stars of his slumbering children, floating toward him.

When the souls gathered at his feet like a vast ocean of light, the king walked through the glittering sea and closed his eyes. Humming a tune, he waved his hands and parted the sea of souls, separating those who carried the light from those who carried darkness.

He would see to it that those who had fallen would have the opportunity to be redeemed, and that those who had not lost faith would guide the way. Regardless of free will, they could still be saved. Smiling at the twinkling orbs, Aramis sang a hymn, waving his hands as if composing an orchestra. Forming the heavens and Earth once more, he set the stage for his new creation. The first aeon had ended, but another had just begun.

REBIRTH

Millions of years after the creation of man

"SHE'S five pounds, eight ounces, and very healthy. If you can't tell, she's got a strong set of lungs," a nurse in blue scrubs announced cheerfully. The newborn let out several raspy cries until the nurse swaddled her in a pink blanket. "There now, sweet girl."

She bounced the baby lightly before leaning over and placing her in her mother's arms.

"Oh, Robert. Isn't she beautiful?" The mother, Amanda asked her husband.

Robert bent over, grinning wide at his newborn baby. "Hey there, baby girl."

The baby stared at him with her big round eyes.

"I've never seen green eyes before, at least not at birth. Newborns always have blue."

"Eyes like a field of spring clovers." Amanda kissed the baby's forehead tenderly.

"What's this red mark on her wrist?" Robert asked, tracing his thumb over the long red line.

"Oh, that's just a birthmark." The nurse assured. "It will darken up in a few days. As she grows, it will get smaller."

Robert kissed his wife on the forehead and gazed at his little girl as she yawned.

"What's her name?" the nurse asked, taking off her gloves.

"Claire," Amanda replied, with a proud smile. "Claire Evelyn Grace."

ACKNOWLEDGMENTS

A big thank you to my writing coaches, Megan Barnhard & Ella E. Barnard, & my Tribe, my Lloyds and Ladies of Author Like A Boss Academy

To my peeps on Twitter #WriteFightGifClub. You guys made me laugh during those rough days. The endless threads of GIFs are the best procrastination *ever*.

Thank you my amazing CP's and BETAs, & ARC Angels. You helped me more than you could ever know.

Kristy, my BFF

Thank you to my kids. I'm glad you are old enough to read this. Yes, Mommy totally gave you a shout out!

Thank you to my amazing husband, my rock, my soulmate, for supporting me, dealing with the late nights, talking about this work, and the occasional writer's hangover. Most of all, for making my dream come true. This was made possible because you believed in me.

Above all, I thank my Creator.

THE STORY CONTINUES...

THE
AEON
CHRONICLES

BOOK II

Excerpt from THE AEON CHRONICLES Book 2

Claire glanced up slowly, finding Aven's fixed gaze. "Why do I feel like you're talking about me?" she asked softly.

"Because," Aven said, leaning forward, "I am."

Claire swallowed as Aven narrowed his eyes, tilting his head.

"Did you dream about me before you met me, Claire?"

Something's wrong. Very wrong.

The dream Claire had on the plane flashed in her mind again, then the vision she'd had in the hotel room. She closed her eyes, pressing a hand to her chest as it caved in on her lungs.

Not now.

"Claire . . ."

When Claire lifted her gaze, she found Aven's full of concern. She could see him, the real him behind the storm of grey. There was no trickster, no playful joker lingering as he reached for her hand. Her shoulders fell in relief at his warmth, but when something skittered behind his shoulder at the piano, she pulled away.

Sucking in a sharp breath, Claire stood up, knocking her chair back and jumped as it smacked against the floor.

"We should get some sleep," she mumbled all too quickly. "We can talk more tomorrow." She rushed to pick up the chair and darted to the steps.

"Claire, wait." Aven's voice was almost pleading.

She didn't want to see the shadow again, didn't want to believe what Aven had said about his demons. If they were real, if they were what kept him up at night, they were now after her too. She forced herself to turn around, eyes closed.

"It was a little more than twenty-five dollars. But I knew you liked it."

Claire opened her eyes, finding Aven holding something from the antique shop.

The music box.

She steadied her wobbly legs and ran her fingers over the smooth carved wood until Aven turned the key and opened the top.

The tune was sad but beautiful, and Claire's eyes welled as the ting of metal plinked to the tune of *The Lonely Ballerina*. She had played this song on the day after her father had died, the last song before she closed her piano top and never played again. Not until the night with Aven, when he had asked her to bare her soul.

As she clutched to the box, Aven slid his thumb across her cheek and wiped the tear. "I told you we would face those beasties together."

Claire shook her head, pressing her lips hard. The memory of the fire and the casket of her father pounded the haunting guilt against her chest. Her body quivered with waves of emotion. She was drowning, gasping for breath, sinking deeper as the anxiety flooded her.

"I wish there was a way I could walk into your mind and take it away," Aven whispered, cupping her face. "Erase the memory of the fire reaching for you, how you tried so hard to hold on to that gutter, the sickening sound of your body as it hit the ground—"

Claire's gaze snapped to Aven's. "You saw it?"

Aven's throat bobbed as if he hadn't realized what he had said at first. "Yes."

"But you told me you weren't there, that—"

"You're the first person I've ever Mind Walked with that I could see what was happening."

"How is that possible?"

"I don't know," he answered, sweeping the hair from her face. "But I do know there's something between us we can't explain. Something buried so deep, that our souls are calling us to remember."

Our souls. A connection. The tug.

"What did you see, Claire?"

Claire stared at Aven blankly. She wanted to run away, wanted to escape his sympathetic stare. But as she drew back, the tug, the knowing of their connection, drew her toward him again.

"What's troubling you?" He whispered.

An image of the dark haired angel came to Claire's mind.

She squeezed her eyes shut trying to banish the vision.

"You'll think I'm crazy."

Aven lifted her chin. "We're all mad here."

Claire exhaled at his words, teetering on the edge of telling him, of confessing everything.

"Did you see me in your dreams before we met?" Aven's gaze was pleading again. "Did it feel like a memory?"

Like a memory. How do you know? Are you him?

"Yes," she managed to say.

There was no hesitation, no other words spoken as Aven pressed her against the banister. His kiss was urgent, passionate, and Claire found pleasure in every tendril of her body, replacing the fear she once had.

"Come to my bed." He breathed against her lips. "I'll tell you everything. No more secrets, no more games."

Claire answered yes with a kiss but jerked away, startled at the opening of the front door. She covered her burning lips in shame and met Will's defeated gaze as he stood at the threshold.

DISCOVER MORE

Visit the Website

www.aprilmwoodard.com

Signed copies are now available

 @Author_April_M_Woodard

 @April_M_Woodard

 #THEAEONCHRONCILES

 authoraprilmwoodard

ABOUT THE AUTHOR

April M Woodard was born and raised in small town in Virginia. She now lives in Georgia, near the big city of Atlanta with her husband and three kids. She spends her days writing young adult fiction with three kitties at her feet. Scratch that. Two kitties, and a mogwai. When she isn't typing away on her laptop, she is sitting on her back porch, sipping sweet tea, and reading a good book.

Photo taken by SHANNONTHOMPSON

Printed in Poland
by Amazon Fulfillment
Poland Sp. z o.o., Wrocław